Adriana Books
The Complete Blog
2010-2021
Vol 1

Adriana Books
The Complete Blog
2010-2021
Vol. 1

by

Dwight Cathcart

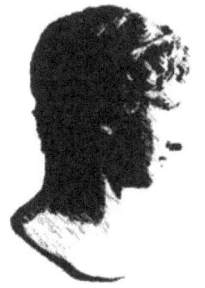

Adriana Books
Boston, Massachusetts
2021

ISBN:978-0-578-94194

Adriana Books *adrianabooks.com*
publisher@adrianabooks.com
Boston, Massachusetts

Cover design: Dwight Cathcart
Backcover photograph: Bill Chisholm

Printed: CP20230218textvol1.pdf
         CPfullcover20220503vol1.pdf

for

Courtney Furno

Preface

These blog posts collected here as *Adriana Books: The Complete Blog, Vol 1 & 2,* were originally published on Adriana Books—during the period November 2010 to November 2021, a decade of rapid change for the gay community. They are mainly printed as they appeared on the web. The links are usually suppressed, but a few give a URL in the text. All the posts with *Earthrise* in the title were separately published in paper last year by Adriana Books.

Terms like LGB, when used in this collection, were expressive of the time when they were written. I considered changing them all to 2022 usage—LGBTQ+IA—and decided against it. The collection as it stands has the value of expressing some of the changes occurring in our community during the period of the writing of this blog.

Volume 1 contains pages 1-332. Vol 2 contains pages 333-675.

All of these posts can be found on *adrianabooks.com/blog.* Scroll down to the search engine and type in the name of the post given in this collection.

Table of Contents

Table of Contents

Table of Contents

Table of Contents

Table of Contents

Adriana Books
The Complete Blog
2010-2021
Vol 1

1

The un-finality of finishing something
November 3, 2010

We are working hard on the last jobs getting our website—
http://www.dwightcathcart.net—up and running. We ask ourselves
questions. Are there enough pictures? Do you have more pictures on
your HD? What did Apple do to Photo 11 so that it won't do what
iPhoto 10 did easily? I seem to go by the Apple store once a week,
asking for help. As it turned out, I don't think the staff was very familiar
with the latest upgrade to iPhoto. I cropped more than a hundred photos.
There were design issues, particularly on the first several pages, and
then Edward worked on the Shopping Cart and Checkout pages. I think
all that's done, now. At one point, I went through the whole website
looking for copy-editing type things. A comma here or there. Clarity.
Tomorrow we'll make some changes to the text of the excerpts of the
three novels. Then, at some point, I suppose late in the afternoon, one of
us will say, "Is there anything left to do?" And the other one will say,
"No. I don't think so." And there'll probably be a silence for a second or
two, and then somebody will say, "Uh—well. Um. What now?" And the
other one will say, "Put it up, and let's see if it'll fly."

This is the way it's always been when I've finished a book. I write all
the way through to the end, so that I know what the last sentence is going
to be, and then, after several days of decompression, I go back

and edit the whole text. Usually, while I'm writing a book, I begin to collect subjects in my head that I know are going to need reworking after I finish, so now that I am header through, I get organized about these subjects. I make a list. I pick the one I am going to look at first, and then I start to work. Sometimes this subject requires that I read a book—find a book, and then read it—and then rewrite scenes. If I am lucky, there is only one scene, but sometimes I rework every scene a character appears in over 300 pages, or 500 pages. Major effort. And then when all this is done—sometimes it takes six months—then I print out a fresh copy and read it through again. I am either unhappy with all the edits I made, or I am happy. If I am happy, I can go on and go to the beach. If I am unhappy, I have to go back to work and do those things again, or do them better, or differently, or something. And then I can go on to some other issue. I repeat this process until gradually the list of things to be looked at gets shorter and shorter, until one day, when I read through a freshly printed-out text, I realize I have read thirty pages without making a single mark on a page. Then the suspense begins to grow. How many pages can I go without making a mark?

But I never say to Courtney, who is my partner, "I finished my book today." Because I don't know if today was the day I finished it. I could be reading it and realize, "I finished this last week." Or I could realize that, "I don't know. I am unsure about this thing. Ask me again next week. I don't know if I finished it." And then I'll read it again. I may do this a number of times, until finally I can say, "There's nothing more to do," and, then I'll grin at Courtney and say, "Now, it's finished," and that now it's OK for me to get Courtney and go to the beach.

In that way, writing a book is like freedom for gay people. At some point in the future, long after we all have gay marriage and DOMA and DADT have been repealed, and many other things have been dealt with, somebody is going to say, "What next?" and somebody else is going to say, "Uh—um, I don't think there is anything else." There's going to be silence for a moment, and then somebody is going to say, "Are we free now?" And the other person is going to say, tentatively, "I think so. Maybe." And then, we can all go to the beach.

2

The myths we tell ourselves

November 9, 2010

I was halfway through *Ceremonies*, when I began to get the feeling that there weren't many other gay books like this. Books that placed their characters at the heart of the gay predicament—we live in a homophobic culture—and then listened while they told us how that was. This is such an important story, how could it be that not many other writers have written about this?

The same thing is true about *Race Point Light*. I think that the pattern my life has taken is a very common pattern—education and coming to adulthood, with marriage and children, before Stonewall— and yet not many of our writers have taken up this subject. We say, *those people were not being honest with themselves,* and then we ignore their lives. All of that manifestly did happen to hundreds of thousands of gay men and women, and I would guess that few of them think they were not being honest with themselves. They knew exactly what was happening. They were coming to terms, as far as they were able, when they did what they did where they did. But these people, for the most part, are not inhabitants of our literature.

Then there is *Adam in the Morning*. We tell ourselves about Stonewall that there were the Dark Ages for gay people, and then the guys rebelled, and it's been getting better, day by day, ever since. Yet there is another story that says there may not have even been gay people before Stonewall, much less the separation between homosexual and heterosexual that we seem to know now.

We understand our lives by the stories we tell ourselves about ourselves. Some narratives are better than others, closer to reality for more people, more profound, more universal and at the same time more diverse. Some are more clearly myths that we tell ourselves not to explain ourselves to ourselves but to explain away difficult aspects of our lives. Sometimes our myths simplify to the point of lying. During the years when I was writing the three novels of the Stonewall Triptych, I came to think it is terribly important for the gay community to explore deeply the narratives it tells itself.

3

The Pictures
November 16, 2010

Since 1982 I have taken many hundreds of pictures of the sites in which these three novels have been placed—Cardiff, Maine, a fictional version of Bangor, Maine, Commercial Street and Race Point in Provincetown, and Christopher Street in the West Village in New York. But when it came time to find a photograph we could use for the cover of each of these novels, I realized that all of my pictures were taken in the daylight, and the significant actions that made those places memorable all took place after dark. Charles Howard was drowned in the night, the crowds at the Stonewall rioted at night, and at the end of his long life, Fair Shaw walked with his friends in the surf at night.

So I went to New York September 20, 2010, getting there in the late afternoon, leaving my bag with my son and going back over to Christopher Street about 8:30 in the evening, with a tripod and a camera. I took pictures principally in three places—the "corner," where Christopher Street begins on Greenwich Avenue, the intersection of Christopher Street and Gay Street, and the stretch of Christopher from #55 Christopher to the Stonewall Inn and a few buildings beyond on the north side of the street, across from Sheridan Square (which is what the inhabitants called it in 1969). Many of the pictures showed the edgy confusion of New York that I like. I chose the cover of *Adam in the Morning* to be one of the pictures of Christopher at Gay Street.

The Bangor pictures differed in the way Bangor differs from New York. New York streets never really get dark. Bangor streets, even one as close to the center of town as the State Street bridge, are badly lit, and do get dark, and make taking pictures without a flash difficult. I started just at dusk, October 13, 2010, at six o'clock. The sky was still light. There is a small bridge, slightly lower than the State Street bridge, a little downstream. I aimed my camera upstream to get the State Street bridge. Then I took pictures in the other direction, downstream, looking out to the Penobscot River—less light, fewer people. The cover of *Ceremonies* is of the State Street bridge, where Charles Howard died. All of my pictures of Bangor were of the Kenduskeag Stream, where Charlie drowned, except a few, which were taken in the daytime, of the granite monument to Charlie. I have been told that people in Bangor keep the monument and its plantings in good shape, and it was a shame these pictures of it had to be taken just at the end of the growing season.

I got to Provincetown in the late afternoon, October 26, 2010, checked into a B&B, and went out on Commercial Street at dusk. I started at the intersection of Commercial and Johnson Street and walked west or southwest through the center of town down to Carver, then I turned around and walked back toward Johnson. The sun had set in the southwest, making the sky over that part of the landscape lighter. These pictures indicate the kind of place Commercial Street is and the way it may have looked when Fair Shaw and his partner Chris and Julio and David walked down Commercial toward the west that night in 2004. I would like to have chosen the days for my photography by the number of people on the street, but it was the beginning of autumn, and the weather was controlling. During September and October, I watched the calendar and visited these places when it didn't seem like it would be raining.

These are not photographs of places in my novels, but they are photographs of places I was thinking about when I was writing my novels. So, enjoy.

4

Feeling Trapped
November 22, 2010

I saw a play the other night, a new play about a family in crisis over a question of forgiveness. Can they forgive the man who murdered their daughter? This led me to consider whether a dramatist could write that kind of drama about a gay family. Say, two gay men and their children, home for the holidays, forced to deal with whether to forgive a man who had murdered a daughter of the family. What makes this problematic is that the two gay men and their children live in a bigoted world. At almost every turn, the attention of the audience would be drawn from a sharp focus on the grief or anger or sorrow or confusion that one or the other member of the family is feeling, onto feelings called forth by the character's life in a bigoted culture.

In the drama I saw the other night, the surviving daughter brings home a man she has met, who, it turns out, is a cop. For a time, the audience wonders whether the cop is going to discover crimes other members of the family may have committed. But he slides into an inconsequential place in this family in crisis. I couldn't imagine the daughter of two gay men bringing home a cop without first having vetted him on the issue of two gay men. If he was OK'd by the daughter, he would become known to the audience not as a cop but as a *progressive* cop, altering the dynamic of the narrative the playwright had been building. There would be no danger from this cop.

I think it's hard—it may be impossible—to write a story about a gay character without dealing with his or her context. This person can't serve in the military, can't get married in most states, until fairly recently was liable to being arrested for violation of the sodomy laws, is being preached against by preachers all over the country, is seven times more likely to commit suicide as a teenager, etc., etc., etc. And once you start dealing with these issues, or even introduce them, they take over the narrative, and whatever you had wanted to write, about grief and sorrow and anger and confusion resulting from a murder, gets subsumed under the bigger effects of homophobic discrimination and abuse. Writing a story about a gay character is just very, very hard to do. Of course, if you push the gay character off to the side and make him or her ancillary to the principal characters, in which case you can fully describe the gay character's life in America without having it overwhelm the narrative of the principal characters. The point here is that, because of our culture, writers in America don't have the same freedom to create stories around their gay characters that writers have around their straight characters. This is another consequence of the bigotry in our culture.

We don't deal with the effects of bigotry on our characters because if we dealt with any of it, since it's so overwhelming, we couldn't deal with anything else. It is somewhere among these factors that we find the causes, I think, for the literature gay people have. If we are going to write novels or plays about gay people, and put them front and center, there is only one story to tell, and that is the story of bigotry and its effects. This is terrible, and it's going to stay with us until we change the culture we have, but until then, this is our story.

*

Check out my website, *www.adrianabooks.com*, and see for yourself.

5

Life and Death

November 22, 2010

I think, the way this blog is developing, at least for now, that I will keep a few subjects running. Two more holidays to get through before we can get back to work. Thanksgiving was fifteen or twenty of my partner's family in a beautiful home on the coast of Connecticut. Last weekend was Holly Folly in Provincetown and the Boston Gay Men's Chorus singing, and we had dinner with friends at a good restaurant to celebrate my partner's birthday. The weather in both places was warm for the season and the sun was out. Christmas will be here in Boston because my partner will be working around the holidays. I am going this weekend to my daughter's house where everybody is gathering— including my son and his family—because one of my daughter's children will be dancing in *The Nutcracker*. With all this holiday cheer, it is important to note that earlier this week, the Circuit Court of Appeals for the Ninth Circuit heard arguments in *Perry v. Schwarzenegger*, the case brought against Prop 8 in California. We don't know yet. The cloture vote on the Defense Authorization Bill which included the repeal of DADT has now taken place and we have lost. Some say repeal of DADT is dead. Others say our single best hope for reviving it is Senator Lieberman. DOMA is still alive, and nobody seems to be taking any steps to kill it. Carl Joseph Walker Hoover is still dead, as is Tyler Clementi. And Charles Howard is still dead. I didn't mean to turn bitter, here, in the middle of the holiday season, but there it is. It's like remembering all the men who died during the Reagan and Bush (1) administrations who wouldn't have died if those presidents had been willing to fund and push prevention.

6

Memory
December 29, 2010

Saturday, December 18, 2010, the Senate of the United States voted twice on the Lieberman-Collins bill, once to bring cloture to the debate on the bill, and therefore to end the Republican filibuster, and once on the bill itself, at 3:00 pm. The first passed 63-33, and the second 65-31. It is not often when these things happen—when civil rights are recognized or restored or expanded—and, when it happened, I was in front of CPAN2 watching.

The greatest share of the victory belongs to President Obama, who has been beating a drum on this issue for the last three years, creating a climate in which it was possible for it to happen, and to the Congressional leaders, who effectively marshaled their forces in the Congress. But many people have been saying that the hardest push was made by grassroots activists, who kept up the pressure on Obama and on Congress, and who made it happen.

So it is going to be repealed. But in this moment, it is important for us who are here to be determined to remember all those who are not here, who fought for this and other advances of gay rights, and who died or were killed before those advances could be achieved, the men and women who were hounded out of the Armed Forces or were murdered by anti-gay homophobes, or who died from AIDS because the federal government was not pushing prevention programs.

It is important to remember that the damage that DADT did to gay people between 1993 and today is still affecting people, the psychic and physical hurt still causing pain, the experience of many men and women still part of the sum of human suffering. We can't say, as we have said about other things, *We don't hurt people that way any more*, and expect to move on to other issues. The men and women who survived that period, many of them, still live, and it is certain that those men and women still suffer their wounds from that time. We can't leave those men and women to be the only ones who remember how bad it was.

7

Heroism
January 1, 2011

But if there is suffering that cannot be forgotten, there is heroism, too.

The mythic narrative that we tell ourselves is that we suffer, and then we rise up and refuse to suffer any longer. This is the great narrative of the American Revolution and of all subsequent revolutions. It is also the narrative of the AIDS years. We were dying, and nobody seemed to care. And then, because nobody cared, the gay community set about caring for itself. It was when Gay Men's Health Crisis was founded in New York, and when AIDS Action Committee was founded in Boston.

It is also the narrative of the Stonewall Riots. We suffered abuse, and then on the night of June 28, 1969, we refused to go quietly into the paddy wagon, and we rose up and fought back, and we've been fighting back ever since.

It's the narrative of the summer of 1984, in Bangor, Maine, after Charlie Howard was murdered. Gay people who had suffered quietly walked out of the Unitarian-Universalist Church and walked down to the center of town letting everyone know that they were there and were not going away.

14

Most of the people who walked out of the church in Bangor, straight into the glare of the lights of television cameras, had not come out before, and were now choosing the most public possible way to come out. There were many people who weren't, and none of us knew what we were walking out into, when we exited the church.

There is drama to that narrative, and the gay community has played out over and over during the last fifty or sixty years. The story has everything for the novelist—suffering, anguish, anger, refusal, heroism. Every time someone comes out, he or she acts out this narrative again. It's a universal theme, and it's another way we show our common humanity.

8

What was it like for you there?
January 7, 2011

There are, I guess, as many reasons for writing a novel as there are novelists, but one of the principal reasons is to tell what it was like there—in Atlanta in 1864, in Meryton in the early nineteenth century, in Yoknapatawpha County in 1928. What was it like for a particular young woman in Rouen during the third and fourth decades of the nineteenth century? For an Irish advertising canvasser in Dublin in 1904? For a beautiful and beautifully educated and mannered young man named Anthony Malone on the lower East Side in New York in the early seventies? What was it like to be the people they were where they were when they were? A novelist may have formal concerns or want to attack the Romantic movement or seek to examine the effects of time on memory, but at some point the novelist always seems to attempt to answer the question, What was it like there? Not so much What did you do? or What happened? but What did it feel like to be you in that place, in that time? What was it like to be young—thirty years old—and male and gay with a lover, at two o'clock in the morning on June 28, 1969, in Greenwich Village in New York? What concerns did he have? What pictures did he like? What posters? What movies? What Broadway shows? What did he think of? What was he afraid of? What was he not afraid of? How did he feel, seeing *Boys in the Band?* How did it feel to walk west on Christopher Street, going home at six to have sex with Joseph? What was it in all this that brought this thirty year-old man to the point where he was willing to fight the cops, to wade into the riots on Christopher Street, his fists clenched together, and to swing them back and forth like clubs at the cops?

All this is central to novels, and, I think, to my own novels. Whatever else is going on, one of the main things these books address is this: *What was it like to be gay in America in the last half of the twentieth century?* How it felt, and how it made a man think, and what it made a man plan to do.

9

Present at the creation
January 12, 2011

Like many men and women of my generation, I was interested in the Stonewall Riots. Like most men and women of my generation, I wasn't there. I was in Ann Arbor, Michigan, during the summer of 1969, but I read the initial reports in the Times, and then I watched the national press as the story developed and then later as the story about gay liberation began to develop.

Many of us seemed to understand, even in those early days, that what was happening was new, entirely new, and our lives were going to be different because of it. But it was not until much later that we began to understand something else, that a new world was being created in those early meetings in the West Village in people's apartments, in churches, and in the meetings of the Gay Liberation Front. We were creating our world.

The Stonewall Riots need to be studied just because they are the beginning. We need to know more about the men who were present at the beginning. And we need to know more about what their options were and what their decisions meant, because we are still living in the world they created.

10

Looking for love in the places that are available

January 15, 2011

My novel, *Race Point Light*, is about a guy who knows from childhood that he likes men. He never wavers about that, all of his life. He has a magical affair with another soldier in 1959 in the most beautiful meadow on earth, on the higher slopes of Mt Rainier. He goes to graduate school and has sex with a graduate student in psychology, and he is passing out leaflets to integrate a greasy spoon when John Kennedy was shot. Later, in 1965, when he is about 25, he gets married to a woman he met in a Victorian Literature seminar. He and his wife have children. He gets his doctorate, they live in a big house, his children are beautiful, but he never forgets the men. Then, after about eighteen years of marriage, my guy says his marriage is over, divorces, moves to Boston, and finds himself surrounded by the AIDS epidemic, with its great commandments, *Do no harm,* and *Help*. He spends the next twenty-five years writing gay novels. In 1990, he meets a guy in the local leather bar—he is one of those sexy bartenders with a leather armband and a harness—and they go home together. They never promise anything about what they feel for each other. They don't swear to be together always, or to be monogamous, and they never ever try to control the future. But they are together ever after, and their love for each other spells Freedom for them.

My guy—he is the narrator of *Race Point Light*—is named Fair Shaw, and he spends all his life looking for love, not in the wrong places, but in the places that are available to him. And during his life, he does what he has to do, he loves his children, he writes his novels, he holds his sexy bartender, and, at the end of the novel, very late at night, he is walking in the surf on Race Point beach, near the lighthouse, when one of the others says, "Fair?" And the novel ends.

Fair's life is the life of hundreds of thousands of American men and women of his generation, filled with conflict, filled with anguish, filled with drama, confronting the big questions of civil rights, personal failure, work, doing what has to be done, and, from time to time, touched with transcendent happiness. And through it all, he never stops loving his partner, and he never stops loving his children. Fair?

11

Christopher Isherwood, grief, loss
January 21, 2011

I read *A Single Man*—about George Falconer's grief—when I was in graduate school in the late sixties, and I don't think I liked it much. At twenty-five I didn't know what grief was, so I didn't know it when I stumbled on it. I also didn't know what this story had to do with my own life, even though I was losing things all around me and part of the huge burden I carried around with me every day was grief. On Tuesday I was in Border's, looking for DVDs. I had a list on my phone, and I worked my way down the list, seeing what I could find. Not a one. Then, as I was about to leave, I saw Colin Firth's grief- stricken face on the cover of the DVD for *A Single Man*.

I told Courtney, my partner, that if I had read this book when it first came out, in 1964, and had been receptive to it, my whole life might have been different. This book is about George, whose lover, Jim, an architect, went to visit his parents in winter. Driving on an icy road, Jim loses control of his car and is killed. The book is about a day in the life of George Falconer eight months later, as George goes about the ordinary things people go about—he gets up, he fixes breakfast, he sits on the john, he notices the neighbors, he teaches a class at the university, he notices the tennis players' sweaty torsos—while devastated by the loss of Jim and losing his grip on his own life. In my early twenties, I hadn't read a book like this, that treated the love of one man for another so tenderly, so respectfully, with such understanding and caring, and with such importance. The book came out in 1964, and that was exactly the year that I most needed to read this book. I needed to be taught that there was a man who believed that the love of one man for another could be treated tenderly, respectfully, with understanding and caring, and with importance. Some years later, when I did read it, I still wasn't ready to hear what Isherwood had to say about the love of men for each other. I still wasn't grown-up enough.

When I saw the DVD in the store on Tuesday and watched it when I got home and then watched it again, then went to the store and bought a copy of *A Single Man* and read it, I differed from my earlier self in that *now* I am aware of loss and *now* I know what grief is, and it seems as if George Falconer is speaking directly to me, making it possible for me to know *now* why my life would have been different if I had read this book with understanding *then*.

12

Christopher Isherwood, George Falconer, the book and the movie, 1961

January 25, 2011

People in chat rooms say the movie of *A Single Man*, starring Colin Firth and Julianne Moore, is "completely different" from the book. The small group of lines from page 28 in the book—where George is thinking of what the neighbors must be thinking about him and Jim— turn into a significant addition to the big scene with Charley (Julianne Moore) in the movie. In the movie, it is Charley who asks whether he ever thinks of what "we could have been to each other, having a real relationship, with kids?" George answers, "I had Jim." And Charley says, "What you and Jim had together was wonderful, but wasn't it really just a substitute for something else?" George asks, "Is that what you really think, that Jim was some kind of substitute for real love?" Charley backs off. Tom Ford, who directed this movie, wants to be sure the moviegoer knows what he is seeing. This change from the book to the movie makes clearer how hostile George's world is to George's love for Jim, how hostile and how ignorant. Even his only friend has no idea how to value George's love for Jim. *Only friend*. In the movie, George connects, briefly, with the Spanish hustler he meets outside the liquor store and with Kenny, one of his students. Kenny pursues George after class, across campus, across town, and to the neighborhood bar near George's house. "What do you *want*?" George asks.

Kenny is unsure. Both of these men waltz around one another, unwilling or unable to reach out to each other. Why can't Kenny, who seems to want to be taken, tell his teacher? And why can't George, who seems to want Kenny, actually say, "I'd like to make love to you." The moviegoer, watching these scenes at the bar, nude in the surf, and at George's home, aches for them that they can't do what they need to do, to give themselves to each other. The changes the movie makes to the book are all there to make George's loss clearer to the moviegoer, who may not have a sense of *how it was for you then in 1962*. George lives in a place where his culture is indifferent to his grief, and his grief is harder to bear because his culture is determined to make him bear it alone.

13

A different kind of gay novel
January 13, 2011

Joseph Roche was active in voter registration drives in Mississippi during Freedom Summer, in 1964. He was from Los Angeles, and in 1961 he volunteered for Freedom Rides after he saw the first one on TV and saw young people beaten by racist mobs. His mother had taught him about Marcus Garvey and black nationalism, and Martin Luther King had taught him about non-violence. Later, he went to UCLA, fought in the Watts Riot in 1964, and then went to New York, where he got an acting job with the New Lafayette Theatre, a leader in the Black Arts Movement. Joseph had sex with men, and he didn't find that the way he was living made him feel better about himself.

Joseph got a job downtown, in the West Village, as Caliban, in a repertory production of *The Tempest*, and then found himself, early in the morning on June 28, 1969, fighting the cops after they had raided the Stonewall Inn. This was where he met Bo Ravich.

Trying to explain to Bo why he had come downtown, Joseph said, "I was aware of wanting to be in a community of fags. A group of us, six or eight brothers and sisters, would be out going to clubs after some event, and I was aware that people were pairing off, but it didn't seem possible for me to pair off."

Joseph is a character in *Adam in the Morning*, and for a novelist the question raised by Joseph's life is *What kind of literature does this life make?* A literature grounded in the political and racial history off the characters, which inevitably explores the point at which the personal becomes the political and *vice versa.*

Bo talks about these matters with Joseph.

"We don't know many black men."

"No?"

"No. I'd like to know more. There've been other times when I've had a lot more black friends than now."

"Well. Maybe I should seize this moment to tell you that I don't know many white gay men. Let's see how things work out. And if you guys are as cool as I think you are, there are some black dudes I could introduce you to."

"Is it OK for me to ask you these questions?"

"Oh, yeah. It makes us close." He kisses [Bo]. "And I have a lot of questions to ask you too, about being white." He smiles and kisses [Bo] again. "You don't seem like a devil."

14

A beautiful film
February 6, 2011

In *Night Catches Us*, a film by Tanya Hamilton, Marcus, played by
Anthony Mackie, comes back to Philadelphia after being away for ten
years. His father has just died, and he has come back into a family
struggling with the past. Marcus left, and his brother, who had to deal
with his father, is resentful and wants no part of him. Young Jimmy,
Patricia's cousin, is resentful of the cops and thinks Marcus informed on
Patricia's husband, who was killed by the cops in an execution- style
shooting in Patricia's living room. Patricia, who is played by Kerry
Washington, welcomes Marcus home, and Patricia's daughter, Iris,
wants to know what happened to her father.

There is enough stuff here to make a powerful movie. But what
raises the stakes is that the film takes place in 1975, and Marcus and
Patricia and several others of their friends in Philadelphia were members
of the Black Panther Party, and what's happening is that they are all
trying to come to terms with their pasts, represented by the question of
what happened to Patricia's husband. Did somebody tell on him? Who?
Why? Patricia says at one point, "That's not what we were," referring to
the execution of a cop. But if not that, then what?

And even more important for Marcus and Patricia now, *How are we going to live now?*

It is a deeply moving film which closely connects the racism of political Philadelphia, represented by the cops and their allies, both white and black, and the actions of the Black Panthers then, and the kids who would like to do what the Black Panthers did, *now*, with the poverty of their neighborhood and with the questions faced by Patricia and Marcus, *What we are?* And, *How do we live now?* It is a slow-moving, elegiac film, conveyed by slow quiet conversations, punctured by gunfire. At critical moments, the camera simply backs off and watches the water in an urban stream flow or the tangled vines of an urban jungle, blowing in a breeze. Long moments are spent as we watch the principals ponder their lives, staring off into the distance.

Tanya Hamilton has it exactly right. Life is interconnected, you can't be on the streets of Philadelphia without knowing about poverty, the cops and the Panthers, and the fact that Patricia's husband was executed, and that Marcus loved Patricia. To understand anything, you have to understand it all, and you can't pick and choose, and you don't really have the right or even the ability to make it pretty. Any of it. And yet, *and yet*, this is a beautiful film.

15

Literature that reflects us
February 12, 2011

A friend wrote this morning to say that he is frustrated by the state of gay publishing. Most gay books that come out are humorous essays about gay life and gay romance novels. I'd like to read something heftier, in which the kinds of things that affect me also affect the characters—that is, politics, race, class, a sense of the characters' epoch. I'd like the novels I read to answer the question, *How is it for you there?* And I'd like that question to be treated seriously.

But we don't much get that kind of novel. The publishing industry is composed of agents, finders for agents, publishers, distributors, booksellers, journals that review books, reviewers, writers, and, finally, the book buyer. I am sure there are others. Most of them don't seem to know how to deal with a big serious gay book. They are clueless. And, of course, the book buyer going to the bookstore at the end of the food chain to buy some serious novel is unlikely to go to a gay bookstore, because he has learned that gay bookstores don't carry serious fiction. Gradually, over recent decades, our whole literature has gotten dumbed down. As readers, we don't know any more what to demand of serious gay fiction than the rest of the publishing industry.

We are serious people. We confronted AIDS. We survived Reagan and Bush (1) and Bush (2), we have learned to work the political system, we have gotten gay marriage in some places, and we have fought against DADT and are fighting against DOMA. We are transforming what marriage means in this country and what this country considers a family. As gay people, we have fought in the great battles of our time. We have been heroic and successful. We have been fighters. We have preserved those aspects of ourselves that were unique. But our literature does not reflect these things.

16

Narratives, change, violence
February 20, 2011

Bo Ravich opens *Adam in the Morning* lying on the steps of the
theatre where he works, on Sixth Avenue, and in the next two or
three hours he becomes a different person. Narratives—stories—
seem to require that characters change in some way, either suddenly,
like Bo, or even more suddenly, like Fair Shaw in *Race Point Light*,
who opens the Sunday paper on June 30, 1969—he's reading about
the same riots that are affecting Bo—and discovers that his life is
transformed. But more usually, change comes gradually, over
decades, somewhere between one's twenties and one's forties, or
between one's forties and one's sixties. The biggest change people
seem to experience is acceptance— of themselves, of other people,
of their place in the scheme of things.

This may sound bland enough, but what is interesting about this
process is that what people often come to accept is the need to fight.
It is relatively easier to go on the way one has been going since one
was born on the first page of the book, to allow inertia to carry one
from day to day, avoiding the issues that are going to disrupt one's
life. As Derek says, in *Ceremonies*, "I wanted a good part with one
good scene—Macduff, say, weeping for his children—and a pretty

boy in my bed," but whatever it was he wanted, he's caught in the middle of a fight he didn't start but can't walk away from, even though he tries.

He's gay, and he can't walk away from that, and when the bigots come out to fight, Derek finds there is no where safe to go. His change is his acceptance—of the need, in this case, to shed blood. This is a tough one. Some people come to this acceptance early. Jack screams, "Fight, you son of a bitch! Come back and fight!" as some drive-by bigots get away. Some wait until the last possible moment, running from place to place until events and bigots catch up with them, and, their backs against the wall, they have to fight, have to transform themselves into something heroic. It may be that there are many heroic people who might not have chosen to be heroes if they had had a choice.

17

Never give in, we own the street
February 27, 2011

Today, here in Boston, I was at a rally at the State House supporting the demonstrators in Madison and supporting our unions and theirs. It was not very big, somebody said a thousand people, and it was orderly. Everybody seemed to agree on the basics—unions and collective bargaining are essential to the kind of culture we have in this country—and the crowd was cheerful and energetic, applauding the speakers at every popular line. The police were respectful and kept a low profile. We had a sense of the other demonstrations—we were told that these demonstrations were being held across the country in all the state capitols—and I don't think people felt very embattled, but even so, it was inspiring to be there with others who felt as I did and to feel that we represented a larger movement than had actually shown up on Beacon Street.

Another rally I went to in front of the State House was several years ago, in favor of gay marriage. It was after the Supreme Judicial Court had construed a new definition of marriage—"two persons" rather than "a man and a woman." The legislature was considering whether to allow a vote by the people on amending the constitution to prevent same-sex marriage. The legislature was inside the building, and we were outside chanting and singing and carrying signs. It was very cold then, too, just like today, and the demonstrators felt very embattled. There were many opponents of gay marriage on the street with us and many strident arguments from people who wanted to quote scripture to us. We had no idea which way the legislature would go. It was going to be one or two votes in either direction that would decide the matter. In the end, the amendment was turned down, and gay marriage as decided by the SJC was saved, and we were saved.

I have spent most of my time since January 2008 studying and writing about the Stonewall Riots, which was another way that American citizens have come together to petition the government for redress of their grievances. The police raided the bar, the customers were thrown out on the street where they ended up rioting, and the police trashed the bar. The police, in three nights of rioting, were never able to control the streets. Some people have asked, "Why didn't the police use their firearms?" I suspect that the answer lies in what is happening in the Middle East. Once the police or the armed forces start firing on unarmed citizens, they have lost the battle. And what the citizens have to do— whether they live in Madison or in Tripoli or Cairo or in Boston or New York—is to be persistent, to keep coming back, to never allow themselves to be permanently run off the street.

Citizens, actually, no matter where they are, own the street, despite the cops and the soldiers. In the end, the gay men and women on the streets of the West Village after the raid on the Stonewall Inn never gave in, and they proved a more powerful force than the cops and the politicians. We have our lives as proof.

18

I think what they said was, "Power to the People!"
March 5, 2011

There are two great areas that are subject to the changes brought by the ebook. First, we now have the ability to publish books without moveable type and without paper, which means we don't need the elaborate methods of shipping and storage that paper books need. We also don't need warehouses, distributors, booksellers in their stores, and paper journals and reviewers. Second, and this is a consequence of the first, we are now liberated from the control of the publishing houses, for now we can buy our books directly from the writer herself, without an intrusive intermediary.

For gay people, these transformations are stupendous. During the last forty years, New York publishers have gradually narrowed our reading to a small range of subjects, and gay people in consequence have stopped buying gay books. A gay man, a "finder" for a literary agent, wrote me last summer that the market for gay literature has "vanished." I don't think gay people are any less interested in gay literature than they used to be, nor are they any less intelligent, but I do think that their refusing to buy gay fiction is a result of the damage that publishers have wreaked on our literature in the last forty years. There is just not a lot of interesting fiction out there.

But now we are free. A writer can write the book he wants to write and, with a minimum of expense, can reformat the book into ePUB or DOCX, thus making it readable on all ereaders. We know how to put these books on the web, and we will find on the web the books we want to read, and sites will grow up to provide us with reviews of new ebooks. This will happen because the ebooks will be there, and the readers will be there, and the need for a site for reviews is already extant, so we will have them.

What we see right now at the beginning of 2011 is the old publishing model trying to retain its old power over the publication of books. Random House just made the news signing a contract with Apple to present its books on iBooks. Neither Random House nor Apple understands the future like we do. We already know we can buy books from anybody. And Apple and their iPad are going to learn to sell books by any writer, too, and not just those under contract with Random House. *Any book by anybody.* We don't have much to wait for, either. Certainly not as long as Johannes Gutenberg. I don't suppose paper books will completely go away, nor will bookstores for the purchase of paper books. But I suspect they will gradually come to be seen as a niche market, there for a certain kind of book or a certain kind of collector. Meanwhile, for the rest of us, the future is already here.

19

It's hard, and we're here to help
March 11, 2011

I read it again last night on Towleroad. The story is about Adam Lambert's track "Aftermath" and quotes Adam's words "about finding the courage to be honest with yourself." We hear this so much that it doesn't raise any comment. We even *say* this, without thinking what it means. The language—*the courage to be honest with yourself*—has been around since the earliest days of gay liberation, and it means that, *if you had courage, if you were honest with yourself,* you would come out now. This implies that the person you're speaking to is not being honest with himself, and the only possible meaning for that is that this person is pretending to himself that he is not gay.

I don't know anybody like that. I think people who hear lines like this know well enough that they are gay. Their question is *What do I do about it?* For many people, perhaps for everybody, *doing something about it* means dealing directly with a dangerous world—in your family and in your community—and that is what is problematic. A kid may not be old enough or strong enough to deal with that dangerous world. Even older boys and men or girls and women could get killed out there or could become so stressed by what is out there that he or she wants to kill himself or herself.

If you had courage. If you were honest. Even though we hear it everywhere, this is totally inappropriate language to apply to teenagers who are struggling and who deserve our support.

20

Worm turns
March 21, 2011

Barney Frank thinks gay marriage is a wedge issue for the Democrats, and ABC reports that 52% are in favor of gay marriage. People say this is a water-shed moment for gay people.

So, we sleep well at night, believing as we do that if you hang in there long enough, the worm turns. Has this worm turned? What are the first signs?

If the goal is to get to a politically-protected class for gay people, then that worm does seem to have turned. There are high-profile indicators, DADT the best one. Gay marriage would be another. The lifting of all inequalities in the INS is another.

But the bigger goal is to get to a point where we don't have serious need for protection, that is, when we are more fully accepted. How close are we to that? An indicator would be the decline in the anti-gay violence statistics. Short of that, we are given polls regularly. What do people think, first, about the various laws and regulations which delegitimize gay people, and then about the more difficult-to-measure issues like attitudes. How do they feel about us?

What is happening here, I think, is the gradual getting-into-alignment of our legal system and our biological and social reality. This is true: our choice of gender object is not a significant factor in defining who we are for the legal system, but right now it still matters a lot to a lot of people, how many we don't know. And of course it matters to us. At some point down the road, it will be possible for us to look at the kinds of differences we bring to the table—everything the gay community has learned about marriage, for example, during its several hundred years in the wilderness—and to see how much respect those differences are given when we begin to talk about them. We are not near there yet.

21

Building a new world
March 28, 2011

When the four principal characters of *Adam in the Morning*, who are, many of them, connected through a local repertory production of *The Tempest*, come off what is for them a world-transforming moment, they sit on the roof outside Bo's bedroom window and watch the sun go down, talking, considering what they want the world to be like now. They've fought the New York cops to a standstill for two nights running, even if they don't know what they want yet.

Bo and Andrew, who are lovers, have been experimenting, since they first met in a class on *What is a man?* at Alternate U on 14th Street. Andrew had said in that class, "The gender roles most of us have been taught enslave us to ways of thinking and acting that aren't native to us. We want to be free. I want to be free, but I am not free, and that is why I am here at this class. I want to be in a room with other men, and I want to talk about how it feels, not to be free." This suggests their method: ask questions, discuss possibilities with each other, take risks, reject the orthodox, see what works.

But this isn't easy, and Bo shows how hard it is. It is really natural to want the other man to make a promise. "I don't know. I think it is hard because I want to control the future, be together always, have this always. I want you to promise me that this will never change." They resist the effort, because it is their freedom that defines them.

Bo and Andrew gather friends, an actor who plays Caliban in *The Tempest,* another who plays Ariel, a woman, Belle, who wants a baby, and a street kid, who hasn't had a home since she was kicked out when she was thirteen.

They press on. They have another night of fighting the cops, and then they have huge questions to answer. How are we to conduct our relationships now? What do we attack first, the NYPD? the SLA? the federal government? Or do we attack the idea of monogamy?

What we see, during the five days of the Stonewall Riots, is four men and two women beginning the process of constructing a new world for themselves.

22

Singing our songs
April 2, 2011

Last Sunday night I attended a concert by the Boston Gay Men's Chorus whose title was *Our True Colors*. The concert was influenced by the *It Gets Better* movement, and during the concert four different men told stories of their youth and coming to adulthood and of the difficulties they faced with unloving families and bigoted, bullying schoolmates. One man told of being pushed to the point of putting a gun in his mouth. The last half of the concert was given over to the extended piece, "Prayers for Bobby," based on the book by Leroy Aarons, music composed by J. A. Kawarsky. Bobby didn't make it. The question was raised by a man I was sitting next to, *Why does the gay community spend so much energy on narratives of pain and sorrow?* This man wanted more positive narratives. Since so many people have survived their horrors, and are now living successful, even triumphant lives, that is a legitimate question. In fact, there was a good bit of positive narrative in the concert Sunday night. "Beautiful," by Linda Perry, and "Firework," by Katy Perry (and others), and the whole thrust of "Prayers for Bobby," and, finally, the energetic and very beautiful encore, "Celebrate." As the concert developed from song to song, I began to realize that the chorus and its director, Reuben Reynolds, had pulled off a very difficult feat. Their concert was closer to the heart of the experience of the gay community than almost any other works of art that we have access to. For the concert had its full measure of pain and sorrow, but it also had its full measure of celebration. Nothing was stinted. It was all there, and, as I told my partner, Courtney, it was like a richly woven tapestry with all the threads, light and dark. Or like a choral piece, in which every singer had something to add. Nobody's story was left out. We seem to find that difficult to do in the gay community.

23

The future arrives before we are ready for it
April 10, 2011

Fair Shaw, who is narrator of *Race Point Light*, finds that each new phase of his life is not what he expected. Shaw has an education, and he has some experience—he was in the Army and on the fringes of the anti-war movement and the civil rights movement—but each time when he finds himself thrown into a new situation, he feels unprepared. The Army, graduate school, marriage, Stonewall, the city at the middle of AIDS. His world seems to change radically every eighteen months. It would be possible to break up *Race Point Light* into at least two novels, and perhaps more, divided after Fair receives a divorce at the end of Part 4, to make an entirely separate novel about a man's life in the city in the middle of AIDS. But that is to make of these two novels, narratives about distinct subjects—a gay man who gets married, and a gay man living in the city in the middle of AIDS— and those subjects have been written about.

What needed to be written about, because no one had done it, is a man who experiences all these things during one lifetime, which is what actually happens to hundreds of thousands of gay men and women in our culture. What would make a gay person get married? What is it like being married? What would make a gay person leave a marriage? What wounds, what scars does he or she have afterward?

How would he or she live after divorce? What would he or she find in the place he or she went after divorce? What are the years of AIDS like in the city? The compelling quality of such a narrative lies in the fact that all these things happen to *the same person*. And the question such a novel would answer would be, *What would that be like?* It would not be a novel about a gay man in a marriage so much as it would be a novel about a gay man who leaves his marriage and moves to the city in the middle of AIDS, and then makes a life for himself in the city with all the memories, objects, relationships, scars, decisions accumulated from earlier decades and earlier lives. It would be in that accumulation that the power of such a novel resides.

Everyone just has to keep going in their lives, from one day to the next, one decade to the next, down to the end, and I didn't want to structure *Race Point Light* in such a way as to imply that anything is ever a fresh start. Before Fair Shaw has gotten over the trauma of his divorce, he is face-to-face with a man who is breathless with pain because he has found out that he has Karposi's sarcoma. One loss is experienced simultaneously with the other loss. After Fair Shaw has made a commitment to a marriage in a pre-Stonewall time, gay men riot in the streets of Greenwich Village, and gay people are now *out and proud*. The gay person finds himself living in two distinct worlds simultaneously, the past and the present and maybe even the future. The future arrives before we are ready for it, and we bear the scars of living in our time. This is uniquely stressful on gay people who came to adulthood in the ten years before Stonewall. They made commitments and promises, and then Stonewall called, "Come out into the street with us!"

24

Getting to safety: 1
April 19, 2011

Today, the paper and the blogs carry the news of the Oregon Study out of Columbia University, funded by the National Institutes of Health and the Fenway Institute in Boston, and published in the journal *Pediatrics*. The study, by Professor Mark Hatzenbuehler, Psychologist at Columbia University, shows that suicide rates among teenagers are dependent upon which county a teenager lives in—the prevalence of same-sex couples, registered Democrats, liberal views in the community, schools with gay-straight alliances, schools with policies against bullying students, schools with anti-discrimination policies that include sexual orientation. The ranking of various counties by these measures is called a social index score. Teenagers who live in counties with the lowest social index scores were 20% more likely to have attempted suicide than gay teenagers in counties with the highest social index scores.

Several years ago, I attended a panel discussion in Cambridge on Gay Youth. One of the panel participants, a young man who was editor of a "youth oriented" magazine, said that the trouble is that if any of us were over thirty, we knew nothing about the lives of gay youth today. He said that the determining factor in the lives of all gay youth up to now was the sense that *I am alone*. There is no one else like me. At least one of the things that coming out meant was coming out into the gay community and the breaking down of that sense of being alone. Today's youth, according to this editor, have the internet. They are never really alone and never even think they are alone.

The teenager in the family with easy access to the internet still may spend his most vulnerable pre-teen years—that is, ten and eleven or twelve—on the internet unaware of what the internet can be used for, still looking for cute cat videos on You Tube. For the internet to be useful in the coming out process for the much younger children, many things have to have come together—the changes in the child's feelings, his having learned what words to apply to his feelings, his discovery that the web is a place for him to look for answers, his learning how to use the web—and different children put all this together in different ways and at different times. I would guess that, if a child has hostile parents, knowing that it is possible to find something different on the web is not going to be very helpful. And if the home is not a welcoming place, then a child faces harsh years before he can get to the safety of that gay-straight alliance in high school.

25

Getting to safety: 2
April 24, 2011

I don't remember being bullied for being gay when I was a kid, but I do remember being given a hard time because I was a sissy. This happened when I was less than ten. I was pretty and wasn't any good with a ball on the playground, and other boys didn't want me on their side. The cruelty never got very bad. What was the worst was my realization that the other guys on the playground pitied me for not being more like a boy, which meant for not being able to play games with balls. In grammar school, I don't think any of us knew what being a "sissy" was, if it had to do with more than the failure to play games with balls.I was aroused by men before I was ten—my dick got hard— but I didn't know what caused it, and I didn't know what to call it. I don't think there was a sexual component to my treatment on the playground. Before about ten, it was all about gender. Later, I figured out that getting hard was always caused by the same thing—some man or boy—and even later I found out what to call it. In high school, what had been called "sissy" in grammar school was called "queer," or "faggot." There was a sexual component, and people knew what it was. Whether the word was "sissy" or "queer," or "faggot," I understood during those early years that I was failing at some basic requirement of being what I was supposed to be. I didn't know exactly what the requirement was—I knew it was bigger than merely playing ball—but I did know I was failing at it. Attempts to help teenagers, who are being bullied or treated cruelly, with programs like *It gets better*, are not addressing the whole problem. Children are being treated cruelly over gender/sexuality issues a long time before they get to high school.

26

Hearts and minds and buckets of blood
May 3, 2011

The Stonewall Riots have been in the news. PBS ran the documentary, "Stonewall Uprising," on American Experience last week. I got out my copy of David Carter's *Stonewall*, originally published in 2004, to compare notes. It's cool seeing gray-haired men, talking about the riots, and then realizing that this gray-haired man is the one in that picture in Carter's book. Forty years ago he was a street kid screaming at the cops. The most powerful memory many of the participants have is of gay people on Christopher Street chasing the cops into the Stonewall and scaring the shit out of them. What came out of the riots was the zap, which was not so much a way to persuade as it was a way to terrorize. Gay liberation also came out of the riots. On the web, I found a story about Larry Kramer and the revival of *The Normal Heart* on Towleroad. I found an interview with him on Salon. Larry is pissed, as usual, and it's us he's pissed at. Present-day gay people are not on the front lines, fighting AIDS or creating new paradigms for community medicine or new ways to take down the establishment. Larry was never one to make his points by persuasion. ACT UP made its points by pouring buckets of blood on the Harvard Medical School front steps and humiliating the Dean. They changed public health as a result.

Then there is the Atlanta law firm, King and Spaulding, who quit the defense of DOMA last week. In a posting by Ari Ezra Waldman, the legal commentator for Towleroad, we are told: "This hiccup in the

House's defense of DOMA illustrates the progress we have made in the court of public opinion and the reason why persuading hearts and minds is the real battle."

Well, maybe. I suspect that, in all these cases, "persuading heart and minds" has worked only after the gay community has used force on its opponents. In the case of King and Spaulding, "persuading hearts and minds" worked only after the very powerful gay lobbying organizations called in all their chips from other big corporations that were clients of King and Spaulding.

The point here is that persuading our opponents to change their hearts and mind is sweet, but in these cases, our opponents didn't actually change their behavior until the gay community got tough.

27

When everything changed, and how that began

May 9, 2011

At about one o'clock in the morning, June 28, 1969, the New York police raided the Stonewall Inn, a seedy gay bar on Christopher Street, which was run by the Mafia, the second time this week. The cops checked the ID of everyone in the bar, and those who had proper identification were released. Each person had to be wearing clothes proper to his or her gender. Those not wearing gender-correct clothes were arrested.

The Stonewall was one of the few bars in all of New York that allowed dancing between same-sex couples. It was a gay bar, right in the middle of the gay neighborhood, and gay people in the Village thought of it as their bar even though it was owned by the Mafia. What the cops were doing was taking away from a disadvantaged population one of the few places where they could be themselves.

At first, as each person was released, she went to the door of the bar and greeted friends already on the street with posing and some camp witticism. Most of the patrons of the bar had been through this before, but tonight the patrons didn't go home. They gathered around the door of the bar and cheered and clapped as each new one came out. Tension was rising.

Then cops dragged out a large woman who resisted the harsh treatment from the cops—they beat her with their billyclubs—and wouldn't go quietly. She fought the cops all the way from the door of the bar to the police car across Christopher Street. When they got her to the door of the car, she put her feet on each side of the door and pushed hard, and the cops couldn't get her in. She broke loose. They recaptured her, beat her, got her into the car again, and she slid through the car to freedom on the other side. The whole large crowd in front of the door of the bar watched silently, tensely. They could hear the sounds of breaking glass as cops used sledgehammers to break up the cash registers, the glass ware, and liquor bottles. Then one voice spoke up, "Why don't you guys help her!" (p. 151). The crowd went insane. The cops got the large woman into the car and drove away, tires slashed.

*

This is just the beginning of the first riot on Saturday morning. I'll pick it up at this point—just as things get insane—in my next post. Hang in there. This is the most important thing that has happened to gay people in a hundred years, or maybe forever. This account was based on David Carter's *Stonewall*, St Martins Griffin, New York, 2004. Page numbers in parentheses are to this edition.

28

More on the hours when everything changed and how that began
May 13, 2011

Around 2:00 AM, on June 28, 1969, the crowd in front of the Stonewall became a mob. They threw things at the cops and at the Stonewall—rocks, paving stones, bricks, empty cans, glass, full cans, trash can lids. There were only ten cops now, facing a mob of five or six hundred very angry men, and gradually the cops retreated toward the door of the Stonewall Inn. Gay people followed them closely, throwing rocks and breaking all the windows facing on Christopher Street. Four gay men managed to pull up a parking meter to use as a battering ram against the Stonewall's main door. Inside, the cops heard the screams of the mob and the shuddering thuds of the parking meter driven into the door. Now the cops trapped inside realized that the enraged gay people on the other side of the door were trying to burn the building down. They were using lighter fluid at first, and then they were trying some kind of fuel—those inside the Stonewall didn't know which kind—in bottles that they tossed inside whenever the cops tried to open the door.

The police didn't have enough gunpower to defeat 600 men. They had visions of being burned alive or of being battered to death by a mob that vastly outnumbered them. The cops were led by Deputy

Inspector Seymour Pine. During World War II, Lt Pine had written the US Army manual on hand-to-hand combat (p. 101) and said later of the riots that he had never been as scared in his life (p. 160). Danny Garvin, one of the rioters, said, "It was like a war" (p. 171). Out in Sheridan Square, the rioters weren't led by anybody. They were the street people, homeless, transsexual, and transgender kids, and they were also what David Carter calls, "conventionally masculine men" (p. 192)—political agitators, troublemakers, and students. They were not the gay people Lt. Pine usually confronted who were so frightened of being exposed as gay people that the cops could do whatever they wanted with them.

These gay people were way out, way sick of the way the cops treated them—why were they raiding *their* bar twice in one week, when everyone knew the cops were paid off? They were determined to terrorize Lt. Pine and his men. Michael Fader, one of the rioters said, "We felt we had freedom at last....The bottom line was, we weren't going to go away. And we didn't" (p. 160). What happened at Stonewall is that gay people, who had never before been demanding and who had always been meek, suddenly turned nasty. Just about all of gay liberation came out of their determination to try to hurt the cops. Before there was a theory of gay liberation, or a gay political movement, there were men in the street fighting cops to be free.

*

This account was based on David Carter's *Stonewall*, St Martins Griffin, New York, 2004. Page numbers in parentheses are to this edition. See also my novel, *Adam in the Morning*, about the six nights of the Stonewall Riots. See the website, *adrianabooks.com* for a full presentation of *Adam in the Morning*.

29

"We lost that wounded look."
May 19, 2011

What's important is how hard we had to fight to get where we are now. There was fighting on Christopher Street very early—from one A.M. to about four A.M.—on Saturday morning, June 28, 1969. And then again that night, and then light skirmishes Sunday, Monday and Tuesday nights. On Wednesday night the *Village Voice* published a couple of homophobic articles about the first night's riotings. Gay men and women were out on the street, fighting the cops again.

Up to the moment of the riots on Christopher Street, what seemed to have defined gay men and women was that terrible things were said about us and *we never fought back*. We never answered the terrible things that were being said about us. We allowed a whole range of psychiatric treatments on ourselves, and that included torture, and we almost never said, "Stop."There were individual voices. Walt Whitman was one, and Gore Vidal was one, and Allen Ginsberg, particularly in *Howl*, was one. There were a few small organizations, such as the Daughters of Bilitis and the Mattachine Society. But what is clear now, looking back, is that there was nobody speaking for our community.

And then, starting with Stonewall, *we fought back*. We got into the street, we jumped on the backs of cops, we threw bricks and paving stones. The men and women on the street seem to have all worked together, even without a leader. Within a month, the Gay Liberation Front was formed, which was big enough and strong enough, and it attracted enough participants to be able to speak for gay New York. Six months later, the Gay Activist Alliance was formed which began solidifying the power of the gay community.

Within a year, both the *Village Voice* and the *New York Times* came around to treating the gay movement seriously and respectfully. Later, the GLF and the GAA led the drive to force the American Psychology Association and the American Psychiatric Association to change their diagnostic manuals by removing the definition of homosexuality as a mental disorder. These changes were not the result of gentle persuasion. They were the result of the gay community having made of itself a power to be reckoned with. On Sunday, Allen Ginsberg went into the wrecked Stonewall Inn. He was quoted in the *Village Voice* in the article by Lucian Truscott IV saying, "The guys there were so beautiful—they've lost that wounded look that fags all had ten years ago." What had happened? How had they lost the "wounded look" they had ten years ago? *They fought back.*

30

How was it there?
May 29, 2011

I intended that the three novels of the Stonewall Triptych be gay novels. When I was writing them, I imagined writing for men and women who had experienced what I was writing about, or something similar. I was going to tell the story of what was happening to the gay people in the small town of Cardiff or to the gay man who grew up in Columbia, South Carolina, or to the gay men and women in the Stonewall Inn on Christopher Street in Greenwich Village, in New York. And when it came time to choose the plot of the novel, I formulated it this way: *Given the murder of my friend Bernie Mallett, what am I to do? Or, Given a homophobic culture in America in the 1940s and 1950s, how am I to learn to live? Or, Given brutal policemen in a homophobic city in 1969, how am I to behave now that the cops have come to Sheridan Square?* I thought that most gay men and women would find all three of these novels familiar—and fertile— ground.

I wanted to write these three novels without reference to heterosexual persons, insofar as that was possible. My characters, for the most part, live inside a gay community or else they live alone. When a gay person picks up these books, I hoped he or she would feel that the world of each of these novels would seem familiar, and he would be acquainted with the issues the characters face and would recognize the outcomes at the end of each of these novels. I wanted *Ceremonies*, and *Race Point Light*, and *Adam in the Morning* to be about the lives of gay men and women who live today. And I wanted gay people to be able to say, *That's the way it was.*

31

Where I found my freedom
June 1, 2011

Mitzi, fifteen years old, transgender, homeless, a fierce fighter, has always known that the private, intimate details of her life seamlessly become public every time she goes onto the street. "I think," Mitzi says, "every time I go on the street I'm giving the finger to everybody in power, and I know that, and I think they know that too." She knows that in 1969 the policies of the Mayor of New York are designed to eradicate her and other street kids like her, but she defeats the Mayor, this fifteen years old girl, every time she walks out on the street.

It's eight o'clock in the evening, Saturday night, June 28, 1969, and Mitzi is walking up Christopher Street with Bo Ravich and Bo's partner, Andrew, and their friend Joseph, going to the second of the three big riots that we know of as the Stonewall Riots. They're talking about their own slowness in getting out on the street and demonstrating their dissatisfaction with the American contract. Bo says, "I never thought there was a gay question that was subject to politics—organizing, speeches, demonstrations, bills in Congress. The gay thing has always seemed to be about something like our freedom to suck cock, and I think I have been embarrassed to put that up for public discussion. It's odd. I didn't think there was any way to change the way things were. Now I do. In just twenty-four hours."

Joseph says, "I remember having a strong connection with the people in Mississippi. We were related, and everybody knew it. They were my brothers and my sisters in Mississippi, and I was going to help them. We were all black, but also we were all getting screwed by the system. The same thing is true here. We're brothers and sisters— we're all fags together—and we all get screwed by the system in just the same way." Joseph continues, "Oppressed people always end up taking to the streets. Through violence. Fanon says that. '*The colonized man finds his freedom in and through violence* '(p. 86). That's what we're doing."

"I like that," Andrew says. "I find my freedom through violence. That's nice. Come on, guys, let's see how much freedom we can find tonight."They walk on up Christopher Street to Seventh. They join the riot, and all of them fight, and they are all of them bloodied, and they find much freedom that night to suck cock.

*

Frantz Fanon, *The Wretched of the Earth*, New York: Grove Press, originally published 1961.The quoted sentence is from this edition.

32

The king, the king's to blame
June 6, 2011

Hamlet, to set things right in Denmark, kills the king. Whatever he has going on in his life with respect to his mother and her second husband, and to the woman with whom he has fallen in love, he has to act against the king, and that is regicide. The audience to that act shout "Treason! Treason!" Since Shakespeare wrote the play in 1601, regicide has become *the* political act of our time. The English did it in the seventeenth century, the French (and Americans) did it in the eighteenth century, everybody did it several times in the nineteenth century. Albert Camus wrote about it in *The Rebel* in 1951.

Today we call it revolution. President Muhammad Hosni Sayyid Mubarak knows about it, President Muammar el-Qaddafi knows about it, President Zine El Abidine Ben Ali knows about it. As each successive dictator in the Middle East has become the object of angry citizens, they learn about it. And what they learn is that the individual citizen feels a hurt, and he connects that with all the other hurts he has felt—and all the hurts his friends have felt—and all these private hurts become a very public hurt which mounts all the way up to the foot of the throne, or, in the more recent cases, all the way to the seat of the presidency.

Not every hurt has a political resolution, but my hunger, joined with yours, becomes a public problem, and, as Laertes says, *the king, the king's to blame*. And he is, too. The Stonewall Riots are our moment of regicide. It is the moment we rebelled, and all these private hurts became very public hurts, and instead of taking the blame on ourselves, as we had done before, we said, *the king, the king's to blame*. And then we deposed the king. Gay men have been speaking truth to power ever since, and we have refused to let *them* tell *us* what to think about ourselves.

33

Pride
June 11, 2011

Today is Gay Pride in Boston. This celebration marks the forty-second commemoration of the Stonewall Riots, and the forty-first Gay Pride march. The first was held in New York in 1970 and was called Christopher Street Liberation Day march. In successive years, other cities held their own Gay Pride marches, most of them on some weekend in June to commemorate the Stonewall Riots. On that first march, people assembled on Washington Place and Waverly Place and then, at two o'clock, walked up Sixth Avenue to Central Park and then to the Sheep Meadow. Good accounts of this first march are in books by David Carter and by Martin Duberman.

A parade or march had never been held before, and the first organizers were very afraid no one would show up. They thought that even if only one thousand people showed up, that would still be the largest gay demonstration ever (as opposed to the size of the Stonewall Riots, which were several thousand people) (Carter, p. 253). Craig Rodwell, the owner of the Oscar Wilde Memorial Book Shop, assumed that they would never get a thousand people to walk from the Village to Central Park. When the march started, participants were intensely afraid of violence.

There were many more people on the sidewalks than in the march, as people hung back, afraid, or unsure whether they wanted to come out publicly. Then, gradually, people stepped off the sidewalk into Sixth Avenue, joining the group in the middle of the street.

The first banner read "Christopher Street Liberation Day 1970" (Carter, p. 253). The first group, with its own banner, was the Gay Activists Alliance. They had two hundred marchers. Other participants had come from Philadelphia, from Washington, and from Baltimore. The Daughters of Bilitis, and the Mattachine Society of New York were there. The Gay Liberation Front marchers included some of the homeless street kids (Carter, p. 254). There were also groups from colleges and universities in Manhattan. In all there were about twenty identifiable groups (Carter, p. 254).

The march was fifteen blocks long by the time it reached 22nd Street (Carter, p. 254), and Carter describes how participants, when they realized how big the march was becoming, became more and more excited. Their excitement—and their joy at being out in the middle of Sixth Avenue among their gay friends—caused others to join them from the sidewalks. Apparently, as their numbers increased, they experienced a kind of euphoria—about themselves, about their community, and about what they had come to do.

The story of this first march is a thrilling one, almost as thrilling as the story of the riots themselves, and I recommend both. In reality, these are small events, even as they seemed huge to the participants, and getting to know them is to get to know a fairly small cast of characters— Craig Rodwell, Sylvia Ray Rivera, Jim Fouratt, Tommy Lanigan-Schmidt, Jackie Hormona, Arthur Evans, Marty Robinson, many of whom appear not only in the histories of these events but in *pictures*. The identities of many others are, unfortunately, lost to history.

It is important to remember today, on Gay Pride Day, that all of this began in a successful application of violence, as gay people resisted the attacks of the New York police. And what we commemorate today, when we march, is that we *fought back*. We should never forget that.

*

David Carter, *Stonewall: The Riots that Sparked the Gay Revolution,* New York: St Martins Griffin, 2004

Martin Duberman, *Stonewall,* New York, A Dutton Book, 1993.

34

Ennis del Mar
June 16, 2011

I watched *Brokeback Mountain* a couple of nights ago and then read the story again, and I noticed how carefully Annie Proulx lays out Ennis del Mar's predicament.

In the summer of 1963, when Ennis del Mar and Jack Twist met, Wyoming and Texas still had sodomy laws, and Ennis and Jack were subject to prosecution for what they did together in the pup tent.

In 1967, when Ennis saw Jack for the first time after Brokeback, he tells him about his dad and his brother T. E. and about the tire iron and the bloody body in the ditch (p. 29). Whatever Jack thinks about this story, for Ennis the danger is real. He says, referring back to their kiss on the staircase, "We do that in the wrong place we'll be dead" (p. 27). At the end of *Brokeback Mountain*, both the movie and the story, Ennis listens to Lureen tell him about Jack's death, and he concludes, "They got him with the tire iron" (p. 45).

Even before Ennis met Jack, he already knew what he was going to do with his life. "In 1963 when he met Jack Twist, Ennis was engaged to Alma Beers" (p. 5). That was settled. "In December Ennis married Alma Beers and had her pregnant by mid-January" (p. 18). The reader isn't told what Ennis actually thinks about what he's doing. He does this, and then he does that, what's expected of him. "The second girl was born" (p. 19), and he's trapped. He doesn't struggle.

Lying in bed with Jack, Ennis says, "I like doin it with women, yeah, but Jesus H., nothing like this." Then Ennis describes his problem. "Took me about a year a figure out it was that I shouldn't a let you out a my sights. Too late then by a long, long while" (p. 26). Too late. But it's too late in a different way than the one Ennis means. It was already too late by the time he finds Jack at the beginning back in 1963.They can't change what they are, and they can't change how they feel, and they can't get away from Wyoming—"All the travelin I ever done is goin around the coffeepot lookin for the handle," Ennis says (p. 40)— and Ennis sums it up, "I'm stuck with what I got" (p. 29). It's a mistake to read *Brokeback Mountain* as if it were about a man who made a mistake. Ennis did not make a mistake. When the guy came who presented him with an erect cock, Ennis knew what it was and what it was for, and what it meant. His tragedy is that he also knew he couldn't do much about it. And he knew this from the beginning.

*

Ann Proulx, *Brokeback Mountain,* New York: Scribner, 2005. Originally published in *The New Yorker,* October 13, 1997. Page numbers in this posting are to this Scribner edition.

Brokeback Mountain, Director Ang Lee, Starring Heath Ledger, Jake Gyllenhaal, Anne Hathaway, Michelle Williams

35

Jack's Narrative
June 20, 2011

A friend said, on reading some story I had written, "Your character missed the whole sixties."

What my friend meant was that my character had missed my friend's idea of the sixties. My character lived through the sixties in a heterosexual marriage, in middle-sized cities in the upper South and in the Midwest. My friend lived through the sixties as a gay man in Boston, and he wanted my character to come out at a certain point, be activist leftist politically, be anti-war and pro civil rights, do drugs, and have uninhibited gay sex.

That is absurd, of course. There are many ways to experience any decade.

There is some evidence that Jack Twist had a more stereotypical time of the sixties than Ennis del Mar. He smokes marijuana, he seems more experienced in sex than Ennis, and he seems less tied down to one bit of geography. When Jack presents his erect cock, Ennis knows enough to know what to do with it but he has already been deeply enough rooted in his times to refuse Jack's invitation to the rest of it.

What we're getting to here is the narrative we tell ourselves. Men experience their times individually, as Ennis and Jack show us, and it may be that this is getting more and more true. There are rumors that "coming out" is not universally necessary any more. Imagine the freedom of being able to live your life without owing that particular action to anybody. That leads to another freedom—the freedom to refuse to say whether you are gay or straight, as some people refuse to fill in the blank *male or female* as an intolerable intrusion of privacy.

Imagine what Ennis's life would have been like if he could have done what he did do, without feeling that he was doing something wrong—or that he needed to declare anything. What if he could have worked out a shared devotion to both Alma and Jack? Or left her for him without the fear of the tire iron? What if we gave each other the freedom to live through the sixties—or any other decade—in the way each person wanted, as he explored his feelings and took on the obligations and responsibilities that he chose and personally assumed? In short, what would it be like if I could write my own narrative and didn't have to live *your* narrative?

36

"We were outgunned."
June 28, 2011

On Saturday and Sunday morning, the images of the celebrating crowds in front of the Stonewall Inn reminded many of us of the images of the very angry crowds in front of the same inn, almost exactly 42 years earlier. Then, there were no professional photographers, and the black and white images were grainy and out of focus, and nobody was posing for the photographer. The commentaries on Friday night's vote pointed out that, at last, we have come from the Stonewall Riots to Gay Marriage, from the initial eruption of gay liberation to the final fulfillment of gay liberation. This linkage invites a comparison and emphasizes that the first was violent, and the second was a legislative act. I saw in some places (but can't find them now) pictures of the Stonewall Riots, side by side with pictures of the celebrations on Friday night on the same block of Christopher Street. How far we've come, it was easy to think, from anger to celebration!

And yet, look at how the Times describes the series of actions that took place to bring about victory. In "Behind N.Y. Gay Marriage, an Unlikely Mix of Forces, by Michael Barbaro," the reporter describes the changing dynamic, "where Wall Street donors and gay-rights advocates demonstrated more *might and muscle* than a Roman Catholic hierarchy" Later, Barbaro says, "it was clear the church had been outmaneuvered by the highly organized same-sex marriage coalition, with its sprawling field team and, especially, its Wall Street donors." The emphasis in these paragraphs is on the use of force, use with a military tinge. "'In many ways,' acknowledged Dennis Poust of the New York State Catholic Conference, 'we were *outgunned*.'" Instead of a discussion of moral issues or even of legal issues, the "road to gay marriage" is being presented in terms of physical struggle, and the Governor, the Wall Street donors, and the gay-rights advocates were stronger. and better at fighting that their opponents. Progress forward has a violent edge, and it is here that the Stonewall Riots and the "road to marriage in New York" belong in the same sentence.

It is hugely satisfying to me that our side proved stronger and better fighters than the Republicans and the Roman Catholic Church. That's just so goddamn satisfying. One of the lessons of the Riots was that the days of our being weak were now over, and from now on we were going to be the fiercest son-of-a-bitch to walk down Christopher Street. And sometimes we are. And when that happens, I thank my good luck that I live in these times when gay people are fierce as well as free.

37

Betraying the great history of gay people
July 4, 2011

There is a range of ways men can array themselves with one another, but most of the traditional forms of relationship depend more or less absolutely on the concept of ownership. The two people in the relationship own each other. They can't have sex with anyone outside the relationship, they can't spend time with someone outside the relationship. These forms of coupling come at a high cost, as men wander, and as both sides in the relationship levy charges of betrayal.

Some gay male couples avoid this pattern by specifically not claiming ownership. A man is free to go and come as he wants without being questioned by his partner. No one in such a relationship is ever asked, "Why didn't you come home last night?" Or, "Where were you last night?" Each man in the relationship is absolutely free to do exactly what he wants to do whenever he wants to do it and does not ever expect to be questioned on it.

In such a relationship, both men avoid making promises— specifically the promises in the traditional marriage service about monogamy and about staying together till death. The assumption is that these couples will stay together as long as it is good for both of them. These relationships are often opened up to include a third partner or a number of other partners who stay temporarily.

There are, of course, other ways for men to come together. Books have been written on the subject. My point here is that many of us know men whose relationships would have to be described in a whole range of ways. What is notable about the gay community is that, in the centuries during which we have been excluded from heterosexual marriage, we have used our time well. We've explored what was possible, determined to find out what worked and what didn't. Many of us have concluded that ownership of one's partner doesn't work, and all that emotional energy expended on expressions of betrayal and grief because the other person has acted the way many men act is merely wasted energy. We have learned that sex is not the same thing as love and that the quickest way to destroy a relationship is to act as if everything were to depend on *sexual* fidelity.

Now then, at this point, when we are about to start marrying legally in ever-increasing numbers, it would be a shame if any large numbers of us forgot the rich history of gay people, forgot the ways we learned to act when legal marriage was closed to us, forgot that we learned years ago that feelings of betrayal are really just wasted energy, and forgot that we know more about what men are sexually than anyone else in our culture. If we start arranging our relationships as if we were straight people, presided over by a priest, we will have betrayed ourselves and we will have betrayed the great history of gay people.

38

Bear Week in Provincetown
July 20, 2014

I think the whole idea behind Bear Week is that the community is exploring images of maleness. In the past, maleness has had something to do with images of male beauty—think of anything by Michelangelo or Perseus with the Head of Medusa by Cellini—and bears have altered that to something rougher, something less refined, something more mature, bald rather than shaved. Bears and their cubs. It is an interesting, and a sexy, idea.

During Bear Week in Provincetown, bears come from all over the United States, Europe, and Australia and New Zealand to celebrate the look and style. By all accounts, the restaurant staffs find the bears great visitors in Provincetown, friendly, open, easy to wait on, sexy, thoughtful, and generous.

While many of the men present themselves in an exaggerated image of maleness, as hairy bears, there were many other things going on in Provincetown during Bear Week. On Monday night, they hold a contest for the audience's approval for the best drag act, and all three of the judges were in drag, although not all the contestants. On Tuesday night the show was Peter Pansy, with a guy playing Peter. Every night on Commercial Street, barkers were in such costume that a passerby couldn't tell what gender they were—what they had started out and what they aimed for now. Courtney and I stayed in a new house in the West End, and we found that men staying in nearby houses called to us when we hung on the railing of our deck. A warm friendly open community.

Walking into the West End on Commercial Street, late one afternoon this week, Courtney and I passed two men with small children. It was such an ordinary sight that it was not until we had gone another hundred yards that I focussed on the fact that the two men were together and the children were theirs. Provincetown spends time and energy exploring questions of gender, and when a person is there, he's passing among a whole variety of genders without quite realizing it. This is not so much experimenting with gender issues. I think the experimenting is long over in Provincetown. What's happening is those of us at the end of Cape Cod are employing all the varieties of gender we've discovered and are showing them off to each other.

Another important thing happened this week. A panel of the Ninth Circuit Court of Appeals has lifted the stay of Judge Phillips' decision declaring DADT unconstitutional and then has apparently stayed the implementation of its own stay. It's dizzying, I know. A very good commentator on these matters is Ari Ezra Waldman, in Towleroad.

At this moment, the Congress, the Executive Branch, and the Courts are all twisted up over gay matters. They are making fools of themselves. Provincetown led the way years ago and continues to lead the way into the future.

39

That which does not kill us, makes us stronger
July 31, 2011

For the last few weeks, I have been corresponding with a man I knew briefly at a school in the South in 1957 and 1959, and, as may be usual in such exchanges, we attempt to find out how we remember it in 1957 and—very gingerly—to find out how we are today. It is a delicate maneuver. I think he liked the school then, and I didn't.

The school was a conservative stronghold in the South and not a good place to be if you were a gay kid. I knew I was gay, and I needed to figure out what to do about it. I was naive and didn't know this school would not be able to give me what I needed. In 1957, in the South, there were just damned few gay men out there on whom I could pattern my life or that I could learn from. In that, this school failed me.

I left this school after two years. Afterward, I did the wrong things—I went into the Army, and instead of starting to write as I wanted, I went to graduate school. I planned to become an academic. I got married. Looking back on it, it seems like everything I did was a deflection from what I really wanted to do. It wasn't until I was middle-aged that I began to live as I had always meant to live. Since then, I have lived without any reference to that school in the South. I live in a gay community among gay or gay-friendly folks, and I write my gay novels.

But occasionally I am invited to exchange letters with other men who experienced that school in the South. In these exchanges, what I look for is that the other man sees how brutal those years were, and how dangerous for gay kids. And now, today, what I look for is acknowledgment that the people I am dealing with have learned what was wrong about the culture in 1957 and have *changed* as I have.

In the years since that school in the South, I got a doctorate and learned about literature. I taught college for eighteen years—Shakespeare every term—and later, when it came time to write my gay novels, I found I was hugely affected by my experience in the classroom. And I had my children, who are with me still, and whose children are with me still, and who enrich me and my partner still.

Life is interesting that way. If I had been given a chance to think about it, I would have said, "I never meant to get married," but I did get married, and now that I am doing what I always meant to do with my life, I find that I do it better, deeper, with more conviction, because first I did those things I didn't ever mean to do. In that way, the homophobia at that school in the South—because I had to learn what it was and to fight against it—has been a gift that keeps on giving.

*

For a full, fictional treatment of this kind of life, see *Race Point Light*.

40

The easiest way to get into the future
August 8, 2011

Life is tough, but it is tougher if you don't tell the truth about it. The hardest part of growing up gay in the years after World War II was not knowing what the truth was. People lied to us and about us—people and institutions and organizations, governments and religions—and it was difficult to know the truth. Then it got to be hard to determine where those lies came from.

I was ten years old, and I didn't know how to fight against all of them—the president, the newspaper, preachers, the governor, my teachers, my scout leader, my grandparents, aunts and uncles, my parents—who laid down what I was supposed to believe about myself. I was really unsure whether or not I was supposed to fight against any of them. I was an adolescent, and I was surrounded by all these hard things people were saying, and I didn't have any idea what to do, because I wasn't sure that they weren't right.

At first, I thought, my goal was to find a way to make the pain stop. The other was just too big a job. I ran away when I was eighteen, and when I was twenty, and twenty-three. I tried to find a way of living that didn't hurt so much, and then, later, I tried, piece by piece, to find what was causing it. This little bit comes from these people. That little bit comes from those folks. But if you can't get away and you can't make it stop, then you start thinking, I must \deserve this. For decades it has been easy for gay people to think we were somehow guilty.

So it's necessary that we search out the truth and then tell it, every little bit of it and never forget it. This is the world we live in. It's the only way to move into the future. We have to determine and then remember what happened. For example, we can't forget that federal public health officials under Reagan said they had "plenty" of money to fight AIDS. And when we have determined who said what and who did what, we can't forget what we know, that these people—among them the public health people under Reagan, the Republicans who provided the votes to pass DOMA and DADT, and all the sorry lot of them under Bush II—committed great crimes, and they were never charged. We must never forget who the criminals are. If we forget that, we'll have forgotten our history.

41

Proust, publication, and the danger of leaving it to publishers

August 14, 2011

Marcel Proust submitted a manuscript of his novel, À *la recherche du temps perdu*, to the Parisian publisher Eugène Fasquelle, in October 1912. This was the first time the book had been presented for publication. Fasquelle turned it down, saying he didn't want to risk publishing something "so different from what the public is used to reading."

Two more publishers turned it down, and, on the fourth publisher, Proust offered to pay the costs of publication. This fourth publisher accepted the offer, and À *la recherche du temps perdu* was published in November 1913, in an edition of 1750.

What is interesting here is the set of forces surrounding the publication of a book—the writer, the book, the publisher, the book-buying public. The publisher is sensitive to giving the public what it wants, which is a good thing, but if all publishers were equally sensitive to the habits of the public in this way, Proust's book would never have been published. There is also the question of *what does the public want?* It is most convenient for the publisher if it can be said that "the public" wants "best sellers."

If publishers stick too rigidly to their idea of what the public wants, then *different* books will never get published. This is of particular danger for minorities, whose literature may be weakened. Or if "different" books do get published, readers may have forgotten how to read them. Lydia Davis, the translator of *Swann's Way* (Penguin), addressing the difficulty of reading Proust, attributes this difficulty to several factors, "one [of which] is that the interest of this novel, unlike that of the more traditional novel, is not merely, or even most of all, in the story it tells." (p. xvi) She goes on to say, "A reader may feel overwhelmed by the detail of this nuance and wish to get on with the story, and yet the only way to read Proust is to yield, with a patience equal to his, to his own unhurried manner of telling the story." (p. xvi)

This is important, because I think we are in a similar situation, where American publishers hesitate to publish books that are different or challenging and Americans are consequently limited in what they can read. This is important also because this French writer, Marcel Proust, who had difficulty getting his book into print, wrote what many people say is the most profoundly important gay novel of the twentieth century.

*

Marcel Proust, *Swann's Way*, trans. with an Intro. and Notes, by Lydia Davis. New York: Viking Penguin, *p. xiii.*

42

But why should any of us read it?
August 21, 2011

In Search of Lost Time, by Marcel Proust, one of the first gay novels by a major writer, was published between 1913 and 1927, in Paris, in seven volumes and 4,300 pages (in the Modern Library translation into English). It is about a young boy growing up and coming to adulthood among the bourgeoisie and Parisian aristocracy during the period just before and just after the first world war. It moves so slowly that a person might think it had almost no story. In 2011, the gay man in the street might ask, What does this have to do with me? It is so long, it is so slow, it was written a hundred years ago, and I have pressing business.

And yet, in the hundred years that it has been out there, *In Search of Lost Time* has solidified a firm literary reputation. The novelist Graham Greene has called it "the greatest novel of the twentieth century." Somerset Maugham called it "the greatest fiction to date." The question here is why should gay people read it? Particularly in an age of DADT or DOMA or same-sex marriage?

For several reasons. These are good stories—the story of the narrator as he grows up and discovers the truth about his culture. The story of Robert de Saint-Loup, who dies on the Western Front, of the Baron de Charlus and his various seductions, of Swann and of Swann and Odette, of the rise of Mme Verdurin, among scores of others. But the greatest story is that of the narrator as he discovers the soft underbelly of Paris—hypocrisy, lying, pretense, values which will not be unfamiliar to readers in 2011.

Much of it is very very funny, one example of which is the scene at the beginning of the novel when Swann is arriving and Marcel and his mother and grandmother and grandfather are preparing to receive him, and Marcel's great aunts are discussing how to thank Swann for the case of Asti he has sent them. There is this kind of comedy, and then there is the much deeper comedy reflected by the salon of the Verdurins and the reception of the Prince and Princesse de Guermantes when all of Parisian society seems to be exposed.

There is superb writing. Check out this:

> As in that game enjoyed by the Japanese in which they fill a porcelain bowl with water and steep in it little pieces of paper until then undifferentiated which, the moment they are immersed, stretch and twist, assume colors and distinctive shapes, become flowers, houses, human figures firm and recognizable, so now all the flowers in our garden and in M. Swann's park, and the water lilies of the Vivonne, and the good people of the village and their little dwellings and the church and all of Combray and its surroundings, all of this which is acquiring form and solidity, emerged, town and gardens alike, from my cup of tea. *Swann's Way*, p. 48

Here is a bit from the middle of the novel, from the seduction scene between Baron de Charlus and Jupien, the waistcoat-maker.

> The latter [Baron de Charlus], resolved to precipitate matters, asked the waistcoat-maker for a light, but immediately remarked, "I'm asking you for a light, but I see I've forgotten my cigars." The laws of hospitality prevailed over the rules of flirtation. "Come inside, you'll be given everything you want," said the waistcoat-maker on whose face disdain gave way to joy. *Sodom and Gomorrah*, p. 8.

If you care about our history—the history of gay people—this is the one of the first and the greatest contribution we've made to literature, and so it's here for you to read. It's ours. It's us. It's demanding. It will stretch your abilities. It will make you a better reader for everything else you read. And it will show you that most of the novels you read come from, by comparison, a narrow spectrum of literature and are small, indeed.

This giant novel by Marcel Proust is another reason to be proud to be gay.

*

Marcel Proust, *Swann's Way*, trans. Lydia Davis. New York: Viking-Penguin, 2003

—————, *Sodom and Gomorrah,* trans. John Sturrock. New York: Viking-Penguin, 2003

43

Living in the long tail: 1
September 3, 2011

Last week, Ewan Morrison, writing in The Guardian, asked, "Are books dead?" and "Can authors survive?" He was writing in the context of the Edinburgh International Book Festival and his belief that the "publishing industry is in terminal decline." It is an interesting article, different from anything else I've read, and worth wide distribution for the questions it raises.

Morrison says that big sellers like Barnes & Noble and Amazon are now selling more ebooks than paper books. What are the consequences of this momentous fact? Morrison notes that the major publishers are all suffering financial straits and not giving writers their accustomed advances. Many writers already are skipping agents and publishers and publishing their ebooks on the internet. He looks down the road a generation and finds "the book" surviving but writers, oddly, not. If, today, a bookseller can sell a million copies of one book, one of the Harry Potter books for example, in the future that same bookseller may be able to make the same amount of money by selling ten books each from one hundred thousand authors, a situation we are now beginning to approach with the small sales of hundreds of thousands of authors on Amazon. This phenomenon is called the "long tail"—those hundreds of thousands of authors each selling ten books, all on the internet, their sales showing on the "long tail" of the graph. Eventually, he believes, writers will be infinitely numerous and none of them will be paid for their work, a situation which he believes has almost arrived in the music industry.

If he is right, this is as depressing as hell.

But there are some significant omissions in his argument. He says, "Most notable writers in the history of books were paid a living wage." This is not true. In our own history, Emily Dickinson was not, Herman Meville was not, and while Morrison scorns the Romantic myth that writers must survive in a garret, I would guess that most American writers are fairly poor people. There are only a few in every generation who actually make a substantial income from their writing. Writers get by on grants, or by teaching creative writing at the local college, or by some other income-producing work. A writer whose career I have followed since 1963 has never earned a living wage from her writing, but she has been a publishing writer for all of those years. The class of people that Morrison seems to be concerned about—professional writers of literary fiction who live on the income from their writing—seems not to have existed as a class until recently, and it may be entirely the creation of the new mega-publishers.

The questions that Morrison raises—the future of the book and of publishing in the age of the ebook and of epublishing—are important because my blog, the Stonewall Triptych, exists to bring attention to my three ebooks which I have collected under the name, the Stonewall Triptych. Morrison's essay skips over the extent to which the publishing industry of the last fifty years created the situation in which writers like me are doing what I am doing, that is, using the internet to publish their books.

More on all this in my next posting.

44

Living in the long tail: 2
September 9, 2011

The "long tail," as it applies to the book industry, is described as a graph of the sales of books. If there are twenty-two books for sale, the one with the most sales would be on the left, with a tall bar. And then, stretching out to the right, each of the other books for sale would have their bars, shorter than the first, in a "long tail," indicating fewer and fewer sales. This graph could describe the business pattern of Amazon.com, which survives on a few sales each of thousands and thousands of books. In the world of digital books, the seller will sell fewer and fewer copies of more and more books. While the publisher may survive in the digital world, a writer probably couldn't. According to some commentators, the move to digital books means that the economic framework that supports writers is disintegrating. In the long tail, a writer cannot sell enough books to survive economically. Ewan Morrison, in his article "Are Books Dead, and Can Authors Survive?" published in The Guardian, points to the danger in the age of ebooks: "Every industry that has become digital has seen a dramatic, and in many cases terminal, decrease in earnings for those who create "content." Morrison says that "writing has already begun its slide towards becoming something produced and consumed for free."

In what Morrison must know is a demand for Utopia, he says, "Authors must respect and demand the work of good editors and support the publishing industry, precisely by resisting the temptation to 'go it alone 'in the long tail. In return, publishing houses must take the risk on the long term; supporting writers over years and books, it is only then that books of the standard we have seen in the last half- century can continue to come into being."

But the cat is already out of the bag. Even if we wanted to, we cannot return to the world of print publishing that existed before epublishing and ebooks. The advance of technology is unstoppable, and there is the very very unprincipled behavior of the print publishing industry before ebooks. Years ago, my agent said of a manuscript I had submitted, "This is a wonderful book, but no publisher in New York will publish it." What loyalties do I owe to that agent, and to the "publisher in New York" now that times are difficult?

While Morrison's article in The Guardian raises truly interesting and important questions, we are past the time when his proposals have merit. What faces us now is the need to ascertain the questions we should be addressing now, living as we do, in the "long tail." What will keep writers writing and readers reading?

45

"I don't care what you are, gay or straight, I love you."
September 16, 2011

"Mommy!"

"What? What's the matter?"

"I don't know how you can say that."

"What?"

"That you love me, but you don't care what I am." "Well,
I do. I love you, and I don't care whether you like
boys or girls."

"But it's different, liking boys and liking girls. And if you
love me, I want you to know that it's different and why it's
different."

"I do. Of course I do."

"Then you need to say it."

"Say what?"

"That you know how it's different, and you love that too."

"Oh, Victoria, you know I do."

"You tell me you do, but you don't say it."

"Say what, Victoria."

"That you know how it's different and that you love that

too."

"Victoria, you are never satisfied. You are always asking for something else from me. Something more."

"Mommy. I'm just asking you to say it."

"Say *what*?

"That you love what I feel, too."

"Well, I do."

"And not say, *you don't care.*"

"Victoria, what's the difference?"

"It's the way I feel. I'm afraid there's a difference and that we don't know what it is, and that we don't see it and are missing it and that it's really important."

46

This one is gone.
September 21, 2011

Repealing Don't Ask, Don't Tell is a big one for me. I served in the Army in the late fifties, and I remember condescending sergeants talking about the "pitter patter of little feet in the barracks" and claiming to know everything that happened in their barracks. Other soldiers—a few of them—called me "queer." When I asked a man I knew where I could go and be homosexual and also be respected, I was told that maybe I ought to go live in Europe. But in any case, I got through my two years without being put out.

It never did really have to do with unit cohesion. There are too many studies out there telling the Pentagon that unit cohesion would not be affected. What it had to do with was stigma. A certain kind of straight man wanted to keep gay men stigmatized, which put us off limits and made it seem safe to straight men. *I'm a man, and you're a queer.*

The other great stigma from the post war years was imposed by psychiatrists. That one—that we were mentally ill—was lifted in the early seventies through the action of the Gay Activists Alliance.

The goal of gay liberation since Stonewall has been to lift these stigmas and to make it OK to be gay, and we've been doing that, one stigma at a time. The next one, I think, is going to be DOMA, which doesn't have to do with marriage so much as it has to do with their wanting to assert that we're unworthy. It's a way of their saying, *I'm worthy, You're queer.*

The big gay rights organizations have been sending out emails today, all saying, *there's a lot left to do.* They're right. There's still a lot to do, but after today, less than there was yesterday.

47

The Kindle and freedom of choice
October 11, 2011

The direction we should be going toward is toward freedom. We need to remember this at every step, so that when somebody takes us in the wrong direction, we will know it immediately.

In the contemporary world—the one outside my window—I am free to walk down the street and to drop into any bookstore I pass and buy a book, and if I can read the language the book is written in, I am able to read the book. But that world appears to be ending, and something very different is happening with ereaders and ebooks.

On Wednesday, Amazon introduced four new Kindle models—Kindle, Kindle Touch, Kindle Touch 3G, and Kindle Fire—at a range of prices, from $79 to $199. For Amazon to make money off the Kindle, it has to link each Kindle to its resources in the Kindle store *and not let the reader buy his books anywhere else.* Amazon makes money off the trapped reader.

Most manufacturers of ebooks do this—link their ereaders to a book store and *not let the reader buy his books anywhere else.* This is less freedom, not more, than we had under the old publishing.

To get us going in the right direction again, manufacturers have formatted books in ePUB. ePUB is a free and open ebook standard by the International Digital Publishing Forum.This is a significant step in the right direction. But manufacturers add DRM to their ePUB, and now, none of them can read each other's files. This needs to change. What we want is to be able to buy an ereader that can read a book from any source. We want to have these DRMs removed.

At this moment, a writer can take his or her novel and format it in ePUB *without a DRM,* sell it on the web, and all ereaders can read it except the Kindle, which will not read ePUB from any source. But purchased books from the big book stores can still only be read on that book store's ereader. This is not freedom.

As long as we are not free, it doesn't matter how many models Kindle brings out, we are still trapped by the Kindle store and the taste of its buyers. Or the iBooks store. Or the Barnes & Noble store. Yesterday I checked these three book stores for the titles of five books I read during the summer of 2010. Even now, a year later, two of the books were not available in any bookstore in any ebook format. Three of the titles were available only on *Amazon.com* for Kindles. As the print-publishing industry continues to collapse, we are going to be more and more dependent on ereaders and the ereaders' stores, and the ereaders' buyers, and instead of being more free—this is what the digital revolution promised, we thought—we will be less free. There will be just us, our ereaders, and our ereaders' bookstores, and the books their buyers choose for us to read. This is not a situation gay readers want to be caught in.

48

Me and my buddy and the Army, fifty years later

October 11, 2011

I got an email two days ago from a man whose name I haven't heard in fifty years. The email said, "Are you the Dwight Cathcart that was stationed in Yakima, Washington. 1960-1961?" This man and several others and I were in the Army together and formed a little group who went into town drinking and sometimes went on passes together. One of these guys was married, and we spent a lot of time at his house in town. We were close friends. I didn't tell any of them that I was gay.

Now, it's fifty years later, and everything is different. Before this man even found me, he found my web page advertising my gay novels, so when I wrote him back and outlined what I had done in the last fifty years or so, I told him, "In 1983 I separated from my wife and got a divorce in 1984, and then I came out." I told him about my partner for the last twenty-one years.

I was interested in the way I felt about that exchange. I found that I felt apprehensive, a little, about what he was going to say. We were friends fifty years ago. We liked each other. I think we had each other's back, as the saying is. I suppose all of those guys must have suspected something about me, and there was nothing that I knew about them that would lead me to think that any of them would attack me now for being gay. But there was something else. This man might say, "Why didn't you tell me?"

I was surprised at my anxiety. Is this guy going to understand why I didn't tell him back then? I didn't know. He went hiking in Arizona before he could respond to what I had told him.

But what I do know is that, at least in my generation, coming out is still a big fucking deal.

49

Unthinkable ideas
October 17, 2011

Some ideas are unthinkable, then they become thinkable. This happens all the time. I suspect that for the vast majority of people in this country, same-sex marriage was unthinkable right up to the moment they had to start thinking about it. They had never seen it, they had no history of thought about it, no experience with it. This happened to me around the fact of my being gay. I couldn't think that I *had* rights. Every time I thought about my being gay, I thought about the stigmas we carried—criminals, mentally ill, sinful—but Stonewall said gays have rights. This was a whole different story.

I was forced into thinking about these matters by an article on the death of Frank Kameny, the founder of Mattachine Washington, and a participant in the Stonewall Riots and, it seems, in every significant gay rights action for decades after. The article is by David Carter, who has his own claim to our gratitude, since he is the author of the book-length study of the Stonewall Riots, *Stonewall*. Kameny had been a cartographer with the Army Map Service and in 1957 was fired for being gay. Kameny sued and took his case to the Supreme Court. He wrote a classic statement of the case for gay rights under the constitution, but, according to Carter, "in 1961, the Supreme Court was not ready to hear this analysis, and it did not take the case." Carter quotes Barbara Gittings, who was also there at the beginning of

Mattachine, saying, "before I met Frank … I had a very inchoate idea of how we could solve our problems. … Frank came along and he had this very strong, very definite philosophy, and it crystallized my thinking. 'Well, yes, of course. If you take the position that Frank has taken, then you get a very clear view of what you have to do, and you don't have to fumble around anymore." '

How does an idea become thinkable?

One of the important questions of our time is just this one. Even before the governments could think about marriage and the military and adoption and the rest of them, majorities have formed to demand these changes. How did this happen? What did we do? *(So we can do it again?)*

50

Love is never a joke
October 24, 2011

About midway through *Law of Desire,* the movie by Pedro Almodovar (1987), Antonio, played by a young and beautiful Antonio Banderas, asks Pablo, a movie director who is very self-centered and seems always to be doing lines of coke, "Who is the boy in the letter, that Juan?"

It is a moment in the movie when Antonio, who says, "I'm what I should be," is trying to manipulate himself into Pablo's bed.

Antonio continues. "He seems very much in love with you."

Pablo answers. "He isn't." Then he says, "That letter is a joke." Antonio has been stalking Pablo since the beginning of the movie.

He says, "Love is never a joke."

In a culture in which Pablo finds it impossible to treat seriously what Antonio is offering and in which the love between two men is often treated exactly as a joke, the work of this movie is to show how very serious love between two men can be. This movie moves toward tragedy, and its method is operatic.

Eventually Antonio kills Juan, the boy that Pablo has been toying with—throws him off a cliff in the moonlight—and then, after an hour with Pablo, Antonio kills himself—sacrifices himself to Pablo's learning what *love* means.

The concluding image of the story is of Pablo, kneeling on the floor in front of a May Cross, cradling the naked body of Antonio and sobbing.

*

And now, Pedro Almodovar's new movie, *The Skin I Live In,* opened in the US October 14, 2011, but has not come to Boston, so I haven't seen it yet.

51

A moment of love
October 28, 2011

When I saw *Law of Desire*, in 1987, I was a couple of years into writing *Ceremonies*. I think one of the reasons the movie was so exciting to me–so thrilling—was that Almodovar was showing me something that I hadn't seen before. I know now that Proust had written about it in *In Search of Lost Time*, and Christopher Isherwood had written about it in *A Single Man*, and André Gide in just about everything he wrote. But at the time I hadn't read all those books—hadn't read them with understanding—and what I had in front of me was Almodovar's movie, *Law of Desire*, with its incredible concluding image.

In 1987 I was writing my book about what happened to all of us in Bangor, Maine, during the summer of 1984 after Charles Howard was murdered. But aside from the immediate task of turning our 1984 experiences into a book, I didn't have an idea of what I was about. I had always had a sense that the book I was writing was not like any other gay books. But different in what way? How? Why?

When Pablo cradled Antonio's naked body at the end of *Law of Desire*, the image they make—pieta in front of the altar, the one still alive sobbing with grief—echoes back as far as the Bible and the Gospels, and, of course, courses through six hundred years of Western art. Pablo and Antonio do not make reference to a particular religious image or even to anything religious. What they do, when Pablo cradles Antonio's body, is to express forgiveness, understanding, regret, gratitude and grief, in the context of the powerful symbolism of a moment of love, in which the younger person has sacrificed himself for the good of the older.

Law of Desire, with its luminous concluding image, urged me to expand my horizons, seek more, attempt larger things, make bigger bets, and change the kind of literature that gay fiction might be, in my novel *Ceremonies.*

52

Mourn no longer for Malone
November 6, 2011

Sometimes a work of art does not present itself so that we know who it is about. *Maurice*, by E. M. Forster, seems to be about Maurice Hall, and then it seems to be about Maurice and Clive Durham together, and it is only later that the reader discovers the novel is about Maurice, and about Maurice Hall and Alec Scudder. This is important because *Maurice* isn't about failure between Maurice and Clive but about success between Maurice and Alec.

The *Law of Desire, by* Pedro Almodovar, seems at first to be about Pablo, the director, and his love for Juan, and it is only late in the movie that it begins to be apparent that *Law of Desire* is about Pablo and Antonio and what they can learn from each other, which happens in the final minutes of the film. Again, it's not about failure, it's about triumphant success.

The Skin I live In seems to be about Dr. Robert Ledgard, played by Antonio Banderas, the doctor who runs the research institute trying to develop an artificial skin, but it is only in retrospect that it becomes clear that the movie is about Vera Cruz, played by Elena Anaya, and that the "skin" which Vera lives in is the artificial skin of gender and that the movie is "about" her discoveries and not about the doctor's madness.

All this is to say that we have to discover things slowly. *The Dancer from the Dance,* by Andrew Holleran, which seems to be about

Anthony Malone, the principal dancer in this particular dance—Lower East Side and Fire Island in the seventies—is only apparently about the beautiful dancer whom everyone fell in love with. The book is really about the world that Malone inhabits, the dance nobody can separate him from. And it is also to say that we ought to understand these works of art slowly. And not rush. Or jump in, because long after Malone has walked into the bay, men are still writing letters trying to determine what it all meant, and Paul writes the concluding lines of the novel: "No, darling, mourn no longer for Malone. He knew very well how gorgeous life is—that was the light in him that you, and I, and all the queens fell in love with. Go out dancing tonight, my dear, and go home with someone, and if the love doesn't last beyond the morning, then know I love you." It is the dance that we have to see and not the dancer.

53

the Marquis de Saint-Loup-en-Bray
November 15, 2011

Marcel, the narrator of *In the Shadow of Young Girls in Flower,* is in Balbec, a resort on the north coast of France. We read this:

> One very hot afternoon, from inside the dining room [of the hotel], which was in half-darkness, sheltering from the sun behind drawn curtains, which were a yellow glow edged by the blue dazzle of the sea, I saw, traversing the hotel's central bay, which extended from the beach to the road, a tall slim young man with piercing eyes, a proud head held high on a fine uncovered neck, and with hair so golden and skin so fair that they seemed to have soaked up the bright sunshine of the day. In a loose off-white garment, the like of which I would never have believed a man would dare to wear, and which in its lightness was as suggestive of the heat and brilliance of outdoors as was the cool dimness of the dining room, he was advancing at a quick march. His eyes, from which a monocle kept dropping, were the color of the sea. We all sat there intrigued, watching him as he passed, knowing that we beheld the young Marquis de Saint-Loup-en-Bray, famous in the fashionable world.

Marcel is more than "intrigued." The young marquis, in his early twenties, is only a few years older than Marcel, and Marcel is seeing him the first time. In this glowing, highly charged portrait, we see how

Marcel sees the marquis and the beginning of the intense friendship between the two men which, for the next five volumes, is going to totter on the edge of erotic fantasy. Even if we didn't know that Marcel Proust was queer, and even if we didn't know that the marquis turns out to be queer, this description of the marquis—so charged with the beauty of men—is the kind of thing that makes us know *this is a queer book.*

*

In the Shadow of Young Girls in Flower, by Marcel Proust (Penguin, James Grieve, translator, 2002)

54

Ebooks and readers mean freedom to gay people
November 21, 2011

I hear or read how sad it is that the publishing industry is collapsing. People resist ereaders. "I stare at a back-lit LED screen enough already."

There are a few things to remember. The publishing industry has not worked well for a lot of people. It has not worked well for writers who are just starting out. It has not been receptive to writers who write in difficult or unusual styles. It has not been receptive to writers whose subject matter isn't mainstream or doesn't invite broad readership. It has not been receptive to writers who write for a minority population in the culture. In an industry dominated by a concern for the bottom line, there isn't much place for the guy who, from the beginning, never thought his book would sell a lot of copies. In a rich and vibrant culture, many books, which may be very fine books and which may add immeasurably to the depth of the culture, may never sell more than a few copies.

In a culture such as ours in America, in the second decade of the twenty-first century, where publication decisions are usually made on the basis of what is going to sell the largest number of copies, it is the culture of minorities such as ours whose vitality is most in danger. The publisher can't afford to publish a book which is content to remain in its niche. Yet often the book that is most productive of new ideas or of a new take on old ideas is exactly the one that is not a cross-over book and is content to be sheltered within the community from which it sprang. A book written by a gay author for a gay audience about a gay subject, with no consideration for straight people or straight concerns, is much like a dissent in the Supreme Court. It may not carry the day in the whole culture, but it has been written, and it exists, and it enters the discourse of the whole culture, and, if it is a good book, it exerts its influence, which may grow until it becomes dominant.

According to publishers, the market for gay books has "vanished." I can't believe this is because today's gay people are less intelligent or less interested in good books. This is the result of the publishing industry giving gay people sillier and sillier books so that gay people learn that if they want a serious and hefty book, they needn't look for it in the gay section of Barnes & Noble.

We—gay people—are being disenfranchised. Publishers are not adding gay books to the culture at the rate our numbers would suggest, and our reading is being censored.

eBooks in ePUB, like my own novels known collectively as the *Stonewall Triptych*, break through this censorship, give an outlet to gay writers for the publication of their books, and restore to gay people the power of the pen and of the press and restore to us the freedom, which is inherently ours, to choose our reading from all the books that are being written.

55

Thoughts on getting home
November 27, 2011

Courtney and I have just come back from the eastern Connecticut shore where we joined extended family for Thanksgiving weekend. We had good food, good conversation, a good sense of belonging—all the things that are expected of such a weekend—and then we returned to Boston last night, and Courtney returned to his job at a local gay bar.

The interesting thing was how assimilated we were—relatively—during the weekend, at a house owned by a straight couple, surrounded by more than twenty people, also straight, and only one person winced when he overheard me recounting a portion of my sexual history to a straight female relative. In short, I felt pretty much at home with this group of relatives, and I didn't feel constrained in any way by being one of only two gay people out of twenty straight people.

And yet, it was a huge relief when we got home, back to our books and DVDs, to our own things, our cat, our politics, and our community, and this made me think of the long-standing discussion in the gay community over assimilation or separatism. I wondered whether it was ever going to be possible for gay people to totally assimilate into the larger community. Aren't we going to always be to some extent separate, divided from the larger community by all the things that have

always divided us? And this because homophobia isn't ever going to
go away completely? And because the larger
community isn't going to recognize the value of what gay people have
learned while wandering in the wilderness? We're just still so far apart.

56

Alan Turing, suffering, gay fiction
December 1, 2011

The Boston Globe published a long article on Sunday, titled "A Computer That Thinks Like the Universe," by Joshua Rothman. It's interesting—it's about quantum computing—and along the way to its conclusions, it discusses what the computers we use are and introduced Alan Turing, who is "the father of modern computing" and whose "theory of computability" is the basis for all modern computers.

This posting isn't about quantum computing, and it isn't about Alan Turing and his contribution to the effort to win World War II, but it is about gay people and our tendency to forget our past. Alan Turing was a homosexual and in January, 1952, he picked up a man outside a theatre in Manchester, UK. After several aborted attempts at a date, and apparently one or two successful dates, the man robbed Turing, who went to the police and told them about the robbery and acknowledged his sexual relationship with this man. This led to Turing's being charged with "gross indecency." He was given a choice of imprisonment or chemical castration by estrogen injection. He chose chemical castration. In June, 1954, he killed himself, apparently with a cyanide-laced apple.

But it is not enough to learn and to remember that *another* one of the great men of the twentieth century was one of us and whose treatment by British culture in 1954, as British Prime Minister Gordon Brown has said, was "appalling." It is necessary also to remember that Alan Turing was only the most brilliant of all those thousands of forgotten men and women who suffered the same consequences of having been picked up by the police. There were thousands and thousands and thousands of men before 1969 who were condemned to "chemical castration" or worse. Allen Ginsberg tells us something about another one in the opening lines of his poem, *HOWL*, where he declares to Carl Solomon, *I am with you in Rockland.* We have no way of knowing how many lives have been destroyed by this appalling cruelty.

At least one of the questions that novels answer is *How was it for you there?* Our literature is almost entirely devoid of reference to this pain and suffering, much of it government inflicted. *Chemical castration!* There has been a TV movie about Turing's life and a Broadway play, and now *The Guardian* says another movie on Turing's life is planned with Leonardo di Caprio. But there are others besides Turing who suffered, and gay fiction is the art form ideally constructed for addressing this subject. Until it addresses *this* subject, the answer gay fiction gives to the question, *How was it for you there?* will be incomplete.

57

Letting go during the eighties
December 10, 2011

Longtime Companion, the film by Norman René; is about a small group of men who know each other from the bars in NYC and Fire Island—that is, some of them know some of them—who are caught for a moment on Fire Island and at work and at home in the city as they digest the first news of the health crisis beginning to sweep the nation. Before any of them know what this crisis is, one of them dies, apparently of pneumonia. Then, in rapid order, we see one of these men after another sicken and die, until there are only two left—along with "Lisa," played by Mary-Louise Parker—walking on the beach at Fire Island.

    Longtime Companion, first released in May 11, 1990, is about events in New York during the early eighties and the earliest stages of the AIDS epidemic. It is the first Hollywood film about the AIDS crisis and widely released in theatres. It was preceded by *An Early Frost,* directed by John Erman, which was a made-for-TV movie that first played on NBC in November 11, 1985, and by *Buddies,* directed by Arthur J. Bressan, which was distributed to a small number of art houses in 1985. I never saw *Buddies,* but I did see *An Early Frost.* Aiden Quinn plays a gay man who is infected with AIDS, who kicks out his lover, and who comes home to his parents—Gena Rowland

and Ben Gazzara—where he is taken care of as he sickens and then dies. At that time I was volunteering with the AIDS Action Committee, and while I was sure there were persons with AIDS who went home to their parents to die, I didn't know any, and I never heard of any. Men's birth families were largely outside the whole process of dying that gay men with AIDS were going through.

Longtime Companion, as I have said, was the first movie to get wide release, and it told the whole story that I was experiencing during those years in Boston. I remember being moved by it, as one after another of its principals suffered and died. The scene that people remembered was when Sean, whom we have known well since the earliest scenes on Fire Island, is in a hospital bed at the home he shares with David and is suffering badly. David seeks to relieve his suffering. He sends the nurse away, and he sits by the bed, speaking soothingly to his lover, who appears to be blind and to not know what is happening to him, and to be afraid. David speaks to him, "I'm here. I'm not going to leave you," and then he says, "If you want, it is OK to go." While Sean gasps for breath, David says, "It's OK. You can go. You can let go of everything. *Let go. All the pain.*" And gradually Sean's breath calms down—slows down— and the scene ends. David had eased Sean over into dying, releasing him from suffering. Some of us were sobbing. I can't remember now whether I had heard about that happening before I saw this movie, but after I saw *Longtime Companion*, I heard about it happening with other men. In New York, in Boston, in other movies.

All of the men in *Longtime Companion* get to know each other very well by the time the AIDS epidemic is in full blast, by the time the movie is really up and running. The audience gets to know these men too, gets to know them almost *very well*, and I think the audience has a sense of the men going too soon, dying before we have had a chance to really get to know them. That was the way AIDS was. We all felt robbed. In the final scene in the movie, Fuzzy and Willy and Lisa—the survivors—walk on the beach at Fire Island and wonder what life will be like after the plague, and there, coming over the walkway, are all the guys who had died during the movie, restored to us, laughing, coming down onto the sand. It is an amazing wish coming true, at least here, in a dream. I think the scene focussed for many of us what we had lost during the epidemic—the people we had loved—when in the confusion of our lives during that time, it was possible to lose sight of what it was we had lost. This was about people and the loss of people we had cared about. *All those people*.

58

Mme de Guermantes at the Opera
December 18, 2018

Night before last I read something that was breathtakingly beautiful. In *Guermantes Way*, the third volume of *In Search of Lost Time,* the narrator is sitting in the Opéra, observing the beautiful women in their parterre boxes above him. "At first there were only vague shadows in which one suddenly encountered, like the gleam of an unseen jewel, the phosphorescence of a pair of famous eyes…." This is slow-going writing. Take it easy, give the writing time. Much of *In Search of Lost Time* is like this. Give in to it. And remember always that the author of this superb writing is gay.

> "But in almost all of the other boxes [of the opera house], the white deities who inhabited these dark abodes had taken refuge against their shadowy walls and remained invisible. Yet, as the performance proceeded, their vaguely human forms began to emerge in languid succession from the depths of the darkness they embroidered, and, rising toward the light, they allowed their half-naked bodies to emerge as far as the vertical surface of the half-light where

their gleaming faces appeared behind the gently playful
foam of their fluttering feather fans, and beneath their
purple, pearl- threaded coiffures, which seemed to have
been bent by the motion of incoming waves; beyond lay
the front orchestra, the abode of mortals forever separated
from the somber transparent realm to which the limpid and
reflecting eyes of the water goddesses, dotted about on the
smooth liquid surface, served as a frontier.... Within the
limits of their domain...these radiant daughters of the sea
were constantly turning round to smile at the bearded
tritons who hung from the anfractuous rocks of the ocean
depths, or at some aquatic demigod, whose skull was a
polished stone, around which the tide had washed up a
smooth deposit of seaweed, and whose gaze was a disc of
rock crystal. They leaned toward these creatures and
offered them bonbons; occasionally the waters parted to
reveal a new Nereid who had just blossomed out of the
shadowy depths, a late arrival who smiled apologetically;
then, at the end of the act, with no further hope of hearing
the melodious sounds of the earth that had drawn them to
the surface, the divine sisters plunged back together and
disappeared in the darkness. But of all these retreats to
whose thresholds their idle curiosity to behold the works of
man brought the inquisitive goddesses who let no one
approach them, the most celebrated was the block of
semidarkness known as the parterre box of the Princesse de
Guermantes."

The Princesse de Guermantes is one of the major characters in *In
Search of Lost Time*. Her family—what happens to its members, what
they represent for Proust—is one of the major subjects for Marcel
Proust.

"Like a great goddess who presides from afar over
the sport of lesser deities, the Princesse had deliberately
remained somewhat to the back of her box, on a side-
facing sofa, red as a coral rock, beside a wide, vitreous

reflection that was probably a mirror, and which suggested a section, perpendicular, dark, and liquid, cut by a ray of sunlight in the dazzled crystal of the sea. At once a feather and a corolla, like certain marine plants, a great white flower, as downy as a bird's wing, hung down from the Princesse's forehead along one of her cheeks, following its curve with flirtatious suppleness, lovingly attentive, as if half enclosing it, like a pink egg in the down of a halcyon's nest...."

Someone in the narrator's hearing says, "That's the Princesse de Guermantes," and the irony of this glowing portrait of her in public is that *what her family represents* is failure. Failure to produce, failure to thrive, failure to cope, failure to be on the right side of the great issues her generation confronted. The youngest member of her family is the Marquis de Saint-Loup, who is her husband's cousin and who is to die on the Western Front before the end of World War I, before the end of *In Search of Lost Time,* and who is gay.

*

Marcel Proust, *Guermantes Way*, vol. III of *In Search of Lost Time.* Translated by Mark Treharne. General editor Christopher Prendergast. London, Penguin Books, 2002.

59

Lawrence v. Texas'
Co-defendant John Lawrence dies at 68
December 26, 2011

John G. Lawrence is dead. He is the man who gave his name to
"Lawrence v. Texas," the case before the Supreme Court decided June
26, 2003 that invalidated all sodomy laws in the US. Lawrence was in
his bedroom with another man, Tyrone Garner, having sex, when local
police came in and arrested them for committing sodomy. Twice
Lawrence and Garner were tried, and each time they sought to have the
charges dismissed, claiming their constitutional rights under equal
protection of the laws and substantive due process were being denied.
Local courts disagreed and found them guilty. Appeals courts overturned
their convictions, after which the State Supreme Court reversed the
Appeals Court and reinstated their convictions. The US Supreme Court
then took possession of the case, and, on June 26, 2003, issued their
decision in *Lawrence v. Texas,* which voided the Texas sodomy law and
all the other sodomy laws throughout the country and also overturned
Bowers v. Hardwick, So now, we remember John Lawrence, who didn't
need to allow his case to be appealed to the Supreme Court and therefore
didn't need to get the kind of publicity in a conservative state that he
got, putting himself in danger. But he did agree to have his case

appealed to the Supreme Court and to run the danger that implied, and as a consequence, the nation is different now, and every time gay rights in the US are analyzed, historians and the rest of us speak of John Lawrence.

This is an extremely important case for gay people, and if you don't know about it, begin by reading what Ari Ezra Waldman, the legal scholar in residence at Towleroad, has to say about it. Then read about it everywhere. Many people say we wouldn't have gay marriage anywhere if there hadn't been a *Lawrence v. Texas*, and we wouldn't have repealed DADT if we hadn't had *Lawrence v. Texas*. So, in your personal list of heroic men and women of the gay community, please add the name of John G. Lawrence, and remember his courage.

60

The will to assert the right to be different
January 2, 2012

What are we going to work for, after all of us can get married? And
what, now that we have DADT repealed? Will they really accept us
then? And will we be happy? What about the people who don't get
married? Or who don't go into the Army? Who don't want children?
What will be our relation to the larger culture? And what should be our
culture's relationship to us? What is going to happen to our gay bars? It's
already happening to our gay bookstores. And do we like that?
Many of us know that Provincetown is changing. What will P-town be
like when everybody in what used to be called the gay community is
married and has children and serves in the Army? Will there be drag
queens then?

Our culture will be different, sure, but it will also be poorer, less
diverse, less vibrant, less capable of giving its children another way to
be different. Right now, being gay means something radically
important—the will to assert the right to be different. In huge
technological cultures like ours in the US, the *right to be different* is
valuable to the individual and to the culture as a whole. The people who
made Apple Computer were *different* and thought differently and so
made a different and surprising and beautiful computer. But in ways
even more valuable, we will miss Marcel Proust, E.M.Forster,
Christopher Isherwood, Alan Turing, Cole Porter, W. H. Auden, who

are what they are, in part because they are gay. What they added to the culture *because they were gay* was immeasurable.

In 2011, Mark Hatzenbuehler, a Columbia University psychologist and researcher published a study in Pediatrics that asserted that "suicide rates among teenagers are dependent upon which county a teenager lives in." Harzenbuehler said "the results show that 'environments that are good for gay youth are also healthy for heterosexual youth.'" It may be that the mere presence of gay kids is good for straight kids.

This is something that Jane Jacobs, in *The Death and Life of Great American Cities*, in 1961, understood. A good neighborhood was a neighborhood with a cross-section of different kinds of people. And according to Jill Grant, Jane Jacobs believed that "cities have natural advantages over towns and suburbs because size gives them the diversity that generates vitality." *Generates vitality.* It's a goal for all people who care about our culture. In our cities, there should be space for African-Americans, for Spanish-speaking Americans, for Chinese, for other ethnic minorities from around the world, and for those who are a whole range of sexualities and genders. And these citizens should not be assimilated to be called *Americans.*

Men and women who are not married and who don't have children, who read gay books and rent porno videos, who refuse to go into the Army, and who call themselves *queers* instead of *gay* people, who are the least assimilated of our tribe, are important to the culture of America and add to the diversity that generates the vitality of this nation. Meddle with us at your peril. Literally.

*

Reconsidering Jane Jacobs. ed. Max Page and Timothy Mennel, American Planning Association, Chicago: Planners Press, 2011. p. 99

61

All around us are ruins
January 7, 2012

Before 1983, when I announced that my marriage was over, I had always been monogamous.

It was not until 1990, as I was beginning another relationship and still in the first bucking, sweaty throes of it, that I felt I needed to say something that was commensurate with the enormity of what was happening: I promised monogamy, words that came out of my mouth, expressions of an idea buried deep. I remember feeling surprised. I wondered where *that* had come from.

Between these two big relationships of my life, much had changed. I had come out, I had spent the better part of seven years reading canonical texts of the gay movement, and I had begun to think for myself. Also, I was writing *Ceremonies.* In this excerpt Dana is on the way home with her partner, Marcia. Marc is their child:

> Tonight we will make love. She has a long pale yellow silk nightgown, and she will come into the bedroom wearing it after she has brushed her hair. She will be standing by the bedside table waiting for me, taking off her rings one at a time and placing them on the table. She will ask me if Marc is sleeping. Her nightgown falls all the way to the floor, showing only

her white arms and her toes and when I say he is sleeping, she will smile and turn off the light, and we will find our way to the bed by the glow of the moon through the window. Then we will make love.

At the cars, we say goodbye. They [Luke and Arthur] go to theirs, and we stand by ours. I look up toward the theater. Derek [another friend] said he would join us by the lake. I am disappointed. He has been called away to something else. I feel like being called away to something else myself, a cottage on the coast, me and Marcia and Marc and a stack of books. I feel called away to friends who have maintained their freedom in the midst of this ruin. The last lights in the theater are turned off, and the entire landscape is lit now only by the cool platinum light of the moon.

Suddenly I hear their car behind me and, "Goodbye my dearest friends!" I turn around. It is Arthur, leaning out of their car window, waving, blowing kisses with both his hands. Luke waves also from the driver's side. They drive way, Arthur still leaning from the window, throwing out his arms blowing kisses, calling, "Goodbye, my dearest friends!" They drive to the end of the parking lot and enter the driveway to the road, their lights disappearing among the trees. I hear him call, "I love you!" the last long *ooooooo* sound diminishing into the dark distance.

We get in, and Marcia starts the car. We drive home through the deserted country. I slide down in the seat and rest my head. The Republican convention is next month. They will celebrate family values. The first woman candidate for a national office has been under continuous attack all week for her husband's finances. The boys are going to be tried as juveniles [for the murder of Bernie Mallett], and their harshest punishment will be confinement in a juvenile home until their twenty- first birthday. All around us are ruins. We are trapped in a moment in history which allows us almost no freedom, except the freedom to define ourselves inside an utterly oppressive culture.

Marc is five-and-a-half months old. He grows daily, discovering his body and Marcia and me, what he likes, what he doesn't. How will he grow to express himself? How would he be if he were free? How would we express ourselves if we were free? Would Marcia and I be as we are now, in love, committed to one another for all our lives?

The road winds up and down and from side to side among the evergreen trees, the moon sometimes on this side of the road, sometimes on Marcia's. I imagine perfect freedom. Would many women live as Marcia and I live, without a man at all, if they were able? Would many women live together happily and with purpose in communes? their children in common, the men somewhere else, there for the occasional coupling? Would some of us—or most of us—live with men in couples, sharing sex and affection and the raising of children? going to other men or women for primary affectional needs? Would the relationship with men be primarily economic and for the raising of children? Would we resort to serial monogamy? first women, then a man for children, then women again for spiritual values? And polygamy? one woman and many men? or the other way around, one man and many women, whose primary sexual and affectional needs would be met in each other?

If Marc were to grow up in perfect freedom, in a culture without fear of sex, a culture that celebrated all the diverse sexual and emotional and intellectual possibilities of men and women,

wouldn't things be more fluid? less rigid? And
wouldn't it be certain in such a community where
anarchy ruled that there would be no rigidly
defined groups who were constrained to limit their
affections and their desire to members of only one
other group? Wouldn't Marc be free?
Would Marc have to define himself *straight* or
gay?

What of Marc's feelings? Don't his feelings
flow from object to object, person to person,
occasion to occasion without break, a rich
continuum of emotional life, flowing over and
around and under whatever comes into his life?
Don't we feel desire with one—or some or many—
forever or for a little while, at the same time or at
different times? And doesn't our desire take
different forms and different intensities according to
the moment and the object?

Dana sees what freedom in the future is going to be like.

*

Oxford University Press has announced a new book, to be published
this month, January 2012, by Eric Anderson, *The Monogamy Gap:
Men, Love, and the Reality of Cheating.* I have my order in, and when it
comes, I'll review it here. Anderson's book has already been reviewed
by Vicki Larson, Huffington Post.

These quoted pages are the last two pages from the end of Part Two,
"Dana," *Ceremonies,* by Dwight Cathcart, ebook published by Adriana
Books, 2010

62

Freedom to feel
January 13, 2012

Freedom. We are in an election season, and the word is everywhere, but we don't usually feel we have to ask what it means. For us, the big gay-rights cases before the Supreme Court place the word in a constitutional context. That's important, but there are other meanings from other sources besides court cases. It is important that gay people know what meaning we assign to the word, so we know what we're fighting for.

The organization that was formed within a month of the Stonewall Riots in June 1969 was called "Gay Liberation Front." "Liberation" means, according to the New American Oxford Dictionary, "the act of setting someone free from imprisonment, slavery, or oppression; release: *the liberation of all political prisoners*." and also "freedom from limits on thought or behavior: *the struggle for women's liberation*."

In my last posting, I quoted two pages from near the end of Part Two of my novel, *Ceremonies*, in which Dana contemplates Marc, her infant son, and considers what it would be like for him to be truly free. She imagines a time in the future when their culture is characterized by sexual anarchy, when "Marc would be free." Later in *Ceremonies*, Deborah and Sally contemplate what *freedom* means. Sally says, "It must mean something more than the freedom to choose between candidates, or to choose between faiths, or even to choose between

ideas. It must reach deeper than that—" Deborah proposes, *"Freedom to feel without constraint."* It seems these two middle-aged, middle- class women instinctively understand themselves politically in the terms of the sixties Stonewall revolutionaries.

In December, 1969, when the Gay Activist Alliance (GAA) was formed, its manifesto demanded basic rights, the first of which was "the right to our own feelings. This is the right to feel attracted to the beauty of members of our own sex and to embrace those feelings as truly our own, free from any question or challenge whatsoever by any other person, institution, or moral authority."

The sixties revolutionaries understood that the form their oppression took—what they were fighting against—was the loss of the right to their own feelings. This is an intimate—and consequently sadistic—kind of oppression. Most queers today might say that, if they feel oppressed, this is the way they experience it: the loss of the ability to feel freely, to recognize what their feelings are, to honor their feelings, because their feelings have been devalued and mocked by the culture they call home.

I like the GAA formula. When I was a child, I knew that there was something wrong with my feelings. Everyone told me that. There were times when I hated my feelings. I was ashamed of them. I didn't want them to be *my own.* So the first step toward liberation for a kid like me was to learn that I had a *right to my own feelings* and that they were truly *my own,* and they were good.

*

Information on the Gay Activist Alliance and the Gay Liberation Front and related matters is drawn from the following two books:

David Carter, *Stonewall: The Riots that Sparked the Gay Revolution.* New York: St Martin's Griffin, 2004.

David Eisenbach, *Gay Power: An American Revolution.* New York: Carroll & Graf Publishers, 2006

63

A rich life

January 31, 2012

People say of themselves that they "just happen to be gay." I think that's bullshit. I am profoundly, inextricably gay, and being gay affects every single part of me. I didn't "happen" to be gay. I am so deeply gay that if you took the gay away, there wouldn't be anything left of me—or I would be a totally different person.

I was gay, and I *knew* I wasn't going to work for American capitalist enterprise, be an organization man and fit in and take orders and live in a suburb. I was a rebel from the gitgo. So starting in grade school, I gradually accustomed myself to being outside, being a loner, being a rebel, being *against.*

I always felt like an outsider, so no matter what the endeavor, I was going to find a way to do it by myself. Liking boys put me in a different place from everybody else and the forces that drove many other people—get a profession, find the "lovely girl," get married, have children, etc.—usually didn't apply to me. I was in a free fire zone where there weren't any rules. There were times when I had to pretend that the same rules that applied to everybody else were applicable to me when I knew they, profoundly, weren't.

And the times in my life when I tried to join an organization—I got a PhD and became a college prof and got *married*—were notable for how very uncomfortable I felt until I gave in and abandoned the effort. Whatever I had to do, I never lost my sense that I was gay.

When everything else seemed to be just a series of pretenses, a long and difficult acting job I was trapped in, being gay liberated my mind. It gave me a firm foundation to stand on, a history to understand and build on. It gave me a future, a way to think, and, finally, a way to act.

Being gay has meant that I learned something of what other minorities experienced in America—Jews, black people, atheists, native Americans, Japanese Americans, others—and I knew that "We the People" did not include all of us unless we fought for it. Because I was gay, much of Christianity came to feel narrow and discriminatory. Being gay, I watched while people claim privileges for themselves that they tried to deny me. Yet they seemed to want to be my friend. It was an interesting—and distancing—experience.

It's a rich life being gay has given me. Part of our family was just here for a quick visit—Courtney's and my children and grandchildren. We baked bread and did homework and talked for about twenty-four hours straight. We've got it good. But none of this just happened to us. We worked to get what we've got—two queer granddads and our kids and grandkids.

64

The necessity of imposing oneself on one's culture

February 6, 2012

Nothing in my last post should be read to imply that having children is a necessary part of having a "rich life" for gay people. That's it for us, and that came about when I underwent a divorce, and then when I worked for the subsequent years with my children, as they grew older, so that I could be a gay man with children and they could be children with a gay father. As is sometimes the way with these things, my children—a boy and a girl—grew up and became an adult man and an adult woman who eventually got married and had their own children and so, by that time, my partner and I, who had found each other about the time our children became adults, became grandparents. This was at a time when having children seemed to be a relatively transgressive thing to do and didn't seem like anything we were trying to foist off on any other set of people. In fact, the way we got here—finding ourselves gay grandparents with children—seemed at the time like the last thing anybody should do if they wanted to be assimilated into either the gay or the straight communities.

One of the cool things is that I have never lost my sense of gays as transgressive people, which they were when I was first dealing with them, a sense that I have carried right up through *Adam in the*

Morning, my book on the Stonewall Riots. We were always fighting some oppressive force, and if, in my own case, these oppressive forces were also trying to keep me from having children, well, at least I had already learned how to fight them, and to win.

One has to eventually impose oneself on one's culture, not the other way around. In another context, having children might be the absolutely *least* transgressive thing a person could do. But in *my* context it was the *most* transgressive. Now, to bring all this back full circle, I have my being gay to thank for that. I think, for many people, having children grounds them firmly in their culture. For me, and since I am gay, it grounds me firmly in rebellion *against* my culture.

65

At last, the truth
February 8, 2012

Two good places to go for commentary on the Ninth Circuit panel's decision in the *Perry v. Brown* Proposition 8 case are Adam B on *Daily Kos* and Ari Ezra Waldman on Towleroad. I don't know what Proposition 8 supporters are thinking right now—I don't read that kind of stuff—but opponents of Proposition 8 agree that something momentous has just happened.

Adam B's last sentence, commenting on the fact that this decision is not the last word, "No, same-sex couples shouldn't have to wait, but make no mistake: *equality is winning.*"

I'll return in two or three days with more on *Perry v. Brown*.

66

Livin' in a crazy-makin' world
February 12, 2012

"It is enough to say that Proposition 8 operates with no apparent purpose but to impose on gays and lesbians, through the public law, a majority's private disapproval of them and their relationships."   — from the 9th Circuit's decision on Prop 8. We already knew that, didn't we? We knew that there was no *reason* for any of the various limitations that the law has imposed on gay people during our lifetime and that all of those laws were based on lies and were there merely to impose a stigma, like Hawthorne's *Scarlet Letter*

This has had a predictable effect on gay and lesbian people. We have been told at various times that gay men and lesbians are not allowed to serve in the diplomatic corps, in the State Department, in the Armed Forces, or on police forces, or to get married. One of the effects of all this has been that a particular man has been prevented from serving in the armed forces and also that the charge against him—that his presence is a danger to unit cohesion—was not true. Or he has been prevented from marrying and the charge against him—that his marrying is a danger to other people's marriages—was not true.
During some times, the gay person's situation was even more difficult because he or she faces numerous charges *that were not true,* charges that were expressive of the *majority's private disapproval*. For long periods since the end of the second world war, gay people have had to

hold onto their sanity while being deprived of ordinary human rights, at the same time they were confronted with multiple charges that they knew were not true. This is a tough world.

There is no point in our trying to convince anyone that we are not a danger to other people's marriages—or any of the other things we have been charged with. As the appeals court said, these are cases of the *majority's private disapproval.* So don't try to persuade them. Don't try to talk to them. Instead, *bring force to bear on them.* Disrupt their meetings, demonstrate in the street, *shout loudly,* have lawyers who are the toughest, most brilliant lawyers anywhere, and keep this up until the other side admits to being *outgunned.* The point here, when we are dealing with irrational opponents who are willing to lie, is to be *stronger*, to never let down our guard, to never assume, because we are good people, that our opponents will recognize us as good people and give us what we deserve. To the contrary, the history of the last sixty years in America proves that they won't, so we have to take care of ourselves. We have to be fierce to be free. None of those folks who were willing to lie for sixty years are just going to *give* us anything.

For Ari Ezra Waldman's most recent comments on the *Perry v. Brown,* see *Towleroad.*

67

Queer
February 20, 2012

Queer is permanently outside the culture and therefore in opposition to it. Queer does not look for a time in the future when there will be resolution, when the failures of today will be corrected and those outside brought in. Queer neither seeks nor wishes for acceptance. Queer seeks to understand today. Queer accepts today what is—the crimes and the radical failures—and accepts that today doesn't lead to any change for tomorrow. Queer does not mature into anything. Queer is not a transitional state. Queer is final. Queer understands that same- sex is only one aspect of queer. Queer stands in opposition. Queer does not fit in. Queer isn't smooth. And there is some question whether Queer is cool. Queer is not dependent on what anyone else does or even anyone else's understanding of it. And it is certainly not dependent on whether anyone else accepts it. Queer is independent of all that and stands alone. Proud, independent, unmoved. It is enough to learn what I stand for. I suspect that there are a number of ways to become Queer. One grows up and into Queer. One realizes at last that, after one has been everything else, one is Queer. It is therefore a state for old people. It is also a state for kids, who understand instinctively that they don't need to try all those states that aren't going work, because they are temporary. Kids understand, having cut out all the transitional stages, they can go right for Queer and have done with it. *Hey, this's the way I am. I'm not ever gonna be part of that other stuff.* Gay used to be like this. It was way out there. It was not respectable. But Gay started trying to fit in and be respectable. It started being a transitional stage on the road to fitting in. But Queer is truth, right now, until everybody gets used to it, when we're going to need a new word for this old truth. Something to describe those of us not on the path to anywhere. Just me. Just us. Out here. Queer.

68

Another victory
February 23, 2012

Today, a federal district court in California declared DOMA unconstitutional in a summary judgment. Adam B of Daily Kos calls this a "big win," and I recommend his analysis here. Ari Ezra Waldman, of Towleroad, continues his superb job of legal analysis of these court cases here. Ari analyzes what a summary judgment is and what it means in this case. What Ari has been emphasizing for several weeks now is the cumulative effect of each of these judgments. He does that again today. He suggests this is the way DOMA is going to be repealed—one brick at a time.

Read these guys.

69

"It ain't necessarily so."
February 29, 2012

One result of the recent procession of federal court cases, beginning with *Romer v. Evans* and including *Lawrence v. Texas*, and the latest, the Ninth Circuit panel rejection of Prop. 8 in *Perry v. Brown* and *Galinski v. OPM,* is that we can now see that the intellectual foundations of the future are being constructed. I don't just mean the legal constitutional structures that are going to control how we are going to fit into the body of the republic, but also the emotional and psychological structures that will control the way we think about ourselves. The concept of "gay people" is congealing and solidifying. We are, apparently, here. "Gay people" is taking on a definition written by the courts—always a dangerous enterprise—and consequently we are probably headed into a prolonged period of intellectual and psychological error, when biological and legal constructs are out of whack with our felt reality.

The heart of the error that's developing is this: Our constitutional jurisprudence—and journalism and education and medicine and the rest—is beginning to agree that a person has a "sexuality." We seem to agree there are two, or maybe three, sexualities, gay and straight and bisexual. Apparently the courts and the other opinion-makers in the culture agree that there aren't any other possibilities. Sexuality is immutable. A person is either straight or gay or bi all that person's life. And we know what these three possibilities mean. Sexuality, in this view, is like skin color. It doesn't change. Sexuality and skin color both indicate characteristics of distinct populations that must be treated equally under the law. And, implicit in this construct that we're seeing raised in front of us is the demand, written into law, that, to get our rights, we have to come out.

I know how we got here. Before *Romer* we had no rights recognized by anybody that were founded in the constitution. *Bowers v. Hardwick* showed us that we wouldn't get anywhere by claiming there was a right in the constitution to engage in *sodomy*. So, when they had a chance, legal theorists proposed to follow the lead of the great civil rights cases of the fifties and sixties. Gay people would claim to be a "suspect class," that is, a class set aside by one immutable characteristic and by a history of discrimination. It seems to be working. Beginning with *Romer,* and then moving through the other gay civil rights cases, the federal judiciary seems to be buying this approach. Gay people are becoming a suspect class whose rights can only be abridged after "heightened scrutiny."

The problem, buried in all this, is a version of human sexuality that *ain't necessarily so*.

There are many people whose sexuality is not defined by the words "gay" or "straight" or "bi"—men who want sometimes to have sex with another man but who call themselves "straight," and women who sometimes want to have sex, or even long-term relationships, with men, but who call themselves "lesbians." There is no hard line between *gay* and *straight*. A person may breach that line concurrently or serially, and it gets breached all the time, and over and over. It won't do, in trying to understand people, to say, as gay people have long said about those who don't fit its theories, that these people "don't have courage" or "are confused." We should take them at their word, and then see where that leads us. And yet, what we'll actually do is tell them *you don't have courage, you are confused*.

Since this is such a big error that is developing, the consequences are going to be dire and hard to correct. A man or a woman can have a real, deeply-felt, consuming sense that he or she is gay—and yet want to have sex with a person of the opposite sex. And a man or a woman can be straight—and yet want to have sex with someone of his or her own sex. People want to go back and forth, *without* changing any of the words they use to describe themselves, but the ideas that are developing don't provide an intellectual framework for a description of these people. That's the problem. For that man who is straight but who has sex only with men—where do *his* rights come from? How does he feel about himself? Lonely, I'll bet. Nor do those ideas take into account what is happening in people's heads. A straight friend, who has a monogamous relationship with his wife, told me that when he has sex with her, he always thinks of naked men. Jimmy Carter's option—call that *adultery*—won't work for most of us or for that friend of mine.

Our culture is developing an understanding of sexuality—and writing it into the law through these court cases—that is rigid, narrow, confining, and immutable, while our sex is fluid, expansive, *mutable,* and constantly surprising.

The consequence of what's happening is that people who follow their hearts, or their genes or their lusts, are *still* not going to find themselves reflected in the structures laid down by the culture and are going to be told, "You do it wrong," "You *are* wrong to feel that way." We are developing an intellectual framework for our sexuality that is going to be as guilt-inducing as the one we've had for the last forty years, and it's clear that it's the culture, which likes binary thinking because it's simpler, that has gotten it wrong *again*.

70

Dangerous Halls
March 7, 2012

I found a short video on *Towleroad* today, *Man in the Mirror,* in which it is said that a "closeted jock faces outing in Joel Schumacher's short." It is also on PBS.org.

Jason is an athlete, a high school senior, maybe seventeen years old, beautiful, a Puerto Rican, and the movie catches him just at that moment when he is asking, *Am I gay?* He asks, *How can I be gay, if I am so masculine?* He has a girl friend, college scouts are coming by "every day," he appears to be the leader of his little group, he's very "male." His cousin from California is arriving today, there's a big ball game coming up, his mother wants him around the house more. The movie is shot in small bedrooms, narrow school hallways, small locker rooms, illustrating how claustrophobic Jason's life is, how few choices he has. The camera is right on top of the actors. We can't ever get far enough away from them to get any perspective, which may be Jason's problem. Major things happen to the young people because other young people are spying on them, peering through doorways, watching them in the hallways. Nobody seems to recognize any boundaries in this world. This is very effective in showing how difficult it is to come out in high school, how impossible to know how people will respond, how dangerous this world is. There is an out gay student, named Eric, and the way he is treated suggests the kind of danger Jason faces.

The screenplay for this film was written by a high school senior, Treviny Marie Colon, when she was a senior at The High School of Fashion Industries in Manhattan. Ms Colon was introduced to a curriculum at the high school called "What's the REAL DEAL about Masculinity," part of which was a writing contest. This curriculum apparently came from Scenarios USA, which made it possible for Ms Colon to make the screenplay into a movie, directed by Joel Schumacher, the director of such movies as *St Elmo's Fire, Batman Forever,* and *A Time to Kill.* Ms Colon said about her movie, "When people see *Man in the Mirror,* I hope they'll step into the unknown, see what's rarely talked about and understand exactly what's at stake for a gay man of color in the closet."

Man in the Mirror is not quite eighteen minutes long and worth your time for several reasons. It will remind you, as Ms Colon says, that it's still hard for gay men of color, no matter what people are saying about other gay men. It's also a warning not to be glib about "how things have changed" around coming out. I read about young people coming out at earlier and earlier ages and meeting with virtually universal acceptance, and this movie is a necessary corrective. The writer was in high school when she wrote this, which suggests she knows her subject. The difference between this story and my own high school experience was that Jason's sister is prepared to be supportive, and his cousin also. There's something else, though. Jason asks, in his big conversation with his sister about his feelings. "I don't know what to think." "I can't feel that way." "Can I be this?" So that doesn't seem to have changed. A major obstacle to coming out is himself. *He was not what he thought he was.*

71

Dharun Ravi and Tyler's coming out
March 18, 2012

Ian Parker, writing in *The New Yorker*, says about Tyler Clementi, "there was no posting, no observed sex, and no closet."

Writing at the same time, Angus Johnston, of the website *Student Activism,* says, "'Out' is not a binary concept, and it's not at all unreasonable to describe Ravi's actions—telling his friends Clementi was gay and posting the news on a public Twitter account—as 'outing.'"

I suspect that most gay people, reading Ian Parker and Angus Johnston, would agree with Johnston. A person can be in different stages of being "out"—all at the same time, with different groups of people.

Our premier news-and-commentary magazine disagrees with the conventional wisdom in the gay community about a common word—*what does the closet mean*—and somebody ought to be turning to a late-edition dictionary of American English to update themselves. It's worth our trouble to get us all on the same page when we're describing the same thing.

The gay community is lax about the way it uses the word, too. Sometimes, as when we describe Tyler Clementi's life just before he died, we're willing to recognize that coming out is nuanced and has many stages; at other times, like when we describe gay men or women who are married to the opposite sex, or gay kids who haven't yet told *us* that they are gay, we seem unable to use any word but "closeted." That's wrong too.

Closeted, coming out, outed are all powerful words and powerfully useful words. The concepts they point toward are even more powerful and useful. It is worthwhile to use the occasion of Dharun Ravi's trial to contemplate our confusion over these words and concepts.

This is the first of several posts on this subject.

*

See *The New York Times* on March 17, 2012.

See *Towleroad* on March 17, 2012, for the results of the trial.

For New Jersey papers for a detailed, charge-by-charge listing of the verdicts.

72

Everybody is different
March 26, 2012

In *Ceremonies*, a young woman is walking down the street, preparing to attend a memorial service for a friend. She turns the corner and sees TV lights focused on the door of the church. If she continues to the door, she will walk past these TV cameras. She says to her lover, "I can't go past that. I'll lose my job." Her lover says she can't *not* go to the service. So, there in the dark, a block from the church, the couple split up, both of them sobbing, one to go on to the church and publicity, and the other to return to the home they share.

After the memorial service, Mickey introduces his boyfriend to his high school teacher who is also leaving the memorial service. Robbie, the boyfriend, says, "That's the first time you've ever done that." Mickey wants to know what he meant. Robbie shrugged, "You never acknowledge me."

Later that night, Mickey is returning one of the many phone calls from his sister, who says she saw him on TV and wants to know why he went to that boy's memorial service.

"What will people think?"
"I think you should lower your voice—'
"They'll think you're queer!"

This is the moment. Mickey's mother's way is to give him an opportunity, even an invitation, to lie. Marian's is to dare him. She comes on like she's training tigers, chair

chair up, whip trailing. "Lloyd already thinks so. He's
thought that for years, and you have no idea how hard I've—"

"This is hard enough. You are not making it any easier."

"Why is it so hard? Tell me that. What are you hiding?"

Every second Mickey waits now the lie rots the bone.
"I'm queer, Marian." And the release he should feel now is
polluted by his knowledge that she's had to force it out of
him.

In these excerpts from *Ceremonies,* we're watching the moment at
which *being closeted* becomes *out.* What drives Mickey is a need for
greater comfort or less pain or, when Marian goes on the attack, a need to
defend himself. Self-protection also drives the young woman to turn
away from the television lights. The girl on the street and Mickey are
both out—to some people—and closeted to others, and what drives them
cannot really be determined without a close knowledge of just what's
happening in that person's life.

You just can't make generic statements about people and the closet
and being out. Everybody is different. Each time is different.

73

Jesus, another tour group
March 27, 2012

In *Ceremonies*, after Mickey came out to his sister, and then to his
mother the next day, he found he had to come out to his friend at work.
He took his friend Charles to a fast food restaurant on the highway.
After some preliminary talk about cars and tires and politics—it's in the
middle of the 1984 presidential election—Mickey says,

> "You know the boy who drowned?"
> "What boy?"
> "The one who was thrown off the bridge?"
> "Oh, that. Sure."
> "Well, he was a homosexual—"
> [Charles] doesn't say anything.
> "—and it upset a lot of his friends, a lot of the
> homosexuals in Cardiff—"
> "What are you telling me?"
> "It upset me. It made me real angry that somebody—"
> "Why did it make you angry?" His eyes have
> narrowed and he has pulled away a little bit.
> "I'm a friend of his."

I am aware of the children shouting and squealing on the slide.

"You queer?" His face has crumpled up into a mask of disbelief.

"I am a homosexual."

A pause.

"No shit!" He lifts his hands from his knees and then drops them down again and leans on them. "You're a fucking queer!" He starts to laugh. People look at us. "Why are you telling me? You coming on to me?" He laughs. "I know, you're telling me to be careful around you, you can't help yourself, right?"

So, Mickey was out to his little gang—his boyfriend and Jack and Claire and Timothy and Bernie, people who came to his house and ate his food and watched his TV—and then he came out to his sister and to his mother, and now he is coming out to Charles, the guy from work. Later, he will come out on television—by which he comes out to everybody—after the funeral service for Bernie. A television reporter and cameraman stop them as they are walking down the lane from the burial plot:

It is 3:45 p.m. in the afternoon on Friday—the funeral began an hour ago—and the sun is beyond the trees. There is no cloud in the sky. The trees, great elms up against the hillside and willows along the lane, in a light breeze, rustle and cast deep shadows. The cemetery grasses are a deep, rich green, the effect of lavish care, and in the shadows the granite tombstones are gray and cool. The cameraman has turned the camera on me. At first I am aware of this only in the periphery of my vision. And then, drawn naturally toward it, I turn to the camera and face it down, talking, answering the reporter's long questions on Bernie's death and its effect on the gay community in Cardiff, on me and my homosexuality, on grief and loss, staring into the large black round glass eye.

"Bernie was very courageous. He said, *I am what I am.* In many ways, he died of that courage." The camera's lens sees me, and in the broad light of day it takes me in without blinking.

Another friend, Dana, a young woman who is slightly older and has a partner and a baby and a good job, and whom all the kids in *Ceremonies* look up to, says, "I learned, however, that you never get to the end of coming out. On the other side of the glass there is always a new tour group coming through who haven't been here before. They start using language about you that doesn't apply, and if you're not careful, the words will begin to seep into your mind and cause damage, like water in a gas tank. They need it all explained to them, and you have to put down your business and lay it all out in simple terms."

You never get to the end of coming out. You can't ever come out to everybody, even on television or the newspapers. You may have to do it over and over. It's not ever going to be finished.

74

An intensely private pursuit
March 29, 2012

In *Ceremonies*, Mickey gives two television interviews. In the first his face is lit so he can't be recognized, and when he sees the broadcast of the interview, Mickey sees what he has done:

> The reporter, on screen, is a warm and vibrant person with attractive middle-class American middle- aged steadiness. He looks directly into the camera and, with smiles and winks and floating eyebrows, establishes trust with the audience. The person he is interviewing—me— is shown back-lighted, his face entirely in shadow. There is nothing identifiable about his silhouette: the cut of his hair, the set of the jaw, the way he moves his lips when he talks, and most particularly, the absence of moist eyes with lashes. There is no feature that would make it possible for someone to respond emotionally to him, to *grasp* him. His voice seems hostile, resentful, and aggressive. I sound even shrill at moments. This is not me. I feel exposed. I have allowed myself to be used. I feel shamed, and I hate it. I *look* shamed.

When Mickey sees himself on TV, his face in shadow, he says, *This is not me,* and during the next several days, he looks for a better fit between the kind of person he is and the way he is presenting himself.

He grows bold. He comes out to his boss because he needs to go to Bernie's funeral, and he doesn't much care whether his boss likes it, and to the cops who come to his house because someone has painted DIE FAGGOT in red paint on his front door, to his landlord who threatens him with eviction because of the door. He says to his landlord, "I'll get a lawyer and fight you every step of the way. I have money, I want you to know. I'll spread this all over the newspapers too. You'll come out of this looking like a bigot, Mr. Fellowes, because I know what this is about—this is about bigotry against a gay man, Mr. Fellowes. And I am going to fight you every fucking inch of the way and do it as publicly as I can, and I want you to make no mistake about me, Mr. Fellowes. I'm not afraid of you or anything you can do to me—" Mickey is searching for a way to *be*, about which he can say, *this is me.* But it is the two television interviews that indicate how much he has changed.

> On Friday, after the funeral at the cemetery, the TV reporter and the cameraman ask permission to interview Mickey. In a beautiful setting, with Bernie buried only minutes before, Mickey allows the cameraman to take him in completely as he talks "answering the reporter's long questions on Bernie's death and its effect on the gay community in Cardiff, on [Mickey] and [his] homosexuality, on grief and loss, staring into the large black round glass eye.

Whether this suits the bigots around town—or whether it suits the new gay community in Cardiff—what Mickey is doing is suiting himself, finding the *me* in all this chaos. At first, he didn't know that was what he was looking for, and at first he didn't know how to recognize it when he found it, but once he found it, he held on to it like a rock—the *me* in the swift-running, violent, turbulent stream of his life.

People call what Mickey does in *Ceremonies*—these are just a few brief scenes from his rich life—"coming out." It is important to notice that finding the *me* in the chaos around him is an intensely private pursuit. He is the only person who is going to know when he's found it, and the effects of finding it are going to be intensely personal. It's interesting that a process that leads those who go through it deeper and deeper into an intimate knowledge of themselves seems to be describing something very public and is called *coming out*.

75

The very private meaning of "coming out"
April 5, 2012

Tyler Clementi was in the process of coming out when he died. *We* can't know how he felt. Tyler is the only person who could know how he felt and the only person who could know how far he had gone on the process toward *coming out.*

It is appropriate here to ask, what is it that drives a person to move from one stage of the process of coming out to another? For example, in the excerpts from Mickey's episodes in *Ceremonies*, what drives Mickey to introduce the fact that he is gay into the heated discussion he is having with his landlord, and then to say, "I know what this is about—this is about bigotry against a gay man." It is a kind of reckless anger and defiance when he feels himself surrounded on all sides by enemies.

But it needn't be. Dana comes out to her parents in part because she loves them—but also because her brother, Kevin, now knows she is a lesbian and will eventually tell her parents. To protect herself, Dana tells her parents.

And what of Carole, the woman with whom *Ceremonies* opens? Why does this very intelligent, very accomplished graduate student at the Wharton School, turn from Esther and reject all that she offers? Why does Carole choose what is a kind of closet? Perhaps she doesn't like feeling out of control—as emotions so often make one feel. But it is more complex than that. She likes being able to share her life with her father, and she likes playing the game he has chosen, so he will understand her achievement. She says, "Since I left Wharton and Philadelphia, winning is all I have ever cared about." Her tragedy is that, after modeling her life on her father's, he grew old and died, and toward the end, she says, to her own amazement, "I don't think he cared how much money I made. He simply ceased to care." She says, "I am not a fool. I know what I sold and why. I know what I bought. I know what a bed feels like when two people are in it."

The point here is that we don't know what "coming out" means for any particular person. Everybody is different. What is true about one person is rarely true of the next person. This ought not to be difficult to remember in a community so built on transgression and an awareness of difference as ours is.

76

Living on the edge
April 16, 2012

When a person is on the edge between *in* and *out*, he is not often faced with a binary decision, *either* in or out. He is faced with a range of possibilities, only one of which is, in the particular situation, *coming out.* He may decide to do nothing. He may decide to tell the other person that he is gay *and then tell no other person.* He may start a process which ends with his coming out more or less publicly. He also may deny whatever circumstances precipitated this event and attempt to go back in the other direction. And he may do any of these things for a whole range of reasons—defiance, search for safety (conceived of in any number of ways), obligations to various persons, cowardice, bravery, or almost anything else, including love, any one of which is powerful enough to drive a person in either direction over the in/out divide.

While a lot of things have changed in the last fifty years, one thing that still seems to be true for all generations of people who experience same-sex feelings is this: people come up constantly against this question of coming out. Nobody who experiences same-sex feelings can really avoid this at some point, and often that person comes up against it again and again during his or her life.

Sometimes, a person hears somebody say, "I've always been out" or "I never came out." But we have a world in which there are many more heterosexual people than there are people like us, and if we don't constantly tell them to stop, they'll act as if everyone here at this party is straight. It is impossible for me to avoid the moment when I am confronted with the questions, *Should I come out? Must I come out? Can I come out here, without being killed? Have I come out without meaning to, to the wrong people?*

We do not live in a post-coming-out world. The death of Tyler Clementi is only the most recent proof of that. The world is complicated, and it is not helped by our being sloppy in our thinking. Nothing matters more to a person who has same-sex feelings than the process of coming out, because the process—whether going in or coming out or maintaining the status quo—gives you an attitude, defines who you are, your relation to your own past, to your future, your relation to your community and to the culture we share.

77

North Carolina, Dean Tillman, the future
April 15, 2012

On *Towleroad*, Krista Tillman, who lives in Charlotte, North Carolina and is a mother of a young gay man (she's also a dean of her college) explains why her gay son doesn't live in North Carolina. "It's not as open and accepting as other places are." She tells what she thinks will have to happen in North Carolina to get him to come home, "where he can have all the rights and the privileges as anyone else in North Carolina."

North Carolina is deciding on May 8, 2012, whether to adopt Amendment One, which will prevent marriage equality and take away basic legal protections from gay and lesbian couples. "The millenial generation [her son's age group] are all strongly supportive of gay rights and gay marriage, and so strongly support it that they say they want to live in a place that's open and accessible, whether or not they've gay. So [the passage of Amendment One will] affect our business climate, maybe not today, but as we try to attract the future worker, that's how it affects us. The jobs follow workers, workers don't follow jobs. We've got to have that creative class, we've got to have that younger generation, moving here to North Carolina, moving here to Charlotte." Dean Tillman closes with a small riff on how having a gay son and his partner and his partner's family has enriched her life.

Dean Tillman makes a powerful statement against the bigotry represented by Amendment One. but she says something else that's interesting. It is her reference to her son, her son's partner and their friends who, apparently, are a mixed crowd of gay and straight.

We get reports on this from everywhere. During the long public debate over *Don't Ask, Don't Tell,* and recently over DOMA, it has been a staple of progressives to claim that young people are far less rigid about these labels than older generations. Young people who are gay appear to be moving toward a position where *being born this way* does not lead to their being *a separate kind of person* who must define himself as *gay* or *straight.*

The problem we have in front of us is that we have these young people who're doing what young people do—they're thinking and feeling for themselves—and, at the same time, we have the federal judiciary which is constructing an entirely different theory of our sexuality. (See "It ain't necessarily so," February 29, 2012, Adriana Books, *adrianabooks/blog*)

78

The business of this country
April 30, 2012

Another gay teenager committed suicide last week. Apparently, we don't know details yet. Towleroad has the bare facts.

Jack Reese, seventeen years old, killed himself near Ogden, Utah, last week just as his eighteen-year-old boyfriend was about to take part in a panel discussion of the movie, *Bully*. Jack's boyfriend didn't know Jack had died until after the panel discussion was completed.

I don't know what to say. Jack's suicide drives me back to memories of my own high school life and to what it must have been like for Jack in Utah. I survived high school in South Carolina in the fifties, but I don't think I was stronger than Jack or that my high school was less filled with hate. I think when you are there, tottering on the edge between life and death, it is only luck, mere luck, that makes you come down on one side or the other. Jack was unlucky in a whole string of ways. He was unfortunate.

One of the things I hate about our political climate right now is that one of our political parties seems to take it as a matter of high political purpose to deny the existence of misfortune in people's lives. They deny that it even exists. And yet whole political populations in this country are born unfortunate, and without recognizing that, the rest of us can't help them. We can't even feel that they need us.

I hate Dan Savage's "It gets better" campaign. It is a weak, inadequate response. We should be out in the street crying, "Until these suicides stop, until every child feels loved, every person respected, no other business will be conducted in this country."

79

Precious citizenship
May 9, 2012

In North Carolina, returns are in, and we lost, as predicted. Rachel Maddow and Lawrence O'Donnell both pointed out that some version of this issue has come before the voters *thirty* times in various states, losing every time. Maddow also made the point that each time the civil liberties of gay people are put up for a vote of the people, gay people lose. There was a lot of chatter tonight about what this means for Barack Obama, whose views on this issue are "evolving," or doesn't mean. Some say it will have no effect on the November election, and some say that nothing Obama does can affect the movement for marriage equality. It is going to come, they say, with or without the president.

I can say that a whole evening of MSNBC is a painful experience for me personally, with or without bad news from North Carolina.

But the news made it worse. Even after a couple of decades of these elections, I still salivate at the announcement of one, feeling I suppose that *this time,* we will win. When we don't, I get in touch with my ancient cynicism. The American people will always vote against gay people. Except they don't, always. Sometimes they are not allowed to vote. In my own state, the leaders of the legislature repeatedly refused to allow the citizens of the Commonwealth of Massachusetts to vote on the civil rights of other citizens of the Commonwealth. This went on long enough for the citizens of the Commonwealth to see for themselves that marriage between two men or between two women had no effect on anybody else's marriage. I never forget how precious my citizenship in this state is to me.

80

When we needed to hear what Obama said, but there wasn't anybody to say it
May 12, 2012

At ten, in 1949, in the fourth grade, I was aware first of what was happening on the playground. I couldn't play ball. My father tried occasionally to teach me, but he didn't know how to teach me and didn't really know what it was he was supposed to be teaching. I hated recess, because that was when I felt most humiliated.

There was something wrong and the first part of the problem was that nobody knew what it was. It had something to do with playing ball, but it was way bigger than that. It was something about my having done something terrible, *being* something terrible, with my failing at being a boy. At ten, I was just beginning to hear from other kids things I didn't understand. I had no idea what was happening.

My teachers ignored it. The other kids on the playground could see what was going on—I couldn't play ball—but they just had one response, *call him a sissy.* My parents didn't want to hear about what was happening. If they listened to me tell them what was happening, then they would have to do something, and they didn't know what to do. I was already having feelings about other boys, but I didn't know whether these feelings were connected with what was happening on the playground. *Did these feelings have anything to do with being a sissy?*

There was nobody to tell me what was going on. It wasn't on the radio. It wasn't in church. My parents. My teachers. I didn't even know if this was the kind of thing you asked anybody else. I went through my whole life before I graduated from high school bewildered and humiliated.

And now, there's Barack Obama, the President of the United States speaking this week, and I wonder for a moment why I am so moved. It's because I grew up—years, decades, all those years of hurt and bewilderment—waiting to hear what Obama has just said this week. It's so much more powerful coming from him than from the Supreme Court.

Adults get tough and do what we have to do without kind words from anyone. But what we've all been getting in touch with this week is how it felt at ten on some playground somewhere when we needed to hear what Obama said, but there wasn't anybody to say it.

81

Disambiguation among Buchanan, Obama, Clinton, Shakespeare, Cellini, and me
May 17. 2012

Newsweek's cover, "Our First Gay President," has caused people to ask, "Is he really?" Andrew Sullivan used the word in the same metaphoric sense that "black" is used in the sentence, "Bill Clinton is our first black president." It meant that much of Obama's experience has been similar to the experience of gay people. In the words of Joe Biden, *he gets it*.

I think he does too, and he's proven that by being the most gay-friendly president ever. I don't understand gay people like Michelangelo Signorile, who thinks we ought to save the title for an actual gay person. That's silly. Nobody said that when Bill Clinton became known as our *first* black president. Nobody thought to say of Barack Obama, he's the *second* black person, after Bill Clinton. The first one got a metaphoric title and the second one got an actual title, and nobody was confused.

Underneath all this is still lingering bitterness directed against Obama for not directing all his energies against federal homophobic bigotry from the beginning in January 2009. Since he has already done so much of what he promised, I'm willing to cut him some slack and not begrudge him a hyped *Newsweek* cover, which, in any case, was a beautiful cover. In the end, we are going to be able to look back on the Obama years and say, *That was the beginning of the end of official bigotry.*

The other thread from this week has been this one: *But James Buchanan was the first gay president!* That's as silly as Signorile's proposal. Buchanan was president 1857-1861, nine years before anyone had an idea that there was such a thing as a gay person, and nine years before the word *homosexual* was invented. Even though Buchanan wrote that famous letter saying, "I have gone a wooing to several gentlemen," he was never gay because there was never a gay community for him to come out into. He was never out except, apparently, to a few friends and to "several gentlemen," and he had none of the political awareness or self-awareness that we associate today with being gay. Saying Buchanan was gay is as false as saying Shakespeare—or Benvenuto Cellini—was gay. I, on the other hand, am gay. I am deeply in love with my partner, Courtney, I am self-aware, and I am aware of the politics of being what I am. And everybody who knows me, knows I am gay.

82

Understanding our communal present
May 30, 2012

I have been writing to a man who went to the school I attended my
first two years of college. I didn't know him then—1957-1959—and
we haven't written in the intervening years. Then, about a week ago, he
found my page in a leaflet for our fiftieth class reunion. On my page,
in that slot where they ask you what you are doing now, I had said, "I
am writing gay novels" and gave the URL for my website. He's gay,
so he wrote, and I was glad he did. The school was in Tennessee, on
the edge of the Cumberland Plateau.

We've been asking each other questions, *What're you doing now?*
He's a college professor. *What was school like for you?* He had plenty
of gay sex, I had none. I left after two years and went into the Army, he
stayed for four. We asked each other what our lives would have been
like if he had left after two years and I had stayed for four. We
approached the questions, *Why did I leave and you stay?* It is surprising
that such a small school (1300 students) could have given two students
such radically different experiences.

The given, which doesn't have to be talked about much, is how
homophobic that world was in 1959. The question that I raised with him
was this: *Would my teachers have been supportive and nurturing even if
I told them I was gay in 1959?* Or would they have expelled me

from the university, there on the edge of the Cumberland Plateau? Would something worse have happened? Something violent? The stakes were high in 1959, and those were dangerous times, and it is hard now to reconstruct exactly what we were aware of and what we were feeling at that school.

The effort at reconstruction is necessary. It helps my friend and me build a friendship. It helps us determine why we did what we did in 1959. It helps us to understand how we ended up in such different places. Understanding ourselves enables friendship. But it's bigger than that. Accumulating the facts about our gay past enables us to understand our communal present. The effort to recover the gay past has as its goal a new *Descent of Man*.

83

Getting out in the open with our speech
June 3, 2012

Brandon K. Thorp posts on *Towleroad,* about President Obama proclaming Gay Pride Month: "At some point, I'm sure the novelty of seeing presidents speak this way about LGBT folk will wear off. For this writer, it hasn't yet." To get the same sense of satisfaction, check out both the text of the proclamation here, and the video here.

In other news this week, the Illinois Attorney General has announced that she will join the suits being brought by the Lambda Legal and by the ACLU against Illinois civil unions laws on the ground that they do not meet the state constitution's guarantees of equal protection. First, Obama's Department of Justice declines to exercise its traditional responsibilities to defend all the laws of the government when it declined to defend DOMA, and now we have the same thing happening on a state level. We make progress.

On the other side of the coin, Lila Shapiro, writing in Huffington Post, brings notice of a report from the National Coalition of Anti-Gay Violence Programs. More anti-gay murders were committed in 2011 than in any of other year since 1998. Chai Jindasurat, one of the authors of the report, said. "I think we're really just getting the tip of the iceberg here."

One of the difficulties with determining how much anti-gay violence is going on has always been the fact that many of the people most vulnerable to that violence would have to out themselves in order to report the violence.

Despite how dark the new data is, Jindasurat points to a possible positive aspect of the on-going tragedy: "We feel that it's not an actual increase in violence but that there are reasons this kind of violence is being recognized for what it is," Jindasurat said. "One big reason is that now it's more acceptable to talk about LGBTQ communities in general."

That's a positive point. And we can take away this idea: If it is more acceptable to talk about LGBTQ communities, and if that helps LGBTQ people most vulnerable to that violence, then the more we talk, the more publicly we talk, the more likely our talk will increase the ability of those vulnerable LGBTQ folks to seek help for themselves.

And finally, a book. Linda Hirshman has written a book entitled *Victory: The Triumphant Gay Revolution,* which will be published on June 5, 2012. I have read two reviews of this book, and both state what they think is the theme of the book, then they argue with that theme, and then they come around to saying, *She's right, of course, in many ways.* That's an interesting response. I have ordered the ebook version. I'll let you know whether it leads me to say, *She's right, of course,* or *There has been no victory. There can be no victory, despite Presidential proclamations and Attorneys General, while so many Americans are being murdered every year for being lesbian, gay, bisexual, transgender,* or *queer.*

84

But mainly just remember
June 13, 2012

The mixed news from the National Coalition of Anti-Violence Programs, discussed here last post, and the continuing epidemic of gay teenage-suicides around the country—it's hard to find any positive aspect of that fact—may be what caused some of us to find Gay Pride a mixed bag.

I like it that we do it, and I like it that, buried under the glitter and the beads, is a communal memory of the Stonewall Riots. The reason we hold Gay Pride in June every year is that it was in June that the cops in New York mounted a sustained attack on the life of their gay community, leaving three bars permanently closed—the Checkerboard, Tel-Star, and the Sewer. The cops raided the Stonewall *twice* in June 1969, and this, even though the owners of the Stonewall—the Mafia— paid them off regularly. So, there's something heroic happening at Pride, a history of bitterness. I could use a little more of that attitude, a little more militancy on these soft early summer days in Boston.

I understand that it's hard to maintain bravado, an in-your-face attitude, hard to maintain an *edge,* when we seem to be winning all our battles. And yet, the edge was still there on Saturday, underneath the groups carrying banners from the banks and the churches and synagogues from the area, and all the gay-straight alliances. The

Living Center was there to remind those of us who still remember
what the Living Center was—a community center for persons living
with AIDS—and there was a time when it seemed to be the beating
heart of all that was gay in Boston.

I also missed the man on stilts. He was up there, wearing a short
skirt and nothing else, and every time the wind blew, his stuff was
clearly on display. The taste-makers in the gay community decided
that things had gone too far, and Mayor Menino's support was worth
more to us than this particular dude's stuff, so the word was passed
and the community cleaned up its act, with the result being that
everything got boring, which it largely is today.

The float from Machine brought up the rear, as it does every year,
and I thought of that building on Boylston and the gay bar that used to
be called the Ramrod which, like many other things, including the
parade itself, has gotten bigger and slicker, but not better. I remember
the Ramrod when it was only one storefront wide, and we were all fairly
serious about our leather. I met my lover, Courtney, there, one night in
September, 1990, and we went home together that night and have been
together ever since. That's another achievement from that time that is
worth celebrating.

So, standing in the sun on Boylston Street across from Copley
Square, I was bored by the Pride parade—all those banks and churches!
and not enough glitter and not one man on stilts. I suppose I have moved
on from the time in my life when Pride was going to shock me. Now it
just makes me think and remember, grieve and remember, and be
grateful and remember. But mainly it just makes me remember.

85

We live in a world they made
June 23, 2012

Today is Alan Turing's one-hundredth birthday. Alan Turing contributed to the Allies winning World War II by breaking the Enigma codes that Germany used to communicate with its submarines. He had a large hand in inventing the computer that we use today and that today Google is celebrating by the publication of a "doodle," which you must have already seen because it's everywhere on the web today. And Turing is an original gay martyr to bigotry and anticipated gay liberation by decades. He died June 7, 1954, the apparent victim of a suicide after appalling treatment by the British Government for acknowledging his homosexuality. A biography about him, *Alan Turing: The Enigma* by Andrew Hodges, was published in 1983, and last month was brought out again (It is also available as an ebook for Kindles). There was also a Broadway play. Google "Alan Turing", and today see his name on the Google News page, under Technology or Google "Alan Turing Google Doodle."

Paul Mariani published *The Broken Tower* in 1999, a biography of Hart Crane, out of which James Franco made a movie in 2011. Hart Crane was another major gay figure who committed suicide (April 27, 1932). Franco seems to have made it an artistic cause to retrieve into the cinematic canon documents from the gay past. He brought out HOWL in 2010, a movie about Allen Ginsberg's first public reading of his poem.

The point here is the books about these men—*Alan Turing: The Enigma, The Broken Tower.* There has been, in the years since Stonewall, a great interest in the lives of gay men and women in the past, and that interest has resulted in a flourishing of biographies and histories.

The great histories—*Christianity, Social Tolerance, and Homosexuality: Gay People in Europe, from the Beginning of the Christian Era to the Fourteenth Century,* by John Boswell, is one of the first great works of scholarship on our community. Hundreds of others have followed, notably *Stonewall* by David Carter, on the riots themselves. There have been the histories of gay New York that preceded the Stonewall Riots, principally *Gay New York, 1890-1940,* by George Chauncey, and *The Gay Metropolis, 1940-1996,* by Charles Kaiser, and scores more.

All these books pose the question, *Who were the people who went before us? And what did they do?* It is one of the strongest aspects in gay liberation, whose anniversary we are approaching next Friday and Saturday, June 27 and 28, 2012, which is the forty-third anniversary of the Stonewall Riots.

This week I have re-read *Ceremonies*, about events in Maine during the summer of 1984 when Charles Howard was murdered, and have been reminded of one of my goals when writing that book: *What was it like to be gay in Maine in 1984?*

We have inherited the world bequeathed to us by Alan Turing and Hart Crane and the men and women of the Stonewall Riots and the men and women of the summer of 1984 in Bangor. Put another way, *we live in a world they made.* And to know who we are, we learn who they were and why they created the world they made.

86

The Stonewall Riots and me
June 27, 2012

Today is June 26th, and tomorrow is June 27th, and after midnight tomorrow night, one hour into June 28th, we will be into the forty-third anniversary of the Stonewall Riots. If you stay up one hour past midnight, it will be exactly forty-three years since Lt. Pine led his cops into the Stonewall Inn.

I could say I don't know why I am so moved by the story of the Stonewall riots. I choke up just reading about it. I know about the history before Stonewall, about the Mattachine Society and the Daughters of Bilitis and the riots on the West Coast, and I know about Frank Kameny. I've read, over and over, about the big woman and her part in the riots—she was the first person to really fight back—and about the anonymous kid (just about everybody agrees it was a kid) who, when watching the big woman fight her fight so heroically, cried out, "Help her!" And they did, and that's when it started. But that doesn't add up to why I am so moved by the story of Stonewall.

The reason I'm so moved is that I think I know what it must have been like to be a person who had never fought before and was so furious that he waded into that mob and didn't care what happened so long as he was fighting back. When the time came for me to come out, I was afraid that the people I loved most at that time would cease to love me. I felt I was about to lose every thing that mattered to me, and every person who mattered to me, and I was afraid it was going to *hurt,* and I wouldn't be able to stand the pain. Yet I went ahead and did it. I took a breath and laid it all out and refused to waiver. I just refused to say anything but, "I'm gay, and nothing's going to change that." And that gave me courage.

It was days, weeks, months, a year, before the pressure eased up and I began to realize that I'm going to survive. They *fought* at Stonewall, and when my time came, I fought too, and when I read about Stonewall, it's as if I'm back there, and I know how it feels to fight and be afraid and yet to have to fight anyway.

87

Honoring what gay people know
July 6, 2012

I recently wrote to a friend: "Like most peoples who are faced with the possibility of assimilation, many gay people wonder what they will be giving up in the process, and what they will be getting in return."

You see it every day in the city, watching Hispanics, some struggling to adopt English, others not, many of whom are determinedly holding onto Hispanic ways. Blacks have been facing the same dilemma for the last 150 years. And women too, as any woman will understand. While gay people have been discriminated against, they have developed modes of self-defense, which, they fear, will be lost if they are assimilated. It is not all about loss or gain of civil rights. It may not even be mainly about civil rights. What I think people would like most is to get freedom (that is, to get civil rights) without giving up anything. One example: We would like to get marriage equality, but have the "marriage" be an arrangement of our own creation, not the creation of heterosexual courts or the heterosexual congress, or patriarchal, heterosexual churches. I think we want a "gay marriage" that is more profoundly honest for both parties than the heterosexual marriage we see before us. I think we fear getting into a relationship in which we are forced to play out the gender roles that the straight community plays out in marriage.

Many gay people resist giving up what we have learned during our time in the wilderness. A person rarely reads, anywhere in the straight media, anything that would suggest straight people understand that they might have something important to learn from gay people. *And gay people know this*. Gay people think, *we have learned so much*, and straight people don't value what we know.

88

Uncomfortable truths

July 14, 2012

I was on Boston common today talking to a friend. We'd just gotten to know each other and we were asking the kinds of questions people ask, exploring each other's lives. He asked me, "Since you're gay, how did you manage to stay married so long? How did you *do* that?"

I told him, "Even though you're straight, you could do that too, have sex with a man, if you wanted to bad enough, or if you needed to, or felt you had to."

He said, "Not if my life depended on it."

I laughed. "That's probably the wrong kind of stimulus to be brought to bear on this issue. But something else. Look, people do it all the time. They don't change their orientation. You can't do that. What they do is go outside their orientation for a short time. *I* did it."

"No. Nothing can make me able to have sex with a man."

Probably each person requires a different kind of stimulus, but people are subject to external stimuli. Money is a stimulus for some people. Give them enough, and they'll do anything. Other people, something else—respect, place in the community, power. There is a whole range of things that affect how men and women choose the gender of the person they are going to have sex with, and getting turned on is only one of them. Witness the millions of gay men who have gotten married and fathered children in the last hundred years.

And the probably smaller number of straight men over the years who have had sex with gay men under a range of stimuli—often alcohol or drugs. We discussed the opening scene of *True Romance* and Christian Slater's character telling us under what conditions he would have sex with Elvis Presley. *If I had to. I mean had to.* He thought Elvis was as pretty as any woman.

What I didn't say to my friend, but could have, since it is true, is that sexuality is malleable—to an extent and for a short time. I could also have said that a man can't permanently alter his sexuality. But anybody can do anything *tonight*, if the stimulus is right.

89

Our literature, our lives, coming out
July 21, 2012

Some writers have taken "coming out" as the beginning of the plot and then made a novel of it. It might start, "In 1993, when I was fourteen, I came out to my best friend…." Others have taken "coming out" to be the climax of the plot, whose final sentence might end, "And then, in 2006, I came out and lived happily ever after…."

If you're a new novelist, there are several problems with these plots. One is that we've read these novels already. A more serious complaint is that, whether you make coming out the climax of the novel or the beginning of the novel, a major part of a person's life is going to be ignored (or have to be imagined). In some kinds of fiction, that's OK. When Shakespeare's lovers get married in the fifth act, we are not invited to wonder what comes next.

But some kinds of modern fiction, being more realistic, *do* wonder. For many of us, *coming out* happens somewhere in the middle of our lives, after some major event and before some other major event. Even a guy coming out at ten years old has some pretty intense stuff going on, before and after.

When I sat down to write *Race Point Light*, I planned to base this novel loosely on a typical life of a man in my generation, and all the different parts of that life were *real* life, every single part of it—his childhood, the run-up to his marriage, his marriage, his children's births, the run-up to his divorce, his divorce, his coming out, his move to an urban gay community, AIDS, his meeting the man who was going to become his partner, their fighting disease together—and it makes a different kind of novel. In *Race Point Light*, *coming out* is neither the end of anything nor is it the beginning of anything. Much more realistic. There is nothing about this life that is *ever after*.

Race Point Light tells a story that begins a long time before the narrator comes out and that ends a long time afterward. It's the story of a man's life that is typical of many gay men in post-war generations. *Race Point Light* explores the drama in these lives, and it has the added advantage of being close to the way we really experience ourselves. There is no fairy tale here.

90

Boy Scouts, here are our medals
July 26, 2012

When I was thirteen or fourteen in South Carolina—we're talking about the early fifties here—the Boy Scouts were different from all the other activities a boy could do. We went on weekend overnight campouts to some local "woods," and I looked forward to it all week long. At night, after the campfire and after the songs and stories, and after whatever else we did, I rolled out my sleeping bag next to one of the adult leaders, and then, when it was dark, I reached behind me and found the Scout leader's arm and pulled it over me. I loved that. It was the only place in my life where I could snuggle up close to a man. The adult allowed his arm to remain across me for a few minutes and then he removed it. Often I got his arm again and pulled it over me, and after a few minutes he pulled it back. This helped me to go to sleep.

When I had grown up some, I regretted having lost those moments at the overnight camping trips with the Boy Scouts, but the memory of them kept me going until, several years later, I was awarded Eagle Scout rank and Order of the Arrow. I have forgotten what the Order of the Arrow was, but I remember believing at the time that it was important.

I don't believe that organizations like the BSA contribute much to the growth and development of children. I don't think I am a different adult from what I would be if I hadn't gone out for Scouts, but I do remember vividly lying in my sleeping bag next to my Scout leader after dark and feeling warm and protected and comforted, when I didn't get those feelings at any other place in my life. At a time in my life when I felt isolated, alone, fearful, inadequate, Scouts gave me comfort.

It is the memory of lying in my sleeping bag next to my Scout leader—and my gratitude for that memory—that has prevented me from returning my Eagle Scout Badge to BSA. Even though it is clear that the BSA has turned its back on me, I didn't feel I could turn my back on that memory of that man who understood what some boys need and let me get what I needed from him.

In the intervening years, my son was born and grew up and chose not to enter Scouts. Now my grandson is approaching that age. Given the situation, I am going to stay away from his decision to go into Scouts or not. I doubt that he does.

But today, I have mailed off to Irving, Texas, my Eagle Scout badge and that sash that Boy Scouts wear with all the merit badges. My partner, Courtney, asked what I was doing, and then said, "Wait a minute." And in a minute he came back with his badges. He said, "Here, put these in too." And I did.

Returning these badges is a way of coming out to the Boy Scouts of America, letting them know that they have—and had—gay scouts they have to respect. When we have in our culture organizations like the Boy Scouts of America and, up until the repeal of DADT, the armed services, it is important to constantly inform them and everybody in the public that we are gay and that we're here, that, in fact, we have always been here, gay in the Scouts and gay in the military (I was gay in the military from 1959 to 1961), and in all the other organizations that have pretended they could change reality, get rid of us and make us not exist. We've always existed, and we haven't ever gone away, there are still gay boys in the Scouts now, and the Boy Scouts of America can't make us go away, just by passing some silly little rule in Irving, Texas. There are always going to be gay boys in the Boy Scouts of America. Do the Scouts really think they can succeed where the Army, the Marines, the Navy, and the Air Force of the United States of America have failed?

91

Larry Kramer and 200 men taught us how to fight
August 5, 2012

My partner is out of town for the weekend, and this afternoon I went by myself to *Dark Knight Rises*. Much of the outdoor shooting takes place on Wall Street in pitched battles between the New York police and the bad guys. In the first image, Wall Street is cleared of traffic and the cops are crowded at one end of the block in front of the Stock Exchange. The bad guys are crowded down at the other. Powerful image.

It made me think of the first big AIDS demonstration, which was in the same place—on March 24, 1987, in front of the New York Stock Exchange. There were about 200 gay men and women. They stopped traffic, and by doing so, captured the media. Because many of the participants had AIDS, they had manipulated the cops into putting on rubber gloves and masks, and they looked terrible. Our guys were in all the papers the next morning—except the *Times*—and it was clear from the media that the guys with AIDS were the good guys. It was from this demonstration that Larry Kramer formed ACT UP, focussed on the chokehold that the FDA had on AIDS medications.

It was a small demonstration—two hundred men and women—in comparison to all those policemen in *Dark Knight Rises*, and what I was thinking of this afternoon, sitting in the cinema, was how huge the effect of ACT UP had been on vast stretches of American life—on public health, on the practice of medicine, on pharmacology, and, of course, on the place of gay people in American public life.

A friend made the same point about the Stonewall Riots. *They were really very small, weren't they?* Well, yes. But it doesn't take vast throngs of men and women to change the nation, if the few you have are of the right sort. Our few had science on their side, and the Constitution, and, of course, morality. No wonder they were powerful. And another thing. The men and women at this first demonstration of the group that became ACT UP taught us that *decorum* is a weapon the other side uses against us. So ACT UP taught us again (we have to keep learning this) to stop being polite.

*

On AIDS and the transformation of America, read Steven Epstein, *Impure Science: AIDS, Activism, and the Politics of Knowledge,* Berkeley: University of California Press, 1996.

92

Travolta and the failure of our language on sex
August 17, 2012

Last week people wanted John Travolta to come out, and he wouldn't, and then writers retracted their requests, ending up with statements like, "Nobody's personal life is my business." We think very badly about sex in our culture.

Mary Elizabeth Williams, writing in Salon, says "frankly, if being a guy who regularly has sex with other guys doesn't make you gay, I'm not sure what does." She gets close to the heart of the confusion here. She would have "being gay" defined by the man's actions. It's not. Sucking cock does not make you gay. Even *enjoying* sucking cock, does not make you gay. Sleeping with women does not make you straight either. In our culture, during my whole life, we have told ourselves that a series of actions made us a certain kind of person. That is emphatically not so. A man's sexuality is defined by how a man thinks and feels. I have only to look at the humanity around me to see that this is so.

Consider these things: There are more than two genders and gradations of each one, with no clear bright line separating anything, as each story of a transgender person tells us. And how do we find out what gender a person is? That person will tell us. My desire may likewise take many forms—life-long for one gender and for one person or for several people for a shorter period or for many people. I may, in fact, have two or more different kinds of relationships simultaneously—a long-term, permanent relationship based on the totality of the way humans can connect and a series of short impermanent relationships based on sex, or *vice versa*. *In* and *Out* don't describe anything real. I am what I am. I don't need *coming out* as a gateway to myself nor do I need *coming out* to tell other people about such a private thing as my sex. In short, I can be a major Hollywood star, in a long-term marriage, and can have sex occasionally with men, and it's nobody's business but my own. (What I can't do, of course, is be publicly homophobic while sucking cock.)

In these matters, one size does not fit all. The Christian church did humanity in the West a huge disservice by trying to impose one set of vows on all people in the Christian marriage liturgy. Some people wanted monogamy, some didn't. The agreements people arrive at to give structure to their relationships should be open to occasional renegotiation by the people involved. No one else can know the factors that are brought to bear upon any person's choices. *The choice is private.*

I have nothing to say about John Travolta's sex. On the other hand, no public figure has anything to say about my sex, either. I seek what is right for me, with one great commandment governing all—do no harm and allow no harm to be done to us or our children.

93

Focusing on the most important thing
August 22, 2012

Now it is time to focus on the Supreme Court.

Here are the stakes: Ruth Bader Ginsburg was born in 1933, Stephen Breyer in 1938, and Anthony Kennedy in 1936. These three justices were part of the majority in both major GLBT civil rights cases of the last twenty years. It is possible that one of these justices will have to be replaced before the next presidential election. If Romney is elected, and if he has a chance to nominate a replacement for any of these three justices, it is likely that he will choose someone like Samuel Alito or John Roberts, or, even worse, like Antonin Scalia or Clarence Thomas, who dissented in both of these cases.

If that were to happen, this would be the result: *Lawrence v. Texas*, decided in 2003, which overturned all sodomy laws, could itself be overturned. The majority on that decision would flip from Kennedy, Ginsburg, Breyer, Sotomayor and Kagan, to a presumed majority composed of Scalia, Thomas, Roberts, Alito and a new conservative justice. *Romer v. Evans*, decided in 1996 by a 6 to 3 opinion, recognized that gay people must be constitutionally protected. The majority on that case would flip from Kennedy, Ginsburg, Breyer, Sotomayor and Kagan, to a presumed majority composed of Scalia, Thomas, Roberts, Alito, plus the new conservative justice.

The point here is that, were Romney to win the election, the makeup of a court would make it possible for a conservative majority to work its will with our rights. We are *one vote* on the Supreme Court away from being a different kind of nation, and the election of Romney would supply conservatives with the chance to get that vote. See also Daily Kos. Time. and Huffington Post.

When you consider what to do with your support this summer and fall and with your vote, consider this: there is no more important issue facing gay people than the makeup of the Supreme Court.

94

Gentle, Stylish, Astonishing
August 25, 2012

Check this one out. It's a *car ad*, and it's running in Japan only.

It raises the issues we've been talking about here—the beauty of men and of women, the range of possibilities before us which may or may not include sex, the essential need for surprise, a fluid impermanent sense of gender, and, overriding everything, the knowledge that all of these things are more valuable than their opposites. Life is better, now.

Toyota's gender-bending win

A car commercial with a twist plays with gender
expectations—and wins

by Mary Elizabeth Williams

It's not the first time a beautiful, bikini-clad model has been used to sell a car. But this one's a little different.

In a new Japanese Toyota ad, the long-haired 19-year-old Ukrainian Stav Strashko struts toward a car as the camera lovingly follows the model's perfect, red bikini-bottomed butt. A jacket is seductively shed. And then Strashko turns around to reveal – she's a man, baby! Yup, that bare chest is flat, but the bulge in the bikini bottom is not.

It's a novel twist on the old hot chick advertising trope, and while it may have exactly zero to do with why you should buy a car, it has everything to do with the changing way gender is portrayed in advertising. Strashko is the surprise within the ad but, thankfully, he isn't the punch line of it. This isn't some transphobic BS trying to sell the notion of what makes a "real" woman (apparently it's menstrual blood) or some hardy-har-har challenge to distinguish the "stallions from the mares" or a joke about how gender identity is something one whimsically takes on and then regrets. In a making-of clip, Strashko says proudly, "I can't put it in words how excited I am about this commercial and everything I experienced here."

Why is the ad not running in America? No doubt because it would immediately gay indoctrinate all our menfolk and then there would never be any more babies made and Mitt Romney would never become president. Why did Toyota make certain that the comments for the ad were disabled? Um, have you ever read the comments on YouTube? We still have work to be done, people.

Strashko, like fellow androgynous model Andrej Pejic, isn't transgender, isn't doing drag. As he says, "I've never thought about becoming a woman. I feel very comfortable in my own body just the way it is." He represents a new understanding that gender isn't always neatly defined, and that if a man can be alluringly beautiful, that shouldn't be anything to be laughed at or scared of. The jury's out whether that's a concept that can sell Toyotas. But it's definitely an idea worth sharing.

95

The homeless man, his son, and me
August 31, 2012

Right now, I can't escape thinking about politics and our choices. The question that occupies me is raised in my walks around the city by the demands made on me—on my time and energy—by various groups asking for money and support, by a homeless man holding a sign, "For me and for my son." I get home and find emails from the president asking for "$13 before midnight tonight." Then there are the ones closer to home, The Human Rights Campaign and GLAAD and the other gay rights organizations.

I could ignore all this, saying, "Those things have nothing to do with me." And they may not. Gay men normally don't have anything to do with women's issues and don't necessarily have anything to do with the issues of homeless men. It may be that the strongest connection between those causes and me is that I care about the welfare of other citizens, which is a pretty tenuous connection.

So, walking around the city, I search for a stronger connection between me and the malnourished kid, the homeless men, and the women seeking abortion, and the political campaigns. Why do I have to get deeply involved in Obama's campaign for re-election? We're human—me and the malnourished kid and the homeless man, the woman seeking abortion—and we all get our rights from the same place, the Constitution and also from the basic fact of what we are. Not because we are good or kind or thoughtful, but because we are human.

We can't escape the fact that we are all connected, and if I want respect because I am a gay human male, I can't escape giving respect. I can't get it unless I give it.

It is only a short step to being committed politically, giving money and carrying signs for the candidate who is going to do something for the malnourished kid, the woman seeking an abortion, and the homeless man and his son. As gay people, the vision we have is of a world in which, if we are free, all must be free. We can't equivocate on that.

96

The effects of the life I've led
August 31, 2012

I told him I didn't trust therapists. The young man said he didn't know why a person wouldn't trust therapists. I reminded him that half my life the American Psychiatric Association had in its diagnostic manual that gay people suffered from various kinds of mental illness *because they were gay*, and they didn't change that diagnosis until 1971 when the Gay Liberation Front broke into their meeting and stopped the proceedings. Psychologists and psychiatrists were the source of all those things floating around in the culture that said, *gay people are sick.* At the APA meeting, Frank Kameny of the GLF cried out, "Psychiatry is the enemy incarnate. Psychiatry has waged relentless war of extermination against us. You may take this as a declaration of war against you!" And it was *then* that the APA agreed that gay people were OK. The young man that I was talking to didn't know about this and said therapists were not like that anymore. He was sympathetic and seemed interested in what I was telling him. Here in the city, at meetings, and in our bookstores, and everywhere else, gay men and women who have spent half their lives coping with the abuse they got from the APA mingle with everybody else.

This experience—this kind of experience—had a profound effect on the generations who came to adulthood before Stonewall. Many older gay men and women are wary of the recent gains of our community— DADT and what's happening with DOMA and the various court cases around Prop 8 in California and recently even the football players in the NFL. Are these successes going to last? When the Republicans get in next time, will they chip away at our rights? Or revoke them entirely? These gains aren't necessarily permanent. Older people sense the tentativeness of our existence.

One of the effects of the life we've led is a self-protectiveness that characterizes many older gay men and women, an unwillingness to give up the protective styles and attitudes they developed when it was hard and dangerous to be gay. They may need them again some day. I have an anxiety that is difficult to convey to my children or my partner—who is a different generation—or to younger friends, and I have a need to say, *But you don't understand.*

So, aside from the need to re-elect Barack Obama, the gay community faces a fault line between the generations which is going to stay with gay people until the older generation gradually dies off. I suspect this fault line between generations may make us less effective as a community. But then, in our effort to overcome it, we may learn something very valuable about love.

*

For more on the war between the gay liberation movement and the American Psychiatric Association, see:

Carter, David. *Stonewall: The Riots that Sparked the Gay Revolution.* New York: St Martin's Griffin, 2005.

Clendinen, Dudley & Nagourney, Adam. *Out for Good: The Struggle to Build a Gay Rights Movement in America.* New York: Simon & Schuster, 1999.

97

The operative word is *fight*
October 2, 2012

Before AIDS, people got sick, went to their doctors, were told what to do, and got better—or worse and died—and that didn't change until HIV had been among us for five years or so. Since the drug companies weren't coming out with effective medications, and since the federal medical establishment seemed to be in no hurry, and since the government didn't seem to have a *plan,* gay men and women stopped looking to others for a solution in their fight against AIDS. They started making noise, joining together and making a *loud* noise, making charges against the pharmaceutical companies that they were making obscene profits off ineffective drugs for AIDS. They fought against the FDA, which had no sense of urgency about releasing drugs that might be helpful to persons with AIDS, and against the whole medical establishment, which didn't understand that it would practice medicine better if it worked *with* the affected populations instead of only operating *on* them. Gay men and women came together at a meeting in New York in March, 1987, and heard the irascible Larry Kramer make the charge that if AIDS was a medical crisis, it was also a political crisis. They formed AIDS Coalition to Unleash Power (ACT UP) in March 1987, and on March 24, 1987 stopped traffic on Wall Street to demand greater access to experimental drugs and a coordinated national policy to fight AIDS. This was the beginning of AIDS activism. It happened during the Reagan Administration and during the George H W Bush administration, both of whom had allowed conservative attitudes against gay people to infect their response to AIDS.

How to Survive a Plague is a documentary by David France that opened last Friday in New York and on Thursday here in Boston. It appears to be made up of videos made by participants in these meetings and demonstrations, using handheld videocams. The documentary is about ACT UP and its fight against the federal government. The documentary is messy, immediate, clear, and extremely powerful. If you don't know this story, you should see this documentary. If you want to be reminded of it—it's been a long time—then get yourself to this movie.

Much of what happened as a consequence of AIDS and ACT UP and Larry Kramer proved that Larry Kramer was right. He was the nearest thing we have to an Old Testament prophet. It's never comfortable living at the same time as an Old Testament prophet. People get tired of being bullied by a man who says he speaks for God. But when Larry Kramer shouts out into the middle of a meeting of ACT UP that has lost its way, "PLAGUE!" and all go silent, it is clear that Larry Kramer was right, The reason our medical research establishment operates the way it does today and the reason clinical research is conducted the way it is today, is, in large part, because of Larry Kramer and ACT UP. They didn't mind being rude if they could save our lives. *How to Survive a Plague* makes clear that there are millions of people who are alive today because Larry Kramer and ACT UP learned how to push the federal medical establishment, including the FDA, and the pharmaceutical companies, to keep searching for effective drugs that would save our lives. The ACT UP motto is ACT UP, FIGHT BACK, FIGHT AIDS. In case you missed it, *FIGHT* is the operative word.

98

Come out!: 1
October 11, 2012

As long as our culture is homophobic, many gay people are going to feel they have to come out. It's an act of courage, self-defense and self-respect.

But I don't think we think often about what we do when we come out and about what it means. Few people think about the fact that straight people don't come out, although my children and grandchildren—all straight—individually came out to me several years ago. I take it that one difference between my children and grandchildren, on the one hand, and me, on the other, is that we continue to live in a mainly homophobic society, and it is necessary for me to declare myself against that bigotry and to take a political stand. While children and grandchildren aren't required by the politics of their time to take a stand, they came out to me and to Courtney, my partner, because they love us.

A diary by STEVEinMI's in Daily Kos today discusses the effect of coming out on the people around Steve in Michigan who are not necessarily gay. Another diary from Daily Kos, from Billeh, quotes Harvey Milk: "Gay brothers and sisters, you must come out. Come out to your parents … Come out to your relatives. Come out to your friends, if indeed they are your friends. Come out to your neighbors, to your fellow workers, to the people who work where you eat and shop.

Come out only to the people you know, and who know you. Not to anyone else. But once and for all, break down the myths, destroy the lies and distortions. For your sake. For their sake."

The trouble with all this is that Harvey Milk and Steve in Michigan are both telling me I *must* come out. In a free society, in which it is just as easy to be gay as straight, it should be a personal choice. I am aware we don't live in a free society, and it is not just as easy to be gay as to be straight, but we shouldn't forget that a free society is our goal. In a truly free society, my sexual orientation is an entirely personal fact. All of us ought to remember that, while we give money to candidates and to HRC and work to get out the vote. The more we are successful, the less permanent will be our present patterns of thought.

There's going to come a time when people don't have to come out and don't have to think about the good of all mankind and can think only of themselves. That's what we're going for on such a personal subject.

It's also true that, even today, the language we use doesn't fit the present reality of people's lives.

*

There is a lot more to this subject. I will post Come Out! (2) and Come Out! (3) tomorrow and on the weekend, all as part of celebration of National Coming Out Day.

99

Come out!: 2
October 14, 2012

Conventional wisdom would have us believe that the period *before* we came out, was a terrible place. *The closet.* Billeh, in the Daily Kos, quotes Paul Monette, who calls it a "hidden life," and "half a life." This is the way gay writers and politicians think about what went before coming out. I am sure that is true for some people, but it is not true for many others. I got married in 1965 and I had children in 1969 and 1970, and while that life was difficult, it was not impossible and it was emphatically not "half a life." During that time—a period that began for us in 1965 and ended finally twenty years later in 1984—I earned a PhD, my wife and I bought and sold three houses. I wrote a book that was published by a major university press. We raised two children, and I got a promotion and tenure, we established ourselves in our community, and we did all of this even though the conventional wisdom in the gay community was that I was closeted, living half a life. That's outrageous.

I have been gay my entire life, beginning when I was about ten. I have never been bisexual. I got married because I was looking for a way to live, and at that time the gay people that I knew seemed to be rebels and I wasn't yet able to rebel against my culture. At that time, I thought I wanted to be a college professor and to live the life I did, in fact, live for almost twenty years. I met a woman, and she and I fell in love. We shared an amazingly rich world view. It is not true that if gay men fall in love with women and marry them, they are at least bisexual. These terms are dependent upon the subject's self-perception. They are not dependent upon who or what gender he is having sex with. I never had any sexual responses to any woman even remotely comparable to the sexual response I have had to men. But the gender of the person I have fallen in love with was infinitely less important than the kinds of things she and I both found important—the paintings we liked, the furniture, the design of houses, our children at every stage of their growth, the books we liked—but I never lost my sense of myself as a gay man, and, during the almost twenty years of my marriage, I told many, many people, both men and women, that I was gay. I was gay, I was also monogamous, as I had promised at my marriage, and I was about as happy as most married men of 44.

But what astonishes me is that nobody is really happy with the way I was living my life. Certain people on the political spectrum didn't like it that I had, in my mind, images of sex with other men while having sex with a woman. And after Stonewall in 1969, there were plenty of gay men who would have called me the dread word, *closeted,* and didn't like it that I was living with a woman and fathering children while professing to be gay. And yet I didn't think I was unique. To the contrary, I thought I was pretty typical of gay men of my generation, some large percentage of whom had gotten married and had fathered children. What was coming clear to me was that our sex lives were not nearly as clear as our language seemed to imply, with its short list of binaries: men and women, gay and straight. Things are messier than that, yet not less interesting, or valuable, or moral, or healthy.

100

Come out!: 3
October 18, 2012

Coming out—both the action and the word—differs depending on where you live. It seems it has always been easier to come out in coastal California and in the Northeast than in the South and the middle parts of the country. It has been easier in New York, Los Angeles, San Francisco, and other big cities, and it can be really difficult in small towns around the country. It also differs by your age. A man born before the Second World War would have been an adult for ten years before Stonewall changed everything, but a guy born in the early fifties might experience the sudden changes of Stonewall as if *these things have always been this way.* A guy born in 1990 might see Stonewall and all it meant as ancient history. Yet we all end up in the same Gay Pride Marches.

What's interesting is that in the same hundred-thousand-person crowd, someone may say, "When I came out," and mean something very different by it than the man walking next to him. Or, a person may say, "I never came out," and be standing next to a man who has never come out either, but for reasons diametrically opposed to the first person. *He never had to.*

I don't think I ever came out—or else the process was so long and done so gradually that there was never a moment when I was able to say, *and after that I was out.* But the man standing next to me in the parade, who has just graduated from college, can legitimately say, "I never came out, either," because he grew up in an upscale family outside of Boston, and about the time he was discovering the idea of sex, he was discovering that it was all happening because he liked *boys,* and he talked to his dad about it.

I suspect that there will be larger and larger percentages of people who say they never came out. I suspect that the phrase *come out* is going to have a mainly historical interest. Even more, the word *closet* is going to be less and less useful for gay people. It will be applied to a smaller and smaller period in one's life—finally not even to the few month period between a boy's discovering what his dick can do and his realization that it's *boys* and *this is not going to change.* The whole point of the word will be lost.

101

The Court, the Court!
October 25, 2012

Remember the Supreme Court. Remember how fragile is the majority in *Roe v. Wade* and the majority in *Lawrence v. Texas*.

These are essential cases, defining the kind of nation we live in. If the Supreme Court reverses itself in either one, the place of women and of gay people will be transformed, and we will become aliens in our own land.

Do not forget the Supreme Court, when you come to vote.

102

Now it is our turn
November 5, 2012

Barack Obama has proven himself a friend of LGBT people. He's a friend of the families of LGBT people, and he's a friend of friends of LGBT people. He has done more for LGBT people than any other president. He steered the effort to overturn DADT, he directed the Department of Justice to refuse to defend DOMA. He released a fully argued and unprecedented case for giving any legal attempt to limit the rights of gay people "heightened scrutiny," and he announced that he was over his process of "evolving" and that he was now in fact in favor of marriage equality. As scores of commentators have pointed out, by his actions the president has transformed the debate over the place of LGBT people in America. Now, the question is, "Why should *any* rights be denied *any* LGBT citizens?"

This is a huge transformation, and it has come about largely as a result of Barack Obama. Before him, we were still in the position of arguing for one right at a time. Is there anyone who really believes that DADT would have been repealed by *any* Republican and that its repeal would have been effected by *any* Republican so smoothly and without incident? And isn't it necessary to see that *this* president, Harvard graduate and University of Chicago School of Law faculty member, is particularly powerful in his advocacy of LGBT issues *because he is black?*

Many on the left complain that the policies of the Obama administration seem to continue the Bush administration—the drones and the kill-lists and some of the worst aspects of Patriot Act—and it is necessary now for all of us to plot a strategy to publicize these wrongs in such a way as to stop any president from continuing them in the future. But the consensus on the left is that Obama is good at foreign policy. He's cool, he's knowledgeable, and he has good judgment. He's handled Iraq, Afghanistan, Syria, Libya, and Iran. We are less entangled now than we were in 2008, nothing new has started on his watch, and the War on Terror is over. He's not a bully, and the world knows that.

Then there is the economy. All the numbers show that recovery is on track, and while the pace of recovery is slower than we wanted, it is going in the direction we want—toward support for the middle class and more income equality.

I am going to vote for Barack Obama. He's the first president in my lifetime that I could call, with any seriousness, *my* president. It's just very good that, in addition to being for *me*, for *us*, for LGBT people, he's also smart, tough, knowledgeable, has an historical sense, and is not an ideologue. He's the only one running for president who could have written *Dreams from my Father*, and he's the one the rest of the world apparently wishes we would choose.

103

Unresolved pain
November 12, 2012

There is a moment in *Homeland*, on Showtime Channel, when Damien Lewis, as Brody, sits at a table in a cell, supposedly in CIA headquarters, his feet chained to the floor, his hands chained to the table. Brody had been imprisoned for eight years in an Arabic country. Flashes of that experience make Damien Lewis look like Edmond Dantes in the Chateau d'If. Brody had long unkempt hair and beard and wild and suffering eyes. Now, in the CIA prison, Brody is battered by a CIA operative, Carrie, played by Claire Danes. This man was battered first by the Arabs and now by the CIA, and his face is raw with his pain. As the scene moves forward, he begins to weep. *I have never seen TV like this before.*

"Unresolved pain is another recurring *Homeland* theme," says June Thomas, the writer on Slate's online discussion of this program—unresolved pain from the 1947 war, from the endless Palestinian conflict, from 9/11, from Brody's eight-year imprisonment and torture.

None of the characters in *Homeland* seem to have gotten past any of the horrors of their pasts, and none of the histories of these people seems to be resolved. Damien Lewis's face, which seems stunned by his own suffering, by the sheer amount of pain his tormentors are willing to inflict on his body, is the face of that suffering.

And now, four days after the 2012 election, in which LGBT people have won historic victories—marriage equality in three states has won, an anti-marriage equality constitutional amendment defeated, a lesbian elected to the US Senate, and others—it is not time to dust out hands and say, *We won that one,* and move on.

We are in the midst of a great victory, but we cannot forget those who have been damaged and injured by the way things have been. By personal hatred and bullying that left generations of gay men and women psychologically and spiritually and physically damaged. By professionals in the American Psychological Association and in the American Psychiatric Association who, until the early nineteen seventies, insisted without any evidence that gay people were sick and made whole generations of American citizens emotional cripples. By the damage that even now is being done to gay Americans by the churches and by religious people. By the refusal of power brokers in our culture up until very recently to help gay people have children by adoption or by AI. By all those long years when we couldn't get married, couldn't get our books published, couldn't write the truth about ourselves, couldn't express the truth about ourselves, had no political power.

The pain our people have suffered must now be remembered in this moment in which we have won great victories. We must find a way to resolve the accumulated pain from the past. And those who are celebrating today's victories must include those who suffered the pain of the long struggle, but who have not been able to share in its victories. They are us too.

104

The way we are now
November 27, 2012

The most interesting thing in the *Times* article by Micah Cohen, on the gay vote, on November 16, is that, among straight voters, the vote was roughly divided, 49% Democratic and 49% Republican. The gay vote, which was 5% of the total, was approximately 75% Democratic, more than enough to give Obama the ultimate advantage, according to a study by Gary J. Gates of the Williams Institute at the U.C.L.A. School of Law, in conjunction with Gallup. It appears that we gave Obama the decisive edge in the election. It appears, finally, we can claim we have power and the next goal is the Employment Non-Discrimination Act, or *ENDA*.

Carole Cadwalladr announces in *The Guardian* that Nathan Silver has announced he is gay. He's the man of whom Rachel Maddow said, "You know who won the election tonight? Nate Silver." Jon Stewart "saluted him as 'Nate Silver! The lord and god of the algorithm.'" After all, he correctly predicted the vote in *fifty* states, and he's gay.

What else? Well, a gay *Abraham Lincoln.* J. Bryan Lowder, in Slate, writes, "In a particularly poignant moment in *Lincoln*, honest Abe spends a few moments with a handsome telegraph operator, played by a somewhat period-discordant Adam Driver. 'Do we choose to be born? Are we fitted to the times we're born into? 'the Great Emancipator wonders aloud, gazing tenderly at the young man." The scene, and apparently the movie, don't give a definitive answer to the question of Lincoln's sexuality, but it's suggestive in this scene with the young man, and it shows what it would have looked like, had Lincoln, our greatest president, been into men. That's a step in the right direction.

Then there's Daniel Craig, as 007, and Javier Bardem, the sexual object-choice for half the gay men in America, who plays a gay villain named Silva. Mark Simpson writes of their most charged scene, "Whether out of genuine desire or a desire to undercut 007's masculinity, Silva slides up close to his bound antagonist and caresses his thighs: 'There's a first time for everything – eh, Mr. Bond? 'But Bond meets his captor's gaze with his customary implacability and asks, 'What makes you think it's my first time?'" Well, whatever. 007 knows about gay sex, and he isn't uneasy with it, whether it's his first time or his thirty-third. He's not *bothered.*

That's a lot of triumphs for the LGBT team in a short time, which we're not yet accustomed to. We'll remember election 2012 for many reasons, and I have no doubt that we will remember the folks who didn't make it to this point.

*

Mark Simpson, *www.nightcharm.com/2012/11/16/poofy-galore-mark-simpson-reviews-skyfall-for-nightcharm/#jump*

105

What do we want?
December 12, 2012

'Tis the season for it. Wanting things. But the question is really about us gay people and what's happening now as we wait for the Supreme Court.

A commentator this week makes a point about the effect of marriage equality on the behavior of gay people. Apparently we want to be like the straight middle-class.

I once sat in an audience while one of the lawyers who had argued the gay marriage cases before the Supreme Judicial Court of the Commonwealth of Massachusetts, which resulted in the first legal gay marriages in America, said, "Gay people want the same things as straight people."

That is manifestly not true. There are many, many things about straight marriage that I do not want anywhere near my long-term gay relationship with Courtney.

At least some of us want long-term relationships which have room for experimentation. At least some of us want to escape the laws influenced by this nation's puritan past and accept more open display of our bodies, in private and on the beach and in our parades and in our art. What we don't want is to have our long-term relationships defined for us by judges in California or Justices in Washington. I don't think we want to enter an institution whose major framework was determined in the fourteenth century or even the nineteenth or twentieth. We want to do it for ourselves and make it fit our lives now, in the twentieth-first century.

We don't want religious people to impose their beliefs on us in these matters of sex, love, and relationships.

I wrote about this earlier this year:

> Without having determined what we want, aside from "marriage," we are rushing into a situation where the most restrictive of us are going to try to lay down rules for the rest of us about our bodies and our sex and try to make everybody adhere to rules. An emotional loving commitment between two persons necessarily means a commitment to sexual monogamy. "I love you" necessarily means "I am going to promise you." It means, I will love you only and in return you must love me only, which, for many people, is akin to a declaration of ownership and an expectation of ownership and has no place when a man says, "I love you."

The only declaration I feel compelled to make to the man with whom I share my life is that I don't own him or his body, and he doesn't own mine, even though the Chief Justice of the Supreme Judicial Court of the Commonwealth of Massachusetts has declared that, in the Commonwealth, "marriage" means "The voluntary union of two persons, as spouses, to the exclusion of all others." Why should a judge make such a requirement on me and Courtney?

It may already be too late to stop the people who want to control us and to turn us into something we're not. In any case, as these things move forward, it is possible for all of us to say, "Wait. Wait. That doesn't apply to me. We are free. Take your rules to another country."

106

The highway, the dark, the silent bus, the tablet screen, thoughts of a friend
December 21, 2022

Our son called twice yesterday, working out the details of a gift for his children. Our daughter came on Saturday and spent the evening here— I cooked, and she talked—before going to Logan to pick up a friend of hers.

I have been corresponding with a friend in a border state about a twenty-year-old student and coming out and the role of a faculty member in that process. In the last week, we've written six emails back and forth. My friend the faculty member is navigating the shoals of different generations, different geographies, different cultures and the effect of all of these on a person's coming out.

Another friend texts late at night from one of those cheap buses between Boston and New York. "Things are going backwards, not forward," she says. She talks about people in NYC who are gay and who are mixed race or mixed orientation and "are feeling the shit along with me." She talks about racism and homophobia. In the big city men and women who are mixed race and mixed orientation can—and do— find a home, even if they also, sometimes, are "ambushed" and swear they're not going to live in the USA any more.

Courtney and I saw *Lincoln* last night and noted the venal reasons given by the players for being against the Thirteenth Amendment, something that now—once Lincoln worked his work, and we've had one hundred and fifty years for it to sink in—has the clarity and obviousness of Newton's Third Law of Motion.

Robert Bork died this week. The media seems to have adopted the judgment that opposition to his elevation to the Supreme Court introduced politics into the confirmation process for the first time. This is stupid. The Constitution assures that Supreme Court Justices will be confirmed in the middle of a political process by handing the process over to the Senate. Secondly, Bork arrived on the scene trailing his own political agenda, and that seemed shocking for a nominee. He deserved to be borked.

Time Magazine has named President Obama *Man of the Year*. His winning the election is a permanent achievement and to be celebrated, but he still has to fight Republicans, and that means, as *Lincoln* teaches us, getting his hands way dirty to achieve change.

Life's a mixed bag, here at the end of December, 2012—some wins, some losses, all of them big—and it's easy to get frustrated and discouraged. Are we better, now, than we were twelve months ago? *Why aren't things better, clearer, now?* But they're not, and we still have a way to go. We're going to get tired and pissed off, and it may not ever be clear that we have won anything permanent. There's a lot of pain in that. But the story of the Thirteenth, Fourteenth, and Fifteenth Amendments is the story of rights won eventually, partially, over a long period. That realization brings at least partial satisfaction.

What brings more complete satisfaction is a friend like the lady on the cheap bus, who spent part of her trip to NYC texting me about the people she knows in the city. When I got her text, I pictured it. The highway coming up toward her out of the night, the dark silent bus, her tablet's bright screen, and her, punching in the letter to a friend she wants to keep in touch with. *Love.*

107

Goals to fight for and what they mean
December 26, 2012

The goals are *freedom* and *a community that is supportive*.

We've won major legal victories—*Romer v. Evans* and *Lawrence v Texas* and more recent court cases—and victories at the polls and in public opinion polls in the last few years.

I have been searching for freedom all my life, and it may be that I am, right now, as free as I have ever been.

I am supported in this freedom by a small group of people. My partner, Courtney, my son, my daughter, my older grandchildren (the younger children don't know anything about freedom, yet). I have friends, a couple in London, some here in the States, some here in Boston and Somerville who want me to be free and autonomous.

Of course, there are forces that try to deny me freedom. There is the conservative Christian right, and there are those folks who are in the conservative *social* right. These people say abusive things, and sometimes do abusive things. There are some members of my biological family with whom I am not in contact. I've been fighting against these people for the last twenty-five years. But they aren't strong enough to prevent me from exercising my freedom, from being what I want to be.

Last week, Guy Branum, who is gay himself, complained at length on Huffington Post because *Nate Silver*, who is gay, hasn't come out the way he wanted him to. Nate Silver appears to be a wonderful person, successful at what he does, and he told the world about a month ago that he is gay "sexually," but not "ethnically." Guy Branum didn't like that. "Silver's refusal to fully participate in gay identity is the real problem," he says. What Branum means is that Silver's refusal to fully participate *in the way that Branum wants* is the problem. Silver has no obligation to be gay in the way that anybody wants.

We live in a transitional period. There was a time when, in order to add strength to the gay community to fight its fights, we have had to, all of us, come out and increase the numbers of us who demanded our freedom, but we're moving out of this transitional time. We're moving into a period when one of the successes of our movement is the number of people who are able to live uncompromisingly gay lives without actually joining the numbers in demonstrations.

It's OK for Nate Silver to live his life any way he wants. Actually, what he's expressing is what many of us are driving toward. *Freedom.*

108

Resolutions for 2013
January 1, 2013

Courtney and I were in a bar Friday night. I talked to a friend about the difficulties of using an iPad or Nook or Kindle outside its own ecosystem—on an iPad, you need to read books from the Apple bookstore, and Amazon books from the Amazon bookstore on a Kindle, and so on. I think the question now is how long people will put up with this. It's supposed to be about *freedom,* isn't it, this digital revolution? These things are getting more and more technologically advanced, and less and less politically progressive. We're buying books for our ereaders and feeding the corporate giants on Wall Street while doing so. That's not what we wanted, is it? The corporate giants on Wall Street are certainly not feeding us—gay readers across America—the books we want.

Later that same night, Courtney and I went to dinner with two friends and talked about the qualities a man brings to a relationship and which ones have a positive effect on the relationship and which ones not. One quality that we agreed on was his experience with relationships with men. A man can more confidently fall in love with a man who tells him he has fallen in love with him, if that other man has been around the track a few times and knows what he is declaring when he says, "I love you." I have only had two loves in my life—one with a woman and one with Courtney—and six years of screwing around between those times.

Courtney had more than ten years of experience in the gay community before I met him. I think we both knew what a long-term relationship was about.

Courtney and I discussed marriage over the weekend. We've been discussing marriage since 2004, when it became possible to marry in Massachusetts. The Supreme Court says it will rule during 2013 on the constitutionality of DOMA and Prop 8. Most commentators seem to think that the Supreme Court will approve marriage equality to some extent, but nobody knows, and it may be that the only feeling a person can have at this moment is anxiety.

2013, which begins tonight, is almost certain to be a year when gay people experience huge changes in their place in our culture. In a time of uncertainty, it's OK to look back at what has worked in the past—keeping up the pressure and fighting back. What this means in practical terms is to give money to the people who can fight for us, the legal organizations of your choice and the social service organizations. Subscribing to tough gay political journals too. What is not acceptable for gay people in a time of large changes and uncertainty is lassitude. So, it's a time for resolutions, and here are three. Remember Larry Kramer and ACT UP. *ACT UP! Fight back! Fight AIDS!* Get out your credit card, open your computer. Join HRC, contribute to GLAD and ACLU. Give money to your local AIDS service organization and anybody else you know of who has contributed to our successes in this past year and to the betterment of your life. You're welcome.

109

We can't forget our past
January 13, 2013

Here, at the beginning of the year, it is important to remember several things. First, those who suffered during the years we spent in the wilderness. No matter how many victories we experience during this year 2013, we are still going to be living among our LGBTQ brothers and sisters who spent most of their lives not living with victories, but living instead with one defeat after another. Our brothers and sisters lived through the long time between the Supreme Court decision *Bowers v. Hardwick*, 1986, which gave federal constitutional support for sodomy laws, and *Lawrence v. Texas*, 2003, which voided all sodomy laws, and lived with the effects of the Defense of Marriage Act, passed and signed in 1996, and lived with the effects of Don't Ask Don't Tell (1993) until 2011, when the act was repealed. Each of these three laws affected the LGBT communities, but what isn't said much is that the fact they were enacted put a stigma on the individual gay people, whether or not he or she chose to engage in any kind of sex—the sodomy laws stigmatized our *thoughts*—or wanted to join the armed forces, and so these laws were damaging to all of us.In a time of great change, it is critical that we remember what our past has been like, and that we remember those who suffered and were damaged by the stigma we bore.

Second, we are not out of the wilderness yet. Children are the most vulnerable of us. Forty percent of homeless youth are LGBT and forty-six percent of homeless youth are homeless because their *parents* rejected them and their sexuality. These data are from a study made practically yesterday—between October 2011 and March 2012. Abusive teaching of LGBT youth, rejection by their families and by city relief organizations, homeless, on the streets of large cities, too young and with no skills to sell, many of them turn to hustling. The suicides of LGBT youth, random acts of violence against LGBT people, and repeals of congressional acts and Supreme Court decisions in our favor aren't going to change these things, at least for a number of years. *All* bigotry is not going to go away. After all, much of what has driven national politics in the last four years is racism directed at our President. Why should gay people think that a congressional act or a Supreme Court decision is going to make our lives perfect?

Third, we are being assimilated into the culture of marriage. This is dangerous. On the other hand, this week, there is this which is wonderful to read. It's a study that shows something that many gay people have known: *non-monogamous couples are as happy as other couples.* We already know this, and during this time when we are being assimilated so quickly, it is good to be reminded of it. *Let's hang on to ourselves.*

110

Watch it, our freedom grows, inch by inch
January 14, 2013

News important to gay readers came this week. Andrew Sullivan and his blog *The Daily Dish* have left *The Beast* and have struck out on their own. Henceforth, without what Sullivan calls a "sugar daddy" to pay the bills and without advertisements, Sullivan will host his own blog, supporting himself with contributions from his readers, who will be asked to pay $19.99 for a year's worth of access to content. Out of the money he collects from his subscribers, he is going to pay his own salary, the salaries of five staff members, and other expenses of publishing his blog. The reason this is important to gay people is that Sullivan is cutting out all the gatekeepers—all the big publishers and papers—and showing a gay person how to gain direct access to readers. This would be incredibly liberating, if it works.

Sullivan's plan raises a question—Would it be good for journalism and for the rest of us as readers? Would the end product be better than the product produced by a reporter working under the umbrella of the whole *NY Times* editorial structure? Would *we* end up with better material to read? For gay people, more different kinds of writing would be available to readers, and gay readers would have access to a broader range of writing.

There are writers all across the English-speaking world who are following Sullivan's adventure—newspaper reporters, because they wonder if this is going to be one more nail in the coffin of print journalism, and bloggers and writers because, if Sullivan can do it, maybe they can do it.

I used to read Andrew Sullivan, beginning ten or twelve years ago. I was impressed that he had been editor of *The New Republic*, he wrote well, and he was gay. But I quit reading him during the first Bush administration because he was too conservative. See the screed by Mark Ames in the *Daily Banter*. His interest in racial intelligence, among other things, seemed way out of the American mainstream.

Now he's moved left and offers us a plan that may prove that the internet can be a source of freedom for many of us. It may be possible for us to free ourselves of *The New York Times* and *Time* and *Newsweek* and Random House and Vanguard and Penguin and all the rest of the big gatekeepers. Gay people have been shut out for much of the twentieth century by the big gatekeepers, who say, even now, that the market for gay books has "vanished," or "collapsed," and who publish only those books that will fit their business plan for their corporations. But what has vanished is the ability of gay readers to find serious gay fiction. It may be that, if more intelligent gay books are offered to the public, the gay reader will return to booksellers, this time on the web.

It may actually be possible to make this work for us.

111

Leave Jodi alone! Leave Manti alone!
January 11, 2013

First everybody jumped all over Jodie Foster for waiting so long to come out and for not saying what everybody thought she ought to have said, because there were all those people she could have helped, and now there is the mystery around Manti Te'o, which led at least some people this week to say this man is gay and to turn a "mystery" into a scandal and then into a judgment in which Te'o is said to be closeted and using a desperately sick woman as his "beard" and for not helping all those people he could have helped.

Our culture—both gay and straight—makes it clear that we admire gay people who come out and who are not closeted. The more prominent they are—an actor in maybe a third of the greatest American films since the early seventies or a Notre Dame linebacker up for the Heisman and a pro career—the more we demand that they come out and "help everybody else." We don't like it when a person, Hollywood royalty-style, hides behind her privilege or maybe uses a fake girlfriend to keep everyone from knowing he is gay. We want to believe that gay people are heroic fighters for freedom.

But, independent of the needs of the gay community, an individual gay person has needs too, among which is the need to protect her privacy during forty-five years of celebrity and the need to grow up a little when you're only twenty-one, almost twenty-two. *Our* needs are not the preeminent ones, always.

Coming out and being heroic was never the only stance for gay people anyway. Gay people have always been able to make their contribution by living their lives and getting on with the business of it, making clear the nature of their sexuality only to the people who need to know, which was certainly always Jodie Foster's case. Just because w are gay doesn't mean we have lost our right to privacy. These cases— and Michelle Obama's case too, with the criticism of her being mom-in-chief instead of coming out as a major corporate lawyer— show our exaggerated need for heroic fighters. A *major actor!* a *major and good-looking football player!* We don't need this. Leave Jodie alone. Leave Te'o alone. Let them do what they want to do. Come out or not, or come out in any way they want. And we can say, always and welcomingly, *There's always a place for you here when you feel it's right.*

112

We are where we belong
January 21, 2013

Barack Obama said this today:

> "We, the people, declare today that the most evident
> of truths – that all of us are created equal – is the star that
> guides us still; just as it guided our forebears through
> Seneca Falls, and Selma, and Stonewall; just as it guided
> all those men and women, sung and unsung, who left
> footprints along this great Mall, to hear a preacher say
> that we cannot walk alone; to hear a King proclaim that
> our individual freedom is inextricably bound to the
> freedom of every soul on Earth."

...and Stonewall.

We knew Stonewall belonged in that list. We just didn't know
they knew it. Now we know they know, and that's entirely new.

113

The promise of the future
January 29, 2013

The press has not gotten over it. The president, in his inaugural address, included *Stonewall* in the short list of significant moments in the great civil rights movements in this country. He said, "Seneca Falls and Selma and Stonewall." Seneca Falls, New York, was a town where, in 1848, there was a convention of women who effectively started the women's suffrage movement. Selma happened during our lifetime and was the town in Alabama where Martin Luther King began a march to Montgomery. This march would demand explanation for the death of Jimmie Lee Jackson, an unarmed voting rights demonstrator, and publicize the need for a new Voting Rights Act. As the demonstrators marched out of Selma, on Sunday, March 7, 1965, they crossed the Edmund Pettus bridge. They could see the end of the bridge and a crowd of cops and of state police waiting there. The marchers knew they would be beaten if they proceeded. They proceeded, and the police attacked the unarmed marchers. All this was caught on film and televised nationally. "Bloody Sunday" in Selma, Alabama, became one of the great defeats of southern segregationists. Selma became the staging ground for two more marches later in the week, with the number of marchers increasing from 525 in the first march, to 8,000 in the third. In response, President Lyndon Johnson and the Congress passed the Voting Rights Act of 1965.

To these grand and compelling images in the American consciousness, President Obama has now added a third, *Stonewall,* reminding Americans that the movement for gay rights began at the Stonewall Inn on Christopher Street in New York, on the night of June 28, 1969, and with the Stonewall Riots, which occurred when New York police raided the Stonewall and arrested customers, and gay people fought back. Many say this is the beginning of gay liberation. This is thrilling.

Everybody noticed what Obama had done, as soon as the word was out of his mouth. *He listed Stonewall with Seneca Falls and Selma!* The press specifically focussed on the fact that Obama "used the word gay!" Talking heads kept saying on all the networks, *No president has ever done that before.* The talking heads fooled around with what that meant. These talking heads were principally straight people, so what they had to say had all the subtlety of white people, in 1965, whispering in the Court House in Selma when a black citizen walked in to register. Now the gay community is weighing in on what Obama did and on what it feels like to have the President of the United States refer to *our* iconic moment of revolution. I would say, for one thing, it is hard to feel like a revolutionary when the president takes *our* moment of revolution and makes it his own.

But there is something else. We have long since forgotten the anguish and struggle and pain that caused Seneca Falls and Selma to be what they are today in the national memory. Today we remember mainly the heroism of the women and of black Americans, and those who opposed them hardly matter anymore. We remember these times and these places as triumphs in movements that changed America.

So, what Obama did in his speech—by putting us where he did— was to make an implicit promise to gay people, that there will come a time when those who opposed us most of my life will be hardly remembered, and gay people, instead of being seen as deviates who demanded way too much, will be remembered for their heroism. That's the promise contained in his putting us where he put us in his address. We will finally end as feminists and civil rights demonstrators have ended—as American heroes. A person with a long memory may remember with what skepticism I have thought of "American heroes." I don't like the concept very much. But when our President, an African- American himself of mixed race parentage, tells us that this is how we are going to be remembered and puts us in such company, I am willing to accept his promise with gratitude.

114

Interesting times
February 12, 2013

Race Point Light doesn't end when the narrator comes out. Like most LGBT persons, the narrator of *Race Point Light* still has at least half a lifetime to live after he moves into the gay community. He has things to do. He has to find a way to live. He has to support himself and has to choose a place to live where he can connect with a gay community and where he can continue to be in contact with his children. He has to find out which of the friends from the first half of his life will also do for the last half. What relatives does he still have? And he has to do all these things in a world where AIDS has taken hold, where the president of the United States, a pleasant, grandfatherly type, smiling, says it's "Morning in America," while LGBT persons, almost every one of them, would agree that our culture is fast approaching *midnight.* This is only partially a novel about the culture of the US. It moves through the forties to the first decade of the twenty-first century, when gay men and women started marrying legally for the first time, but that's not where the focus is. We're reading about a man determined to think well of himself and at least one of his goals while a teenager and young adult is to find out *how.* As a young person, he is not ready to be a rebel—what his cultures, gay and straight, offer him is alternatively seductive and repellant—until he tries their offerings and finds them to be failures. He is ready to create a new life. He gets off the Interstate down from Maine

Labor Day, 1984, and finds himself in the middle of AIDS.

"Coming out" is a theme that occupies the narrator all through his life. He asks questions. What is it? How do I do it? When? Where? *I am out now, but I don't remember how I got here.* He wonders, Is the question of *Coming out* too steeped in sixties radical politics to be applicable to anybody's life in 2004?

Race Point Light is a big novel, epic in scope, a narrative of a culture in crisis, and yet the focus is intensely on the narrator, who thinks about the intimate issues of his life and lays them out for the reader to see and feel and understand, and who moves toward a quiet resolution. He moves in no strict chronological order from Commercial Street in Provincetown in 2002 to the South Carolina beach when he is three or four years old to Race Point beach, when he is sixty-five, moving from idea to idea, wars, the deaths of presidents, impeachment and conviction, presidential indifference to his obligation to attend to the health of citizens, the scandal surrounding the discovery of the AIDS virus, feeling and understanding the impact of events in his culture. It is a giant novel about what the narrator comes to see is the most interesting—and powerfully important—sixty years for gay people in all of western history. *Race Point Light* is a fascinating, absorbing story, alternating between large scenes and intimate, small scenes like a single man crossing Arlington Street alone in Boston, late at night, in deep snow, considering the meaning of the Serenity Prayer. *Race Point Light* has the fascination of some kinds of gossip, where the person speaking is someone we trust and is *willing to tell all she knows.*

And yet, *all she knows,* since this is an autobiographical novel, not only suggests everything about a person we could know, it suggests a serious and comprehensive narrative about the whole culture of the United States during the last half of the twentieth century, its successes and its catastrophic failures. The narrator of *Race Point Light* says, in Provincetown in 2004, *"We've lived in interesting times, for a gay man the most interesting times of all. It may be that there haven't been, since the beginning of the earth, a more interesting sixty years than 1940 to now for gay people."*

*

You can read *Race Point Light* about this man and his interesting times by going to http://www.dwightcathcart.net. There you can buy an ebook copy of *Race Point Light* for your iPad, Nook or Kindle or a print copy to put on your shelf.

115

What we demand
February 22, 2013

The papers and the web have been full of news about Barnes & Noble—they're cutting back on the number of their bookstores—with analyses on why that has happened and what this means for the future. I went by B&N today and was told our local, intown B&N is one of the biggest and most profitable bookstores in that whole chain. The employee told me that the Boston B&N, along with one or two others, are sure to survive if the company survives.

I was at B&N to talk to an employee about the Nook, B&N's reader, and about putting my books on the Nook. I was aware that what I was talking about was one of the cultural shifts that was driving these big bookstores out of business. They were being polite to me and helpful, but the fact remains that I am writing books and selling them directly to the public, and there are no New York publishers or booksellers involved. I suspect there is not room in the playing field for B&N and for me too.

And the straits that B&N and other booksellers find themselves in today is a result of the many book buyers who have been dissatisfied with the job that book sellers have been doing these many years. The corporate structure of many of these big booksellers has prevented them from responding to the market so as to continually offer interesting and important literary works. Money talks, and the booksellers have needed to sell books that are big sellers.

The ecology of publishing—finders, agents, publishers, booksellers and the industry built around the fact that books, once printed, need to be stored and shipped and distributed—is big money, so publishing finds it more profitable to publish one book selling one million copies than to publish one hundred books selling 10,000 copies each. The effect of this kind of fiscal structure is that minorities— people like us, gay people— are placed at particular risk. We don't produce many books that sell enough copies to make it profitable enough for big publishers to publish a wide range of books for us. And so, after decades, smaller minorities stop going to the big publishers when they want certain kinds of books. It is like the markets for certain kinds of popular music and for independent movies. Some moviegoers haven't been to a big-budget movie in decades.

The publishers and the booksellers have turned away from us and left us to our own devices. As it happens, our device of choice is the reader, the iPad, the Nook, the Kindle and the others. Now, what's left is for us to loosen the grip the readers have on the publisher's bookstores. It is possible to find books for readers that don't come from publisher's bookstores. The manufacturers of our readers—Apple, Amazon, and B&N—don't make this easy, but we can learn how to find these books, and we can learn how to put them on our readers. By doing so, we can gain control of our reading again. And this will happen: if we use our freedom to find the books being written for us, then writers, knowing we are out there, will write their books for us and for our readers, and those books will be interesting and important, because that's what we demand.

116

The gifts of time
March 1, 2013

I lived in New York for most of 1963, and one of my best friends was an actress, three years older than I, who had a major part in a major soap broadcast from New York. She was my cousin, and we had much the same background in South Carolina—conservative family and a desire to leave the South. The actress lived with an antiques dealer who had a shop on the East Side. The antiques dealer came from Mississippi, and her family owned a plantation. The three of us sat up many nights, drinking too much, talking about ourselves, our families, politics, and about America at the beginning of the Sixties. We enjoyed being together, going out to dinner, to the movies, and to the theatre. We supported each other. They were gay, but at that time, and in my cousin's profession, it was difficult for any of us to come out, even to each other. They are both dead now

This morning, the headline on the front page of *The Boston Globe,* read, "Firms call Defense of Marriage Act unfair." The lede read, "Nearly 300 companies and business groups across the country, including many prominent Massachusetts firms, are asking the US Supreme Court to strike down the Defense of Marriage Act, saying it forces them to discriminate against married gay employees." In the next paragraph, the article says, "A who's who of corporate America signed on to a friend-of-the-court brief filed Wednesday." I was astonished that a *who's who of corporate America* could be brought together to support such a goal. But as the day went on and I thought more about these events, I began to think about the people who would have been even more astonished than I at such at a headline and grief- stricken that they had not lived to see it.

I know plenty of people who didn't live to see what's happening now, who fought for it but who died before we were this close to victory. The slow march of time presents us with one victory after another, and that same march takes down one friend after another. What we hope for is that we will accumulate more victories than defeats. For decades in many of our lives, it has been just the other way around. My friend the student at the School of the Museum of Fine Arts, coming from Pride one year, said to me, "They are all celebrating, but I don't know what there is to celebrate." He had AIDS, and he saw his life dribbling away at a faster rate than science was accumulating cures. He understood very clearly that he was in a race, and he suspected that he was going to lose that race, and the expression on his face, every day, said, *hurry hurry.*

So, on a day like today, with a headline like today's in *The Boston Globe,* and thinking of the actress and the antiques dealer in New York and that art student in Boston, I know the meaning of *bittersweet.*

117

It's not that they were so nice, it was that we were such good fighters
March 7, 2013

At every step forward in this long process, we should stop and consider how we got here. We didn't get here because we were polite and our opponents were kind. We got here because we were tough, relentless, and fierce. We got here because we knew our stuff and our opponents were merely driven by hatred. We had *tough* lawyers—all of them— and we mastered whole libraries of studies of various kinds proving that we're OK. And, as the *New York Times* said after the NY legislature voted in marriage equality for that state, "it was clear the church had been outmaneuvered by the highly organized same-sex marriage coalition, with its sprawling field team, and, especially, it's Wall Street donors."

In my last posting, "The gifts of time," I wrote about that day's *Boston Globe*, whose lead article's headline was "Firms call Defense of Marriage Act unfair." This did not happen because corporate America suddenly decided gay people were wonderful employees and it didn't want to be mean to its gay employees. Gay people have always been good employees. Those employees have been letting their employers know for years that they wanted to be treated like all the other employees. Instead corporate America has read the future, which was decades of lawsuits from employees demanding to be treated like other employees. We got to this point after suing successfully to have sodomy laws overturned and to have Colorado's Prop 2 overturned.

We got to this point after suing for equal marriage rights in courts at all levels on both coasts and the middle of America, and *winning*. Even soldiers are marrying each other, and kissing each other *on the mouth* on the front pages of the national press, and the republic hasn't fallen and everybody is pretty much over being shocked or even amazed.

Every poll says the people are speaking on this issue moment by moment, and the majorities in favor are getting larger and larger with every poll. Corporate America has suddenly realized it had better get in step and catch up. The *amicus* brief that prompted the *Boston Globe*'s article was an act of self-defense on the part of corporate America. The *last* thing corporate America wants is to be separated from its customers. I think corporate America can see the future: When gay people get finished with the courts and the legislatures, they will start with individual companies and organizations—the recent history of gay people and Chic-Fil-A and Boy Scouts of America springs to mind— and I would think that *no* American organization wants that.

The BSA have ended up on the other side of the argument from the *Army,* for God's sake.

It didn't happen because any of those corporations who signed that *amicus* brief were nice people who had reverence for the Constitution of the United States. They are still driven principally by greed. These victories we are experiencing right now are coming out that way because we are tough and we're good fighters and we don't give up.

Ever. We have good lawyers, and we have big donors, and we know how to get organized. It's a winning combination.

118

Melville, Faulkner, Shakespeare, and me
March 14, 2013

Reading *Moby Dick* when I was seventeen made me want to write novels. *Absalom, Absalom!* had the same effect. I majored in English literature in college, and I went to New York and wrote for a year. A friend said, "The trouble is, you don't know anything about what you're writing about." Bingo.

I didn't know how to learn how to do what I wanted to do. I went to graduate school, concentrated in the English Renaissance Lyric and wrote a dissertation on John Donne. This was the early sixties.

I got married—it was a way of resolving the conflict in my life—had children, was teaching in a university, and finally decided I had to start over on everything but the children. After a long time, I left the university and left my marriage, and in my last summer before moving to Boston, a young friend of mine was murdered by homophobes. His name was Charles Howard.

During the summer after Charles Howard's death in 1984, we all were coming out and organizing politically, and experiencing grief at Charles Howard's death, and we knew all of this was important. We were doing on a local level what writers were writing about on a national level, creating a gay community. I had read enough to know that our history was important to gay people. A major effort of the women's movement and the black civil rights movement had been to

240

recover their history, and I thought we should write this down, the events of that summer of 1984, to prevent them from being lost.

When I started I found I was writing a Faulkner novel. I was a southerner, and most novels by southerners since Faulkner sounded something like Faulkner. A friend said, "Please don't go on this way." I kept at it for a year, then quit, unable to go on. Finally, one night I was in a meeting, and I heard a man talking about himself and his experiences, and the hurt his experience had caused him, and I realized, *that's the voice I need in my novel.* I went home and started to write again. I wrote, *This is what happened on Saturday, the day of the dance.* And after that, I never stopped. I kept writing, hearing that voice in my head talking of the pain he had experienced. *I knew about this.* This became *Ceremonies.*

This is what had happened. Without knowing I was doing it, I had taught myself how to write. The years in college, in graduate school, teaching Shakespeare every year, and all the books I had read. I had completed my apprenticeship and when the time was right, when I witnessed an event to write *about*—the murder of Charles Howard—I was ready to write about it. And I could do it my way. I knew how to do it because I had read all those books and taught all those classes and had all that experience. I never thought about how Faulkner did it. I didn't think ever about the New York publishing industry. I thought, nobody else has ever written a book like this, and I'll write it first, and after I've finished it, I'll show it to the publishers.

There must be other ways to get to where a person has to be to be able to write. I think I had to spend a very long time in my apprenticeship before actually beginning to write. I suspect that other writers can pick up what they need to know sooner, earlier, maybe better. But one of the effects of a long apprenticeship is that I learned the things that are necessary. Shakespeare taught me how to start a scene and to tell a story with a *lot* of characters. Melville and Faulkner taught me how to tell a story characterized by high moral seriousness. I don't think I know it *all* even now, but I'm on my way.

As it happened, the publishers didn't want to see my books. My subject—*gay men and women fighting back*—was one they were not accustomed to dealing with. Even some gay readers were not accustomed to such stories. But it was a good subject, a necessary one, and my book was needed, so I kept on. After *Ceremonies,* I wrote two subsequent novels, *Race Point Light*, about a man fighting back during his whole life, and *Adam in the Morning,* about the Stonewall riots. All three of these books were about their times. What it was like to be gay in 1984 in a small town in Maine, or gay in the West Village in New York in late June 1969, or a nomad and gay between about 1950 and 2005 determined to find a place in America. I ended up publishing these novels on the web as ebooks, unencumbered by the power of the publishing industry to limit our freedom to read the subjects powerful and true to us. I learned in my long apprenticeship how critically important a literature is to a community—serious books apprehended seriously that reflect back to a community its facts, its history, its concerns, attitudes, myths and legends—so it can become what its writers imagined.

119

Criticisms of Will Portman
March 21, 2013

Will Portman came out to his father, Senator Portman, Republican of Ohio, in 2011, which caused his father to announce this week that he had changed his beliefs on marriage equality. Since then we have had a heated debate over coming out and over whether Senator Portman should be admired for changing his views. The culture's confusions over these issues obscure the debate, which isn't leading us anywhere.

Many people say that any recruit to our side in the marriage equality debate is always a good thing. Others add that the Senator should have changed his mind about marriage equality based on legal or constitutional arguments, not his emotional closeness to his son, or that he should have done it years before. Many Republicans seem to believe that there is no good reason for changing your mind about marriage equality.

Today, Josh Barro, the chief writer for the blog The Ticker, on Bloomberg News, puts up a post in which he argues that Will Portman is not to be thanked or admired for coming out because he had in fact done his duty. Listen to this:

> This is why coming out is a duty: Every time a gay or
> lesbian person demands acceptance, they make it easier for
> others to do the same. We have the power to change people's
> political and personal attitudes toward gays simply by being
> present and known to be gay; we can only exercise that

power if we come out. This is an argument that Harvey Milk gave powerful expression to before he was assassinated. Milk said,

> Gay brothers and sisters, you must come out. Come out
> to your parents ... Come out to your relatives. Come out
> to your friends, if indeed they are your friends. Come
> out to your neighbors, to your fellow workers, to the
> people who work where you eat and shop. Come out
> only to the people you know, and who know you. Not to
> anyone else. But once and for all, break down the myths,
> destroy the lies and distortions. For your sake. For their
> sake.

This is an argument that has been put forward by leaders in the LGBT community for the last forty years. But there is something wrong with this. Both Barro and Milk understand that the burdens of coming out don't fall on everybody equally. Barro when he came out: "Announcing that you're gay in a wealthy family in a progressive suburb of Boston as you're about to enter Harvard University is a pretty easy hand to play."

People are different and they are in different circumstances, and the gay community should not set up any general rules that condemn men and women who are different. There are many different ways of *not coming out,* just as there are many different reasons. *If you can come out, fine. If you can't, or don't want to, that's fine too. We'll still love you.* And for god's sake, stop accusing people who don't come out of *not being honest with themselves,* or *of lying.*

I think we have a pretty good thing going here in the GLBT community. We don't need to force people to join us (*if you don't come out, we'll say you're lying*). You're going to be welcome here when—or if—you do decide to join us.

120

The Supreme Court, Tuesday morning
March 26, 2013

On Towleroad, you can read Ari Ezra Waldman, their resident legal expert, about whom they say,

> Ari Ezra Waldman teaches at Brooklyn Law School and is concurrently getting his PhD at Columbia University in New York City. He is a 2002 graduate of Harvard College and a 2005 graduate of Harvard Law School. His research focuses on technology, privacy, speech, and gay rights. Ari will be writing weekly posts on law and various LGBT issues. You can follow him on Twitter at @ariezrawaldman.

Ari has been writing for Towleroad for several years, giving commentary on the legal issues and the court cases the LGBT communities have been going through during the past several years. I recommend him.

You can now (at 3:51, Mar 26, 2013) read his entire two-part analysis of the questioning this morning in the Supreme Court. It's wonderful, and it's very reassuring.

And if, like many people, you get a little overwhelmed by lawyers arguing with one another, you might remember what Frederick Douglas said: *If there is no struggle, there is no progress.*

121

How are we winning this thing?
April 1, 2013

All this is getting hard to take. Chris Matthews was just addressing the question, Why have numbers changed so quickly in favor of equal marriage? His answer and the answer of his guests, was that it had to do with the numbers of gay people who have come out. Every straight body, it seems, knows a person who is gay, and it becomes increasingly difficult to deny basic human rights to someone so familiar. Coming out, in this view, is a tactic for fighting the homophobia of straight people.

I don't believe a word of it. We all know gay men and women who came out years ago—some in their teens, some since then—and whose biological families have treated them like shit, with bigotry and hatred, and who have continued to do so for decades. The people who knew these gay men and women best were completely unaffected by knowing them.

In Maine, during the summer of 1984, after the murder of Charles Howard, the local newspaper considered the options available to the community to restore calm and order. The paper acknowledged that many people in the city of Bangor, Maine, just wanted gay people now marching through the streets of the city*"to return to the closet."* But what are citizens to do, the paper questioned, "if gay people will *not* go back into the closet?"

That gets it exactly right. It is emphatically not true that gay people, coming out, will change the hearts and minds of bigoted citizens. But if we come out *and then refuse to go back in again,* if we pursue our own course, if we know what we want, and if we fight relentlessly for it, then, *then,* we can grasp victory.

This is what has been happening for the last forty years or more. Men and women have come out, and then have refused to go back in. They have fought relentlessly for the things that matter to them. And they have never given in. The whole history of the marriage equality movement is a testament to our perseverance. The fight started in Hawaii in 1993 and moved on for the next twenty years to the sequence of states that have adopted marriage equality since Massachusetts adopted it in 2004. This happened because the gay people who were out were relentless and refused to give up and fought for it year after year after year. We have had more stamina than our opponents. It is likely that we have been clearer about our goals than our opponents. We have been smarter about tactics, and wiser about choosing our allies.

We fought, and gradually the American people have joined us, not because they were finally getting to know gay men and women and found us sweet—we have been their brothers and sisters and their sons and daughters and their fathers and their mothers and their husbands and their wives for the last several hundred years—but because what they began to know about us was that we were fighters and that we wouldn't give up. *We will never give up.* Being nice and unthreatening had no part of it. We had a better goal, a clearer goal, and we had better lawyers, and, as the *Times* said of the New York victory, *bigger donors.*

In the years since Stonewall, if we have come out, I suspect it was to find a more comfortable and safe place for ourselves. My own motivation for divorcing my wife and moving to Boston didn't have anything to do with the gay community's needing me in the fight against the straight world. And that is right. But that made me fight harder and more effectively for my causes. *And none of this had anything to do with straight people.* The fight, the parameters of the fight, the definition of all the terms, the way we were going to fight, and the people we were going to fight with, had long been defined before the gay community had accumulated a significant number of straight allies. *We did this for ourselves.*

122

How things work
April 8, 2013

I was walking back from Home Depot, when I found myself walking almost parallel with a young man in a pin-stripe suit and tie. He wasn't dressed for Home Depot. We nodded. He smiled. I smiled. We walked on, and then I asked him if he was a Mormon. I pointed out that people in our neighborhood don't generally dress like that on Sunday. So, I found myself walking across the parking lot of Assembly Square Mall with a Mormon.

I said, "I don't see how you can stand to be doing what you're doing." I pointed out that the Mormon church had been one of the largest donors to those who brought Proposition 8 to California. The Mormon church has fought against every advance by the LGBT community in the last fifty years. I pointed out that the men and women who opposed integration in the sixties have been forgotten, because the history of the United States has been toward greater equality and greater democracy since its founding. It was important to see the conflicts around us, and it is necessary to choose a side in these conflicts, and it is necessary to get it *right*. It is necessary to know what you are doing when you set about trying to control the future, as these churches are doing. I told the young man in the pin-stripped suit that when his church speaks of religious freedom, it causes real pain and real damage to real people. "What are you *doing?"* I asked him.

My partner, Courtney, laughed when I got home after my trip to Home Depot and told me, I was *"confrontational."* Well, so were the men and women on Christopher Street in June 1969. Look what came from *their* confrontations. It is necessary for us to fight back, all the time, without ceasing, even when we are tired of it. Polite people never get anywhere.

123

Making it cost 'em
April 19, 2013

My last post was called "How things work," published April 7, in which I wrote about my encounter with a young man doing missionary work for the Mormon church, as I walked home after picking up something at Home Depot. The young man was polite and friendly, and I pointed out that the Mormon Church, for forty years, has been in the forefront of the fight *against* gay people, in making my world unsafe for me. My partner, Courtney, told me I was "confrontational." OK. Yes. And then I pointed to the Stonewall Riots, where men and women fought back against the New York cops *who had made their world unsafe for them.* I wrote: *It is necessary for us to fight back, all the time, without ceasing, even when we are tired of it. Polite people never get anywhere.*

But other people felt that the confrontational mode is not appropriate to them. Or is difficult. Or wrong. An old friend writes that she struggles with it. Her default mode is civility, and confrontation doesn't come naturally to her, even when she understands the point of it. Today, in Boston, we are experiencing what seems to be a civic moment where people on both sides are in the confrontational mode.

The point, I think, in my blog, is that *I am fighting back* is a truth that ought to be said but isn't said often enough, even in the gay press. We are weakened by not hearing this regularly. We need somebody--I need somebody--to say *fight, stop being polite, stop trying to get along, stop being afraid.* Gay people have a right to a safe place. I've learned (intellectually) that not fighting, being polite, trying to get along, being afraid, are corrosive of my character and are bad tactics. I need to stop living my life by the easy-way-out. I know I will take the easy way out, if one is offered to me, so I need to pump myself up by saying over and over (this is my way of giving myself courage) *stop being afraid.*

This is what happens to me. I seek safety. I seek comfort. That is my default fallback. So I resort to civility. For years, the ruder, cruder, more appallingly brutal you were to me, the more civil and polite I became. And then one day I realized that being *polite* was not stopping any of this brutal behavior. My tormentors took my civility as permission to continue to torment me. It was then that I came to understand that polite people never get anywhere.

To truly engage with the people in our culture who are conveying hatred and ignorance against me and the people I care about, I have to get down and dirty. I *have* to make it cost 'em.

124

The winning tactic in these wars
April 24, 2013

Violence—bombs, guns, ethnic slurs—has been so close to us in Boston
this week that it's been difficult to think. One of the threads of this blog
has been the need for us to *fight back,* and various people have asked
me what my books are about, and I've said, *They're about gay people
fighting back.* That has been a central fact about gay life— the need to
fight back, to create a safe space for ourselves—since the Stonewall
Riots, and it underlies all of our advances today. Every year our great
community celebration, Gay Pride, commemorates our fighting back in
those riots.

The whole history of the gay community since 1969 has been a
history of us forcing ourselves into the public space—that is, *fighting
back.* It is clear to many of us that we would not have had the recent
victories in the Supreme Court, in the Congress, and. preeminently, in
the polls, if we had not created our activist organizations, developed a
generation of leaders, contributed money to our activist causes,
demonstrated, rebelled, *been rude,* refused to accept the *status quo,* said
over and over, no matter how many people were tired of us saying it, *I
will be safe in my world, I will not be battered, I will have space to live
my life in freedom, I will hurt you if you try to take my safety from me,*
and, of course, most of all, *I will have freedom to respond to the beauty
of members of our own sex.*

It is difficult to talk about violence when a central street in Boston is still closed seven days after the Marathon bombing, but when gay people fight for their space, it is nothing like a person placing disguised bombs on a crowded pavement of a city street. It has almost always been true that gay people, driven to fight against those who would restrict their freedom—who would restrict their *lives*—make publicly clear what they do and why they do it. They *claim credit.*

There is nothing silent or secretive about violence directed by gay people against the actions of homophobes. *I'm here, I'm queer, I'm fabulous, Get used to it.* Queer Nation did not say, *Please.* They told who they were and why they did what they did. The Gay Liberation Front, on May 3, 1971, disrupted a meeting of the American Psychiatric Association in Washington, DC. Frank Kameny, a member of GLF, as described in *The Advocate,* "denounced the right of psychiatrists to discuss the question of homosexuality. 'Psychiatry is the enemy incarnate. Psychiatry has waged relentless war of extermination against us. You may take this as a declaration of war against you!'" As a consequence, the APA, on December 15, 1973, removed homosexuality from the list of mental disorders. Don't believe for a minute that they would have changed that determination if the gay people hadn't been rude and threatened to disrupt every meeting the APA had until they changed it.

The winning tactic, then, is *be rude* and promise to keep being rude until they change. *We'll fight ya, if you try to do that again.*

125

And, for those interested in building things
April 29, 2013

Three days after the bombing at the finish line, something happened of a very different kind, but which got little attention in the press. The Digital Public Library of America opened online and is now available— even if in a limited way—at URL *dp.la*. Type in those four letters in the address line of your browser, hit *return*, and you're there. This is important to us because, like epub, it's going to give gay people—and other minorities—access to documents about their communities which currently reside in research libraries and institutions and museums around the country. On the Digital Public Library of America, gay people will have access that is direct and unencumbered by gate- keepers, and free. To a community whose past has been expurgated and censored by others, and poisoned by the concept of *Don't Ask, Don't Tell,* the opening of the Digital Public Library of America is a step toward freedom.

According to Robert Darnton, the University Librarian at Harvard, in an article titled, "The National Digital Public Library is Launched!" in *The New York Review of Books*, the DPLA has been in the works since October 1, 2010. A small group of representatives from foundations and libraries met at Harvard to discuss making "the bulk of world literature available to all citizens free of charge" by creating a "grand coalition of foundations and research libraries." Since then, a mission statement has been written in somewhat more technical language. "The DPLA would be an open, distributed network of comprehensive online resources that would draw on the nation's living heritage from libraries, universities, archives, and museums in order to educate, inform, and empower everyone in the current and future generations."

They have started with the libraries, and the libraries 'holdings, which are already digitized, but by degrees the DPLA will be able to offer increasingly comprehensive collections from its participating libraries and foundations. I expect that gay people are going to have to wait for a while for useful documents to be available through DPLA. But this is going in the right direction, *free to all*, and comprehensive. Imagine what that means to *us*. Even if what DPLA achieves is only to make it easier for someone on the East Coast to get documents from the Huntington Library on the West Coast, that is going to make a difference in our ability to access our past.

Check out *dp.la*. Explore a little. You'll see what possibilities this has. Then keep coming back as this thing grows. And read about it everywhere. This is going to make our lives—including the lives of gay writers and readers—*better*.

126

What do you say when someone comes out to you?

May 11, 2013

S. L. Price, writing in Sports Illustrated, May 6, 2013, quotes Patrick Burke on the subject of Burke's brother's coming out. "When your brother comes to you and tells you, 'I'm gay,' if you say anything other than, 'Great, I love you, I don't care,' that's where the problem is.'" (SI, p. 46) This is a common progressive response in our culture. A person comes out, and the most common decent responses people make are *I don't care*, and *I've always known you were gay*. SI quotes Jason Collins' aunt giving the second response (SI, p. 36). The trouble with someone saying either of these is that the person coming out has more or less struggled with this issue, gotten up courage, told you he or she is gay, and before he has a chance to get a real response from you, you tell him you don't care about what has troubled him. A better response would go along these lines: *Great, I love you. I bet it's been hard. I want to hear all about it. I want to know everything, because you know how much I love you, don't you? Tell me everything about how it's been for you. I love every single part of you.*

Looking back on my youth and younger ages, I don't think I often actually was subjected to homophobic abuse, but what I did get, very often, was some statement that subtly told me the other person didn't want to know what I knew. Jason Collins' aunt told him, "I've known you were gay for years" (*SI*, p. 36.) Collins tells us that when she said that, he no longer had to worry about his aunt. But he doesn't tell us what happened to that conversation after his aunt told him she had known he was gay *for years*. Why didn't she tell him she knew? Why didn't she help him? Why wasn't she *proactive?* This response leaves the gay person with nowhere to go with his experiences of the years he spent closeted. *But I wanted to tell you.*

I suppose what the person means, who says, *I don't care*, is that *I don't care about those people who disapprove of you.* But whatever the three words mean to the person who speaks them, the person who hears them thinks, *Jesus! What she doesn't care about is a huge part of my life.* And *How can she say she loves me, if she doesn't care about this part of my life?* A person who cares about you, who 'loves ' you, is going to care about every part of your life, is going to want to know about everything that has ever happened to you, is going to feel as full of joy as you do, now that you have come out, because now you are both released to share all of your life, not just the smaller, censored part of it that you could share before.

She's going to care *a lot.*

127

Tim DeChristopher and civil disobedience
May 16, 2013

Tim DeChristopher has just gotten out of prison, having served two years for attempting to disrupt the sale of oil leases of land in Utah. His civil disobedience, which began under the Bush administration and continued under the Obama administration, is welcome news, as is his being able to speak well about what he had done. Last night on Chris Hayes' show on MSNBC, DeChristopher spoke about civil disobedience and its philosophical justifications. He had made a statement to the court before his sentencing two years before. Here is an excerpt:

> When a corrupted government is no longer willing to uphold the rule of law, I advocate that citizens step up to that responsibility. If the government is going to refuse to step up to that responsibility to defend a livable future, I believe that creates a moral imperative for me and other citizens. My future, and the future of everyone I care about, is being traded for short term profits [of corporate America]. I take that very personally. Until our leaders take seriously their responsibility to pass on a healthy and just world to the next generation, I will continue this fight.
> Since those bedrock acts of civil disobedience by our

founding fathers, the rule of law in this country has continued to grow closer to our shared higher moral code through the civil disobedience that drew attention to legalized injustice. The authority of the government exists to the degree that the rule of law reflects the higher moral code of the citizens, and throughout American history, it has been civil disobedience that has bound them together.

I am here today because I have chosen to protect the people locked out of the system over the profits of the corporations running the system. I say this not because I want your mercy, but because I want you to join me.

This is not going away. At this point of unimaginable threats on the horizon, this [i.e. my going to prison] is what hope looks like. In these times of a morally bankrupt government that has sold out its principles, this is what patriotism looks like. With countless lives on the line, this is what love looks like, and it will only grow. The choice you are making today [in sentencing me] is what side are you on.

*

A documentary was recently made of these events called *Bidder 70*, which was the card number DeChristopher used when he was bidding in the oil lands auction. It is currently in release around the country and, while I have not seen it, reviewers say it is worth seeing. DeChristopher is a man worth watching, not only for his effect on the climate-change movement but for what we will learn—or be reminded of—of civil disobedience.

128

Being rude and out-of-control
May 21, 2013

Tim DeChristopher said, in his sentencing statement, "Since [the] bedrock acts of civil disobedience by our founding fathers, the rule of law in this country has continued to grow closer to our shared higher moral code through the civil disobedience that drew attention to legalized injustice." The "higher moral code" is not the same thing as "the rule of law," and the distance between the two is made clear by the men and women who are willing to commit acts of civil disobedience. Civil disobedience has had a long and honored tradition in this country—the Massachusetts residents who held the original tea party in December 16, 1773, those who disobeyed the Fugitive Slave Acts of 1793 and 1850, and, the women's movement, the civil rights movement, burning draft cards during the anti-war movement. Men and women went into the street and did what society had made illegal. *They broke the law purposefully* to call attention to intolerable conditions. They demanded attention be paid *and then refused to get out of the street.*

Gay liberation began on the West Coast, in San Francisco and Los Angeles, when the Committee for Homosexual Freedom brought actions against States Steamship Lines for firing Gale Whittington for being gay (April 9, 1959) and against Tower Records for firing Frank Dennaro for being gay (June 5, 1969). The Stonewall Riots were themselves the most powerful acts of civil disobedience in our history. And then AIDS introduced the nation to AIDS activism. In Boston that took the form of ACT UP pouring 55 gallon drums of blood-like fluid on the steps of the Harvard Medical School until the Dean of the School felt forced to say, "I am not a bigot," to general derision. The ACT UP actions were so successful that the way clinical trials were organized was changed, apparently permanently. The very action that started ACT UP, stopping traffic on Wall Street, resulted in the FDA opening up the approval process for new anti-AIDS drugs.

Lt Daniel Choi, who was thrown out of the Army after he came out, chained himself to the White House fence *three times* since Barrack Obama became president, in March 2010, April 2010, and May 2010, demanding repeal of Don't Ask, Don't Tell. Lt Choi went to Times Square to inform the recruiting office there that he intended to rejoin the Army. The repeal of Don't Ask, Don't Tell finally passed Congress and was signed into law by President Obama December 22, 2010. Lt Choi, who was a graduate of West Point and who had come out on Rachel Maddow's show, was a master at embarrassing the Pentagon. He kept chaining himself to the White House fence, even when it was clear from the record that the White House just wished he would go away. They didn't want to convict him of anything. The last time, it took the government two years to complete the trial of Lt Choi, and in the end he was found guilty and fined $100. No jail time. The earlier charges were dismissed. Apparently, the Army felt, *Jesus, is this over! Is this man never going away?*

Tim DeChristopher's civil disobedience is admirable and effective, but it is not unique. All the way through the history of gay liberation— on both coasts, since the fifties—there have been men and women committing civil disobedience and capturing the imagination of the people and causing change, bringing the enacted law into line with the higher moral code to which they are committed.

Gay men and women have known better than most that there is a disjunction between ourselves—our felt reality—and the way we are experienced by our culture, by politicians, by the churches, by the legal system, the "helping" professions, and by the conventional wisdom of our culture. We have *always* been disobedient. And while some might think that the GLBTQ community has reached a "tipping" point, where no more progress is necessary or even possible, that will be true only when it is as easy to be gay as it is to be straight. That time is not yet. *Let's be rude about it, guys.*

*

Donn Teal, *The Gay Militants*. New York: Stein and Day, 1971. Information on the early gay movement on the West Coast was drawn from Teal's book.

129

What do we fight against, or for
May 29, 2013

We have to fight to improve our situation in America, in order to become, as the character Joseph says in *Adam in the Morning,* "*Americans,*" merely coming out won't do it. The post before last was the second of two on Tim DeChristopher and an elaboration of his thoughts on civil disobedience. According to DeChristopher, it is only through civil disobedience that we force the rule of law in our society to grow closer to what he calls the "shared higher moral code." It is only through consciously breaking the law that we can force the law to be examined in a court of law and in the court of public opinion and therefore effect changes in the rule of law.

But if we fight, what do we fight against? Or for? At the end of the first night of fighting in the Stonewall Riots, Bo Ravich invites the gang back to his apartment for breakfast. It's four o'clock in the morning. There's Bo, his lover Andrew, their new friend Joseph, the handsome actor from South Central LA who plays Caliban in the current production of *The Tempest* and who had experience in Alabama and Mississippi in the first Freedom Rides and in Freedom Summer, and, asleep in the living room on the sofa, is Mitzi, a fifteen year old homeless girl who was a leader of the street kids in the rioting. They are sorting out what happened tonight. *What did we do, when we fought New York's finest cops all up and down Christopher Street?* One of them wonders if this is the beginning of the Revolution. Joseph doubts it. "I don't think the Revolution is going to happen. The people who have the power are too entrenched, and I don't think we can shame them into giving up their power. I think we can fight them, like we did tonight, like you did tonight, but the fight has to be a much, much bigger thing than our battle around Sheridan Square." Andrew, Bo's lover, says, "So the fighting was for ourselves?" And Bo says, "Yeah, I think so. We proved we could do it, that we could fight back, and now we never have to take abuse again lying down. We had to prove to ourselves we can fight—" Andrew smiles, "—even if we don't prove we can win." "Yeah, right." It's Joseph. "We have to learn that, independent of them, we are OK." *So the fighting was for ourselves.* We are different, now that we have fought, even if our opponents aren't. We have found our courage. We have found our brothers-in-arms. We don't ever need to take their abuse again. We are new people.

So, if we fight, we can't lose. No matter how many men—or unjust laws—they throw against us, finding our courage to fight makes us more courageous, stronger, more formidable opponents *just because we fought back.* And when a LGBTQ man or woman says, *I stood up for myself,* whether or not he or she is able to stop his or her opponent, the LGBTQ person *has made himself better, stronger, more powerful* for the next fight and brought liberation one step—one day—closer. We win just by doing it.

*

Quotations to the talk among Bo Ravich's friends on the question of *What do we fight for?*, which takes place in Bo's kitchen after the first night of rioting in Sheridan Square, are to my novel *Adam in the Morning,* Boston: Adriana Books, 2010, an ebook available for purchase from *http://www.dwightcathcart.net.* It is one of the three novels of the *Stonewall Triptych.*

130

It still ain't necessarily so
June 8, 2013

This month, the Supreme Court will decide the Prop 8 case, known as *Hollingsworth v. Perry*, and the DOMA case, known as *US v. Windsor*. An analysis of what these cases are and what they mean for the gay community and the prospects for a gay success can be found on Towleroad, in the writings of Ari Ezra Waldman.

These cases, the Prop 8 case and the DOMA case, are important because the Defense of Marriage Act, which denies federal recognition of marriage equality anywhere may be overturned, and many commentators believe that the Prop 8 case is going to result in legal marriage equality at least in California. People who get married in Massachusetts, and all the other states which currently offer marriage equality, will get all the federal benefits currently withheld from them, and the largest state in the union will join the twelve currently offering marriage equality. The sheer number of persons able to be married to members of their own sex will hugely increase. So this is huge. Because it is huge, the possibilities for disaster are also very great. A defeat on the Prop 8 case would be crushing, and a defeat on the DOMA case would set us back by a generation.

But there is another way of looking at all this. Almost anything the Supreme Court does this month is going to be a setback for everybody. I wrote about this in a post called *It ain't necessarily so*, in February 29, 2012, and that post is worth reading again. What's happening— whatever the Supreme Court does—is that our constitutional jurisprudence is beginning to harden around the belief that a citizen has a "sexuality," that there are three sexualities to choose from (gay, straight, and bi, and you can already begin to see the problem developing here), that a person has a sexuality all his or her life (the same ones), and that to get your rights, you have to come out, which means you have to place yourself somewhere in this scheme and stay there. I wrote then, "Our culture is developing an understanding of sexuality—and writing it into the law through these court cases—that is rigid, narrow, confining, and immutable, while our sex is fluid, expansive, mutable, and constantly surprising."

In that blog post, I talked about people who think of themselves as "straight," but who propose to have sex with men, or who think of themselves as "gay" but aren't gay all the time. People who don't recognize any clear bright line between the two. I know a guy who loves his wife and has never been non-monogamous, but who thinks of naked men every time he has sex with her. Things just aren't divided up into three sexualities. They are very fluid, and they are very mutable, and very expansive.

I concluded with this paragraph: "The consequence of what's happening is that people who follow their hearts, or their genes or their lusts, are still not going to find themselves reflected in the structures laid down by the culture and are going to be told, "You do it wrong," "You are wrong to feel that way." In these court cases, we are developing an intellectual framework for our sexuality that is going to be as guilt-inducing as the one we've had for the last forty years, and it's clear that it's the culture, which likes binary thinking because it's simpler, that has gotten it wrong *again*."

131

Waldman on Towleroad on Supreme Court: 1 and 2

June 27, 2013

Towleroad and Ari Ezra Waldman are aware that the Supreme Court will probably be releasing the decisions in the marriage cases Friday morning, June 28, 2013.

Ari is running a series of explanatory blog posts in preparation for these decisions, which promise to be momentous.

As I have said before, Waldman is good at explaining legal issues affecting gay people for those of us without legal training. Try them out. [I have found that I get different posts depending on whether I link to Towleroad from my iPad or my MacBook Air.]

In this post, Ari explains the state of federal marriage law *if DOMA is struck down. (http://www.towleroad.com/2013/06/ fedmarriagelaw.html)* In this post, Ari explains the question *(http://touch.towleroad.com/tlrd/#!/entry/gay-rights-after-scotus- what- if- theres-no-standing-or,51c326fcc5f0cf15b3773bae)*

132

Waldman on Towleroad on Supreme Court: 3
June 22, 2013

Yesterday I posted two links to Ari Ezra Waldman's posts on Towleroad under the heading of "Gay Rights after SCOTUS." Here is a third. It's on "The Future of Civil unions and Domestic Partnerships" *(https://www.towleroad.com/2013/06/nextcivil/).*

133

Gay men, gay women, the truth, and the Supreme Court: 1
June 23, 2013

It's at the end of the last, the third, night of the fighting, people are drifting away, some of them to go down to the piers for sex and some to the trucks, but our guys are still sitting on the high stoop next door to the Stonewall, watching and listening to things dying down. It's the end of the novel, *Adam in the Morning*, and our guys—it's all guys because Belle, who wants help from the guys to get pregnant left a few minutes ago, and Mitzi, a fifteen-year-old homeless girl who has been on the front lines of the fighting for three nights, has gone back to her gang—turn their attention to final things. *What now?*

"Our guys" are Bo, a carpenter at the local repertory theatre, his lover Andrew who is a waiter and a writer who writes from a radical leftist perspective for counter-cultural rags and is strong, tough, brilliant, Joseph, an actor who has just come from the West Coast and has experience with the best Black Arts Theatre in America and wants to move in with Bo and Andrew and plays Caliban in a Village repertory theatre, Bo's straight brother Billy up from Houston to help Bo in the fighting, and Gus, the youngest and prettiest of them, a fighter from the tough neighborhoods of Baltimore and also an actor, who plays Ariel. These men address the question, *What do we need to put our energies into now?*

"Besides, guys, we need to take time this summer to look at the question Andrew raised," Joseph says.

"What's that? I've forgotten."

"The obvious one, the most basic one of all."

"And what's that?"

"Why this one. Andrew asked it this morning on the sidewalk, going to get Billy's tickets." Andrew is enjoying this. "What are we? What is a gay man? What is he for?"

Everyone laughs.

"I'm serious, guys. That's the most important question of all. And we don't know the answer to it, either." (a couple of pages before the end of *Adam in the Morning*)

It was something their gang had been talking off and on about since the beginning of the riots. *What is a gay man?* Someone who has sex with men. That's for one thing. Everything seems to follow from that, but Bo has been invited to have sex with Belle and father her child. Is he still gay? How much sex with women can a gay man have before he stops being gay? And, of course, Republican lawmakers raise the question, How much sex with men can a Republican have before he stops being straight, or a Republican? Bo Ravich, the narrator of *Adam in the Morning,* doesn't want to take that approach to the problem. "I can do what I want. I'm free." It's the Sixties in *Adam in the Morning,* and freedom is a powerful symbol. *I want to be free.*

The question of a *gay man—what is he?* is important right now in this week between June 21 and June 28, 2013, because a week from today, at the latest, the Supreme Court is going to deliver its judgments in the marriage cases, and it is unlikely that their decisions are going to even mention the science around the answer to the question, *What is a gay man?* The science around the question studies the behavior of a man like those in Bo's group. The actual behavior of gay men on the street is not going to figure in the Supreme Court's decision. It is also unlikely that the Justices are going to mention the politics around the question. The politics around that question divide humanity into two or more groups, name them, and then determine appropriate behavior for each. It is unlikely that the Supreme Court is going to recognize that there *is* a politics around this question. That means that, however the cases are decided this week, things are going to be *more* complicated afterward than they are now. This is always the way when great decisions are made while ignoring great bodies of knowledge.

*

The quoted passage is from the ebook *Adam in the Morning,* Adriana Books, 2010, which is available from Adriana Books (*adrianabooks.com*).

134

Waldman on Towleroad on Supreme Court: 4
June 24, 2013

Ari Ezra Waldman and *Towleroad* published the fourth post in the run-up to the Supreme Court decisions this week. He gives us eight things to keep in mind when we read the decisions. Here is the link. (*https://www.towleroad.com/2013/06/8things/*)

135

Waldman on Towleroad on Supreme Court: 5
June 25, 2013

Ari Ezra Waldman has a post up on Towleroad about the implications of the affirmative action decision for the marriage cases tomorrow.

136

Waldman on Towleroad on Supreme Court: 6
June 25, 2013

Ari discusses the effect of the decisions already announced on the decisions not announced and on the drive of gay people for equality. Watch it here (*www.towleroad.com/2013/06/awaldman.html*).

137

Gay men, gay women, the truth, and the Supreme Court: 2
June 25, 2013

When I was growing up, everybody around me—my parents, my grandparents, my sister and brother, my cousins, my scoutmaster, my teachers, the priest, politicians—thought the same way about how I was feeling. I was definitely aroused by men and by particular aspects of men's bodies, and when I started becoming aware of this, I was aware that I should absolutely not tell anybody else what I knew. My whole culture condemned me for feeling the way I felt. Today I remember how it felt to feel something and to know that everybody thought I was feeling the wrong thing or that I was wrong to feel the way I felt. Part of what I wanted, after I divorced my wife and moved to Boston, was the right to feel without being condemned. It was years after I moved to Boston before I first began to know what it felt like to have my own feelings and to know that other people around me felt those same feelings or respected those feelings.

What was needed—and I didn't know this when I was in my twenties—was some change in the culture that allowed it to accept and to reinforce the feelings I had. At the time, I thought we needed to address the places in the law that prevented me from serving in the Armed Forces or, later, that prevented me from getting married, or that taxed me differently from straight people, or that prevented me from getting into bed with a man without being afraid that I was going to end up in jail. But as we have moved toward success in those areas, we also have had to address the fact that our culture for years has refused to give me and others like me the elemental acceptance of our feelings. This was much more complex than my need for my culture to accept the way I felt about men's arms. It was a need for the culture to accept my sense of the impermanence of feelings—what I both felt and learned—and my sense that *love* was not the same thing as *sex,* and that much of the impermanence of heterosexual marriages and the cause of the high divorce rate among straight people was the consequence of the heterosexual culture always seeming to think that sex was love. What was needed was for us to tell the larger culture what our life was like, to say it over and over again and then to expect the straight world to take seriously everything we said. Taking the Stonewall Riots as a plan, we needed to demand respect.

What makes a gay man is a serious question, and the four men, and two women (one adult woman and one fifteen-year-old girl) in *Adam in the Morning* don't agree on an answer. They don't argue about it—they love one another and respect one another and so don't argue about most things—but they do discuss. Belle, for example, backs away from her proposal:

> 'I think I may get pregnant without asking any of
> you for help. I don't want to be in a position of asking
> any of you men to give up being gay, even for a minute,
> so I can get pregnant.'
> [Bo answers] 'Belle, there is no brick wall between
> gay and straight. Being gay is not something you can
> give up, no matter what you do, but it's also not
> something that governs every single sex act and thought
> you engage in. '[Belle and Bo in conversation, Tuesday
> afternoon, on the roof, *Adam in the Morning,* Adriana
> Books, 2010]

If the affection among these folks is strong enough, he *may* do it, on the other hand he may not, and he'll tell us what he'll do and what he won't, which is the way it should be, and we will respect him.

The courts don't want to allow this. Chief Justice Margaret Marshall of the Supreme Judicial Court of Massachusetts, which declared that same-sex couples should be allowed to marry in the Commonwealth of Massachusetts, also declared marriage in the Commonwealth to be "a voluntary union of two persons, as spouses, to the exclusion of all others." But we, not so committed to the identity of sex and love, know that we can have commitment and love without monogamy, and so even though we can now have marriage in the Commonwealth, it is marriage defined by the Justices of the Supreme Judicial Court and is not *ours,* not defined by us or by our experience.

In the Commonwealth, the Chief Justice defined marriage in a way that conflicts with the feelings and the actions of a significant number of gay people. We've been here before. We're being told, "We're going to let you do this. These are the rules." I expect what will happen is that we will vote with our feet, gradually changing in new and unexpected ways the institutions we now are getting legal access to. Until we change marriage, we will have to live with another version of what we lived under from my birth in 1939 to my heterosexual marriage in 1964, a dishonest contract, imposed from outside.

138

Gay men, gay women, the truth,
and the Supreme Court: 3
June 26, 2013

What we are looking at here is a developing definition of *gay man* that is very porous. There isn't really such a thing. Alfred Kinsey collected data on sexual histories that resulted in his creation of a seven point scale in which he said everyone could be placed. Most men in the population can be placed in the 0 column "if they make no physical contacts which result in [homosexual] erotic arousal [...]." On the other hand, men can be placed in the 6 column "if they are exclusively homosexual, both in regard to their overt experience and in regard to their psychic reactions." [p. 639-641] A man can be placed in 4 column "if they have more overt activity and/or psychic reactions in the homosexual, while still maintaining a fair amount of heterosexual arousal activity [...]." Other more recent scientists have created vastly expanded scales by which to measure human sexual activity, and there are scales that attempt to measure psychic activity of a person engaging in sex, but they have not created anything that successfully attacked Kinsey's work. [See *Kinsey, The Measure of All Things*, Jonathan Gathorne-Hardy, Indiana University Press, Bloomington, Indiana, 1998, p.450-452]

Today, we are in a peculiar situation. Our science comes from Kinsey and his heirs, and our politics comes from the Sixties, the Stonewall Riots, and the Gay Liberation Front's cry, *Come out!* The cry has nothing to do with the accumulation of accurate data. If you are a Republican Member of Congress and are caught having sex with a man in some restroom somewhere, it may be because you are generally *always* wanting a man but haven't ever told anybody, or it may be that you have never wanted a man before now. What is clear is that the self-definition "I am gay" or "I am straight" are independent of the specifics of your sexual history—that is, independent of the data drawn from you. Either "I am gay" or "I am straight" may be true without regard to the data drawn from you that may define you as a Kinsey 1 or a Kinsey 3 or a Kinsey 5 or some other designation.

And now, tomorrow the Supreme Court is going to rule on the marriage cases, and somewhere in the Court's decision may be a reference to the phrase "gay people," and the Justices will not be referring to the science of the incidence of sex. The Justices will not make reference to the percentage of gay people in the culture or they will make reference to "ten percent" of us who are gay, but this will be thrown into the opinion without much regard for where it comes from. As far as gay *people* are concerned, the justices might as well be making up their opinions out of whole cloth. We will be able to get married, or we won't be able to get married, depending on factors that don't have much or anything to do with us. We will enter into relationships which are monogamous—or not—based on factors that don't have anything to do with the Supreme Court. They don't know us. Only occasionally, when one or some of us drift into the same petri dish as something they are familiar with, are they able to get us partly right. *Biologically male.* Well yay. But most of the time, they don't know much about what is valuable to us or what drives us. And when the lawyer in Massachusetts said, "Gay people just want the same thing straight people want," the lawyer said something that was manifestly untrue.

I've written about all this before, when there was a run of court cases at the end of 2011 and the beginning of 2012. Things have not gotten better since then, and the danger is greater, because this time the court is the Supreme Court. I wrote then, "We can now see that the intellectual foundations of the future are being constructed. I don't just mean the legal constitutional structures that are going to control how we are going to fit into the body of the republic, but also the emotional and psychological structures that will control the way we think about ourselves. The concept of "gay people" is congealing and solidifying." And it is almost certain that they are getting it wrong. We are not like that. We are not like straight people. We don't divide our sexuality among three options.

Why get married then? It's fun, it's heart-warming, it makes it easier to live together in our culture, it's great to feel the warmth and approval— and *love*—of friends and family, which is sustaining during hard times, and it is a public expression of what I feel for Courtney, my partner.

Gay people, even those who get married, should remind themselves and each other that their relationships were just fine before they decided to get married, that marriage brings financial advantages, and the approval of the community but does not make their relationship better, or that marriage does not make those who undergo it better in any way than those who don't. Nor are those who have children. And they don't conduct their relationships better than those who don't. All are equal.

In a moment when "marriage" may be vastly expanded, it is essential to remember all those during all those years who were in love but who, because the government prevented it, never married.

139

A demonstration of happy people, the 54th Regiment Memorial, rain, Bromfield Camera
June 26, 2013

I went into town to find a demonstration of happy gay people, but the only demonstration I could find was in front of the State House around a man running as a Democrat for Congress. Everybody seemed happy, but they didn't seem gay. I crossed the street. There were tourists with cameras around the 54th Regiment Memorial. Several listened to a guide telling about the memorial. Not disappointed, I thought the 54th Regiment Memorial was perhaps exactly the right place for me to be after the Supreme Court decisions this morning, even standing alone. Both celebrated moments of changing American democracy, the inclusion of the African-American soldiers among the troops fighting in the Civil War, and the inclusion of same-sex couples among those who must be given their rights under Article 5 of the Constitution—liberty and due process. The soldiers in the Memorial seemed so brave, marching off to war, carrying their rifles, so entirely admirable, and even though most of them died at Ft Wagner, still they were victorious, like all the generations of gay men and women have been victorious in their long march.

It began to rain, and I considered the danger to my camera. I turned my camera off and took out the battery. Bromfield Camera was nearby, and I ran, crossing streets and dodging pedestrians. There were three gentlemen behind the counters in Bromfield Camera, good friends, two up at my end of the age scale, and one way down at the other end of the scale, and we joked. "I'm in danger of getting wet." Being New Englanders, they said that was impossible, that it wasn't really raining hard enough, you know, to actually *wet* someone. I told them I needed a plastic bag to protect my camera. We talked about the Supreme Court.

The younger one said, "Now that we have gay marriage with all the federal benefits—" He paused. "Will you marry me?"

Everybody laughed. I said, "Sure. If this doesn't work out with Courtney, then I'll marry you." Courtney and I have been testing this out for the last 23 years, so I think this may last. But it was nice to be asked.

140

People who were careless and malicious and ignorant
July 7, 2013

It's satisfying, having access to a right that everybody else has access to, and to have that right unencumbered by any factor. These rights are inherent and do not come from the Constitution. Justice Kennedy recognized that. We can get married. Our marriages are recognized by the federal government, and nobody can limit those rights, including the US government. The people who try, like the various conservative churches and religions and the Republican Party, will, I suspect, lose adherents of their own rather than change our behavior. That's already happening.

The recognition of these inherent rights is affecting the gay community in a variety of ways, depending on generation. A young friend, when the marriage cases were being debated before the Supreme Court, said he found it hard to believe that this debate was taking place. This should have been dealt with decades ago, he said, with a noticeable strain of impatience. Others, in the middle generations, see that these victories are the result of decades of work by thousands of activists. Now that we have arrived at the resolution we should have arrived at decades ago, we can move on. For myself, I don't trust it. Our opponents fought too hard to prevent this from happening for us now to arrive on the scene and greet everyone present with good will. I think of all those in my generation who had never had the option to marry—decent men and women who lived their whole lives without basic rights, without marriage and without the right to serve openly in the Armed Services, and without ever being able to be public about their feelings for their own gender. It is hard for me to turn around and to accept as my comrades the people who caused all this, people who were careless and malicious and ignorant of the lives of gay people. I remember the damage that has been done—people robbed of a portion of their lives— and I won't forgive and can't forget.

Two days ago, I read a brief piece on *Huffington Post* by a mother whose son came out to her in 2001, when he was twelve. This mother reacted badly,—she was a religious person—and the son grew up into an alcoholic and a drug addict and ultimately died of a drug overdose. The mother is pictured kissing the face of this son while he is in a coma, apparently before he died. I read this piece, and was almost incapacitated for days afterward, the thing was so painful.

I remember the people who didn't get their rights during their lifetimes, who *died* before they were fully recognized. Now that we are getting our rights recognized, we have to remember the people who went before us. We can't be the kind of people who forget.

141

Chris Matthews, Anthony Weiner, sex, and language
July 26, 2013

I had the TV on to MSNBC, listening to the progressive cable channel chew over Anthony Weiner. Chris Matthews was sputtering with (I suppose) astonishment and dismay, talking to two psychologists, trying to understand why Weiner did what he did. In a very brief exchange, he said, "I just don't get it. I think, I get, I get sex—," by which he meant that he understood sex but didn't understand the motivation of a man like Weiner. He went on, "—like we all do. We get sex. Male and female. Gay and straight—" By this point I am sitting up and listening hard. He is going on, and then he begins that characteristic thing he does. He stutters, searching for his next word. He can't immediately come up with it so he says, "—and—other possibilities." He didn't mean to say that. His stuttering displayed his ignorance. Don't start with *gay*, unless you know what you're going to say after you've said *straight*.

Chris was exploring how and why the sex drives of all of us end up making damned fools of a lot of us, even making some of us call ourselves names like Carlos Danger. But people have never been able to control their sex to any great degree since the beginning of the Earth, and what is astonishing is that Chris Matthews was acting astonished and dismayed by that fact.

If Chris had started with *gay* and ended with *straight*, he would have painted himself as even more offensive than he did when he ended it with "—and—other possibilities." At least Chris recognizes that there *are* others—all the rest of us, men and women who are neither gay nor straight—who have to be acknowledged, even if we are not named. This brief exchange puts his ignorance, and the poverty of our language, on display. He didn't know what to call them, those other possibilities, so it is a pretty fair bet that he didn't know how to think about them, either.

Chris's real mistake was in starting his analysis of sex by thinking of sex as if it were a binary construct. "I get sex, like we all do. We get sex. Male and female." The way he edged into his little discussion is to introduce male and female and sex and the idea of straight, an understandable if parochial mental knee-jerk. He took what he knew best, introduced that into the discussion, and then used *gay and straight* to start a progression. But the trouble with such a progression—*gay, straight, and other possibilities*—is that you can't wimp out like that. You have to name the genders, one by one, once you name the first one. Unfortunately, the human race is built so you can't ever name them all.

What Chris Matthews should have done on his program tonight was open his line of inquiry by asking his two psychologists, "Can you talk about what drives us when we want to have sex with another person?" And then, "What is it about sex that often makes us lose ourselves in it?" And, in that rapid-fire way he has, he should have asked another question, before the psychologists had had a chance to answer his first two, "Why does sex so often make us make fools of ourselves?"

What we need are new words, new ways of talking about these matters, and so new ways of thinking.

142

This is what is essential about us
August 6, 2013

There has always been the danger that the more assimilated we are, the more we will become like them and therefore lose what makes us unique. Assimilate us, and eventually we disappear. This has been a danger for Jews, for black people, for women, for Native Americans, and for every wave of new immigrants to arrive on these shores. It may be that assimilation *means* loss of identity. *Assimilation* has been the technique our culture has used since the beginning to cope with new populations: *It will make them like us.*

This is bad because the gay community has learned how to conduct its romantic and sexual relationships without benefit of the law. That's major, and in that area we have it all over heterosexual people. We conduct our relationships without benefit of divorce, charges of adultery, property settlements. We know the difference between sex and love and can talk about which persons are available as sexual partners without having the state play a part in any of these arrangements. And when necessary, we know the point at which our agreements among ourselves need to be re-negotiated. If we're assimilated—just because there are more of them than there are of us—the probability is that we will drop all this and take up the practices of heterosexuals.

We have developed a way of preserving the freedom of individual persons while enabling that person to form various kinds of important relationships. We know how to conduct *long-term* relationships without any officer of the state anywhere to be seen. Every week, as new states offer marriage equality, we see pictures of couples who have been together twenty, thirty, forty years, who are now getting married. We have been refining our ability to live long and successful lives with no partner, and we show every week that we know how to live *alone.* We already know how to do it. We make a contribution to our culture just to the extent that we don't allow heterosexuals to make us forget that we know these things. We need to teach *them* what we know. We need to say, very loudly and repeatedly, *We know these things.* And then we need to say, *You folks need to learn what we know.*

There's another reason that it's bad for us to assimilate. If we care about the civilization we are a part of, we care about preserving our ethnic heritage—that is, the ethnic heritage of gay people— just as much as we care about the ethnic heritage of the various waves of Africans who were brought here or of European Jews before and after World War II, or of the tribes of Native Americans who've always been here.

What we need from heterosexuals is the equal protection of the laws. What they need from us is *our difference.*

143

What makes good people good
August 17, 2013

This week the news is out of Russia and has to do with the anti-gay laws there, their effects on Russian LGBT people and on the Winter Olympics 2014, and what the rest of the world is going to do about it. First response was from gay bars around the world dumping Stoli down the drain, then from people who said Stoli was made in Latvia and owned by Russians in Luxembourg. What to do? Then came the discussion over whether the anti-gay laws would be enforced against gay Olympic athletes and against gay travelers visiting Russia for the Olympics. Apparently. People proposed moving the Olympics to Vancouver, which has an Olympic site already built from its own successful Winter Olympics in 2010.

People have been weighing in on whether it is right to move the Olympics—or to cancel them entirely this Olympiad. These people speak of the Olympic athletes who have trained for four years and who expect to be given the opportunity to test their skills against other athletes from around the world. People compare the right of these athletes with the right of gay and lesbian people in Russia to be safe. This is a nice argument, if you can ignore the LGBT persons whose rights are being trampled on so that an athletic contest can take place.

I don't know at what point I would think it is legitimate to abandon the defense of the rights of lesbian and gay persons so that some other event can take place, but, so far in my life, I have never encountered such a moment. The people making the decision to abandon the defense of the rights of gay people are all—pay attention here—straight people. I would have some respect for this process if I saw that gay people were being asked to give up the defense of their rights in favor of some other, greater, good. But actually, there is no *other, greater, good* that exists that could possibly justify the gay person giving up his or her human rights. We are being told to give up the defense of our rights, *because this other thing is more important to the whole world than your rights are to you.* But you didn't ask the gay person, before you bartered away his rights. This is blackmail, and the gay community should not submit to it.

Beware of people who want you to make a severe sacrifice *for them.* Good people don't do that. Good people sacrifice *for you.*

144

We don't tell the truth about ourselves
September 9, 2013

What should be the subject of a gay writer?

I ask this question seriously. I have read a recent article in Salon by Daniel D'Addario which seems to explain what is happening now in publishing.

The headline over D'Addario's article is, *Where's the buzzed-about gay novel?* D'Addario knows something isn't working. There are just not enough gay characters in current literature getting the same intense examination that heterosexual characters routinely get. He also says, even the LGBT characters who do make it into books in the bookstores are from a narrow range of experience. D'Addario says,

> "Publishing is not a charitable endeavor devoted to equal reception for all: it's a business catering to the interests of an audience comfortable with gay people but not necessarily comfortable with stories that don't cohere with a mold recognizable from, say, *the most recent Michael Cunningham novel.*"

There seem to be two causes for this present situation. D'Addario quotes Matthew Gallaway, the gay author of *The Metropolis Case*,

"The publishers want to sell as many copies as possible," so they want to stay away from anything that might be controversial. Readers, too, bear some responsibility. Sarah Schulman, lesbian activist and novelist, says readers "have gotten used to a certain kind of white gay [writer] who does not have very overt sexual content in his work, who fits paradigms they're comfortable with." The result of this is that "the gay character must not experience homophobia from middle-class white people, he can experience it from rednecks, but not from people like the reader. He's not allowed to be angry about his life."

Concluding, D'Addario discusses something he calls "minority lit," in which the minority writer will write, in the words of Alexander Chee, "about the difficulties one faces as X minority in the US—and so this becomes the expectation." Chee concludes, "even before you pick up the novel, it can feel like you're about to read a long-form complaint." D'Addario seems to feel that the possibility that a novel is a "long-form complaint" is a terrible thing, driving away publishers and readers.

But something else is happening here too. Twenty or thirty years ago, academic historians started assigning novels to their history students as a way of teaching them about some historical phenomenon. *Intruder in the Dust, Absalom, Absalom! Native Son, Giovanni's Room*, and *Portrait of a Lady*. If D'Addario is right in his assessment of current publishing, where will future historians go, among current gay novels, to find the truth about the lives of gay men and women in the first decade of the twenty-first century? If publishers don't want anything controversial, and if readers don't want anything outside their comfort zone, who will tell the truth?

When I was seventeen, in high school, I came to understand that a writer—we were discussing Herman Melville—was a truth-teller. It was not until twenty-five years later that I was handed, as on a silver-platter, the subject about which I was to tell the truth—what happened to a group of gay people in a small town in Maine when one of us was murdered by bigots.

Later, I wanted to write about the life of a gay man who had gotten married in 1964, then read about Stonewall in 1969, then divorced and moved into the gay community in 1984. There was nothing about this man in literature. In fact, whole important swaths of the American population have been ignored by writers who create America's literature, and *fiction* treated them as if they didn't exist. But they did exist, and we need to know about them.

What was the effect on individuals of DOMA and DADT and the various obscenities of the American Psychological Association and the American Psychiatric Association during the forties, and fifties and sixties, and of the constant assault on the persons of gay people from Christian churches? Where has been the writer who could tell us that the most savage abuse that a gay person experienced during those decades usually came from his own family?

No wonder the buzzed-about gay novel does not yet exist. We have people like D'Addario explaining to us why gay writers need not tell the truth about gay lives. The reason we have the literature we have is that intellectually lazy agents and editors and commentators and critics say over and over to readers and writers that it's OK—even necessary—not to tell the truth about our lives.

145

The validity of the lives we lead
September 18, 2013

"I don't really think that it makes sense for a work of art to take on a social purpose. Just because there are so many constraints that you're working under already—what material is available to you, what your capabilities are with the abilities you have, what will the market bear, what's the nature of your audience—these are the constraints you have to satisfy. If you have a purpose of social reform, I don't think it'd be art."

Caleb Crain, who wrote *Necessary Errors*, said these words, which were reported recently in *Salon.com* by Daniel D'Addario. Reading them, I begin to think of the "social purpose" in novels I have read and of the "social purpose" in three of the novels I have written. In the third sentence above, Crain defines "social purpose" as "social reform," meaning, I think, that when *Macbeth* argues against regicide Shakespeare's social purpose is to support the Tudor myths, and that is impermissible in a work of art. But he couldn't mean that. I guess that a study of literature could argue that half the works of literature are about the causes or the effects of murder of one kind or another.

The sixth commandment, *Thou shalt not kill*, is a kind of tennis net that functions in the literary work for the character to deal with. It exists in thousands of novels, causing difficulties, suffering, illumination, more suffering, and in the end, sometimes, release. A social purpose is a subject like anything else, and it exists to be written about and to be dealt with by the character.

An elaboration of the sixth commandment, *Thou shalt not kill gay people,* exists the same way. We have hundreds of plays and novels about killing the king, but almost none about killing the gay kid next door. Listening to Caleb Crain, it would seem that the former are art and the latter not. He thinks we should not write about the moment when the gay kid next door is murdered or about its consequences, because this would give the novel *social purpose.* This murder is intrinsically important. It is interesting. It has moral significance. In fact, killing the gay kid next door satisfies every one of Aristotle's requirements for tragedy, including, as we have seen in our own lives, the disruption of all society when the victim is found tied to a fence on the prairie outside of Laramie. Or, to choose an illustration closer to home, the murder of Bernie Mallett in *Ceremonies,* the first novel of the Stonewall Triptych, which then disrupts everything in Cardiff, Maine, and destroys the accommodation straight Mainers had made with the gay people in their midst. And nothing is ever the same again.

It's not the *social purpose* that makes bad novels out of gay political events or movements. I doubt that every work of art is, as Craig would have it, *its own thing.* I think of *Guernica.* Of *September 1, 1939.* Of *Intruder in the Dust.* Of *Mrs. Dalloway.* A novelist, dealing with all the constraints that Crain lists in the first paragraph above, can surely find space in his novel to make the point that *Murdering a gay kid violates the same codes that murdering a king or a queen or a president or four little girls in a Birmingham church.*

Now, to be clear, not all novels are about murder. Some are about men falling in love with one another, and, given the realities of literature, it is true that not even most novels have to be about heavy subjects. But it is legitimate—and appropriate—when an author chooses to write about the murder of a gay person, to believe that that event is not a *merely* private event, and is worthy of the effort of both writer and reader.

I don't think gay literature has been dumbed down by writers who have a social purpose. We live among *social purposes* all the time, all day, every day. A novel about my going to the Boston Common at seven o'clock six days ago to join a demonstration against any action

against Syria can be as compelling as anything being published today—
it might be a very long novel, with a cast of thousands, and a very
complicated plot, and, of course, a profound and subtle treatment of its
subject. What is dumbing down our literature is the publisher saying,
Don't write about it. It will offend somebody, including straight people,
and the readers saying, *Don't disturb me.* The result is that we can't find
books about ourselves. Even though most of us—or many of us—live
lives which are deeply political, and even though many of us are deeply
anguished by the politics and the violence of our lives. We are *already*
disturbed.

We can't continue to allow publishers and writers to ignore the
lives we lead.

146

Marriage
October 4, 2013

It is inevitably a political act, for men, for women, regardless of whether they are marrying someone of the same sex or the opposite sex. It is a political act for economic reasons, and, for gay people, it has been a political act since the first gay person asked for a marriage license and was turned down. County clerks were dispensing licenses to some citizens and not to others, which is essentially political. For gay people to get married today, DOMA had to be overturned by the US Supreme Court, and laws had to be passed or overturned in the Commonwealth of Massachusetts.

But it is more than that. My partner, Courtney, and I have been together for twenty-three years. We have a good relationship. We don't argue with one another. We treat each other with respect. We find it easy to give in to each other. We love one another. I have often wondered how *getting married* would make our relationship different from what it has been. I didn't want to do anything that would make our relationship less than it has been.

Since the late winter, my partner and I have been planning to marry. Last Saturday, September 28, 2013, on Race Point beach in Provincetown, on a perfect day—low seventies, cloudless sky—we were married, surrounded by his father and stepmother, by his brother and his wife and their children, by my brother and his wife and by my niece and her guest and my nephews and their wives, by Courtney's uncle and aunt, their son and several of Courtney's cousins, by our children and their children, and by a man and his wife whom I've known for 45 years, by a neighborhood lady and her husband, and by our friends. I walked through the dunes from the parking lot at Race Point beach, along the path with the blue mesh, and when I reached the top of the dune and could see the vast drama of Race Point beach below me, under that intense cloudless blue sky, I could see gathered over to my left around a tall rainbow flag all of the good people we had asked to join us, waiting. Someone was running toward me across the sand. As she got closer, I could see it was one of our granddaughters, followed by another granddaughter, and their mother, all of them beautiful.

Then I knew the difference between what Courtney and I had done for the last twenty-three years and what we were about to embark on. Our relationship has been essentially private. *This* was going to be a relationship embedded in a community of people who cared about us— our relatives and our friends—and drawing support and strength from being surrounded by them, but free, still free. These people love us as we are.

I hugged my granddaughter and her sister and my daughter, and we walked down across the sand toward the flag and the crowd and Courtney, who were waiting for us to arrive, so he and I could marry. We could have stayed the way we were. It was good, Courtney and me, loving each other. But this is good too. Different, but good.
Courtney and me and everybody around the rainbow flag on Race Point beach on Saturday, September 28, 2013, under a cloudless sky.

147

Where we are now
October 19, 2013

Many people—both gay and straight people—think because gay people can be married in thirteen states that we have solved that problem, and, at least in those thirteen states, we can move on to other issues. That's only partly true.

Think of the long fight for our civil rights as a war. During the time when we were actively fighting, many many people were wounded by the experience, by the cruelty of parents and friends and doctors and teachers and politicians. They are, now, similar to the wounded warriors to whom the Wounded Warrior program devotes its energies. That is, the gay people who fought bigotry and received psychic wounds that were crippling or disabling are now walking in our cities and towns and through the countryside, and while these walking wounded may not have lost a limb or bear physical scars, their emotional well-being has been crippled and their psychic health is lost and maybe permanently gone.

So when we consider the events of the last year or two—the revocation of Don't Ask Don't Tell, and the repeal of DOMA, and, for many of us, a more openness to our lives—we must not ever forget how many of us still bear the scars of the way this culture treated gay people fifty and forty and thirty years ago and who walk along our streets with a severe psychic limp.

I said some of this on the beach at Race Point when Courtney and I married, and a straight friend commented, "We don't treat people that way any more." Which is just the point. As the rest of the gay community moves on to marriage and military service and community respect—and the straight community moves back to thinking well of itself again—some among us remain permanently crippled by events forty years ago when we had neither marriage nor military service nor community—nor family—respect. These are the survivors, home from the war, walking with crutches.

We have to remember these wounded, who are going to be with us for decades. They deserve our respect and our memory of their wounds and of the battles they fought which wounded them.

148

Remember them, remember us
October 27, 2013

At the end of the Stonewall Riots, in my novel *Adam in the Morning,* four men are sitting on the high stoop of the building just west of the Stonewall Inn. It is eleven or twelve, the night of July 2, 1969, and the men are resting after fighting New York cops for five or six hours. Other men stop by the stoop and ask if they're OK—they are bruised and have blood in their hair—and they make plans for the coming days. The four men watch the cops and the crowds disperse. They talk about what's happened. They know it was something stupendous, and they agree it was *fine*. Their conversation gets slower, as it does when people, having just had a life transforming experience, are lost in their own thoughts. Then Joseph, the actor from Los Angeles, says, "I'm thinking of all the people not here, who would like to have been here."

"Right," Andrew [the partner of the narrator] says, "we ought to drink a toast to them. *To everybody who couldn't make it. And to all those who survived the time before the riots.*"

"Great," Bo [the narrator and Andrew's partner] says, "Remember our brothers and sisters here and everywhere, now and since the beginning." They hug each other's shoulders.

During the five nights of the rioting, a man who wasn't there the first night, says, "I wish I had been there. " Belle says, "I am aware of all of you having had this life-transforming event last night and everybody is feeling like comrades, and suddenly I feel left out," and makes plans to riot the next time the cops appear. The men tell her she'll have to run from the cops so she should chuck her wedgies and wear sandals. During all the fighting, the people on Christopher Street are aware that they have been given an opportunity which others would like to have had—men and women who would have fought if they had been in New York during the riots or been alive or been old enough or not too old.

It's not complicated. After many of the great moments of recent gay history, there have been people who said, *We have to remember all the men and women who aren't here, but who are one of us.* The gesture answers a human need to think of the others. Humans tend to forget the past, to forget the people who were not here, to forget those who came to the conflict late, to act as if the only gay people who matter are the ones on the street, fighting. But we can't forget our past. In addition to winning the battle for marriage in the Supreme Court and in fourteen states, we have to win the battle for our history and not let it be lost to us. The guys in the street in New York were not the only guys in the gay community in 1969. Gay men and women were everywhere then, just as gay men and women are everywhere now. We do this for everyone's sake—recognizing that everyone contributed to our history—and also for our own.

*

Andrew and Bo and Joseph and Belle are characters in my novel, *Adam in the Morning,* Adriana Books, 2010. You may read about *Adam in the Morning* on my website *adrianabooks.com,* where you may also buy this book for your ereader.

149

It could be a bum trade-off
November 14, 2013

Gay people have recognized for a long time that learning how to live in a largely straight society presents the possibility of assimilation, and assimilation presents problems, different ones at different times. Over the weekend, I was reading *Gay Men at the Millennium: Sex, Spirit, Community,* a collection of essays loosely organized around the questions Where have we been? How far have we come? Where are we headed? Thirteen years ago, these writers were looking around them and trying to figure out where we are. The editor, Michael Lowenthal, collected essays or chapters from various books to look at these questions.

The writers of some of the essays bring up the concept of assimilation a number of times, and usually the dangers of assimilation are spelled out. The danger of assimilation differs from decade to decade. In one decade gay people may fear that they will lose their "edge and their sense of style, their fabulousness." In another decade, they may fear that they will lose their willingness and ability to experiment sexually. And in a third, the fear is that they will lose their relative freedom from class. Almost no one thinks assimilation is a good thing. What this means is that, depending on his age, a gay man may be indifferent to one danger and sensitive to another, and his lover, ten years younger, has a different set of responses. It also may mean that a person's fear of assimilation in the deep South may be significantly different from the fears held by someone in the Northeast.

The fear that we feel in the second decade of the twenty-first century is a consequence of the great social movements brought about by the Obama administration: the coming out of large numbers of gay military personnel and the movement of large numbers of gay men and women into the county clerk's offices to get marriage licenses. Some significant numbers of us wanted these things to happen—the repeal of DADT and the overturning of DOMA—but the anxiety many of us feel is brought about by changes in the gay community whose effect on all of us we don't know. We fear that we are going to lose something that's important. We don't know what we are willing to give up to get something important.

Years ago, in 1996 actually, Gay Pride in Boston began to get boring. It started that year when a man wearing a kilt got up on stilts, and played around in the street, between and among the groups and the floats of the parade. The wind came too, of course, and played around with the man's kilt, blowing it up like Marilyn Monroe's white skirt over the subway grate, revealing that he didn't have anything on underneath. Just his tight ass and his cock. There were other things in that parade that year. There was a bed being pushed through the street with two women making love. The resultant uproar attacked the man on stilts and the women in the bed. The editor of Bay Windows said none of them had any taste. Apparently the mayor said he wasn't going to take part in Gay Pride in the future if it didn't clean up its act. What we should have done is thank the mayor for his participation in the past, and tell him that we could do without his services in the future. Then we should have had our parade. But instead, we cleaned up our act, and we lost something major as a result. Pride got boring, and people stopped coming. Except the banks, who come in droves.

*

Gay Men at the Millennium: Sex, Spirit, Community, edited by Michael Lowenthal, and published by Jeremy P. Tarcher/Putnam, a member of Penguin Putnam, Inc., New York. Sorry, no digital version apparently.

150

The man on stilts in a kilt in the wind
November 19, 2013

I wrote about this briefly the other day. The point was that as we assimilate into the heterosexual world, the gay community seems to pull in its horns, so it speak. It seems to become less flamboyant, less "out there," less extravagant in the way it presents itself. Some might say, the more the gay community is accepted by the heterosexual community, the less fabulous we become.

On this particular day, during Gay Pride, there was a man on stilts wearing a kilt. And of course the wind blew and showed to the 150,000 people who had come to watch the parade that the man was wearing nothing under his kilt. This was wonderful, I thought. Many people thought differently, including Jeff Epperly, the editor at that time of the Boston gay weekly, *Bay Windows.* Epperly surmised that the man on stilts had no taste. Many people weighed in about the man on stilts—no one seemed to know who he was—and most people seemed to agree that the man on stilts had no taste.

I was pissed. I thought the gay community was certainly less a place I wanted to join if there was no room for the man on stilts with the wind blowing his kilt, so I responded the way I usually do, I sat down to the computer and pounded out a response. I thought it was exactly the right thing to say at that point, but I couldn't get it published anywhere. So here it is:

I am the naked man on stilts
by
Dwight Cathcart

Jeff Epperly wanted to know who the naked man on
stilts was, and I am writing this to let him know that it
was me. My name is Dwight Cathcart, and I am a gay
man who has been practicing on stilts for a number of
years so I could pull off this stunt, as all of my friends
know, and, as Jeff and all of your writers have said, I
have no taste.

I do have a good tight butt, however, and my dick is a
greater than average length and girth, as all 150,000 people
at Gay Pride 1996 will attest.

I haven't had any taste for a long time. Probably not since
I came out. Before I came out, I had a lot of taste. I wore the
right clothes from the right stores and married the right
woman and had the right children and went to the right
schools and had the right kind of house, all filled with 18th
century antiques, which are very tasteful. And I liked
Sargent's paintings, which, in Boston, are *very* tasteful,
except when they are *very* obscene and the MFA hides them
for years. I moved among people who also had taste. They
were miserable, of course, in their tasteful houses, doing
their tasteful things, but they didn't rock any boats or offend
anybody, and everybody said of all of us, *They are people of
taste,* even in their misery. None of us ever wrote a novel or
painted a painting, of course, because people who do those
things can't be thinking very hard about *taste.*

But one day, I decided that *taste* was not what a life
should be based on, because I was miserable in my good
taste, all locked inside of a narrow little cage, trying to
follow all these piddling little rules, and wondering all the
time if I was still *tasteful. Taste* is such a trivial *little* way to
judge people and things. *Am I tasteful?* What a waste of
energy even to consider the question. Even to think about
taste makes your lips purse up as if you were sucking

lemons. What I needed, I discovered, was a little honesty in my life, and a little sense of humor, and a little courage. So I bought some stilts and worked on erasing my tan line. And you all see the results. Freedom.

What I achieved, of course, was vulgarity, which was what I had been missing all my life. After I quit being a person of taste, I discovered how many things my dick would do that tasteful people never dream of. And my mouth. And where I could *put* them! I discovered the energy there is in questioning these leaden values people have which they subsume under the tight nasty little word *taste*. *Vulgar*. The word's roots have to do with the common people, and I discovered the energy, the vitality, there is in the common people, the *honesty* there is in the common people, that people who purse their lips and say *taste* never dream of. *Vulgar*. It is impossible even to say the word without coming on strong. *Vulgar*. God, it sounds like the bass pipes in an organ, doesn't it? Name me one leader in any field of human endeavor anywhere in the world whose primary concern is being *tasteful*.

When I got up on my stilts in my vulgar manner, showing my dick and my ass, what I was doing was coming on strong. Coming on against the limits which our society has always placed—and continues to place— on gay sex and style and fetish. I was coming on strong against people in our own community who have lost a sense of themselves as *common people*, who are striving to rid themselves of the dirt of their humanity and bleach out all their quirky, amazing sexiness. I was coming on strong against Arline Isaacson, who thought that everybody at the parade but me was *normal*, whatever the fuck that means in this context. And of course, up there on my stilts, showing my ass and waving my cock, I was remembering how gay people have always had *tasteless* thrown against them and their behavior. I was remembering how *lewd and indecent*

is still thrown against them. Well, here I am, folks,
tasteless, lewd and indecent, having my good time. In
your face. But my lips aren't pursed.

    I saw *Stonewall*, the movie, last night at the MFA.
The most painful parts had to do with the men
and women in the fifties, who thought that wearing a coat and
tie and hats and gloves and stockings and walking around in a
neat little circle in front of Independence Hall would gain
them freedom. So tasteful. So ineffective. Nobody *ever* got
freedom by being tasteful.

    I scorn to be tasteful. I revel in being vulgar, a man of
the people, aware of where my cock hangs, and proud to
call it by its right name, its *ancient* name. You can take
your taste and shove it. And I think *any man*, seeing a
naked guy on stilts at Gay Pride, doing our job, ought to be
proud to say, *Hey, that's me up there.*

151

Tim, Prior, Lt Choi—they present a problem
December 13, 2013

I was on the Red Line here in Boston, going to Cambridge to attend a concert in Paine Hall at Harvard. Courtney was playing the harp in the orchestra. The train was crowded because it was rush hour—six o'clock—and when I pushed onto the car and grabbed a strap, there was still stream of people coming onto the car from the next door down. Just before the door closed, a few more people pushed into the car and stood next to me. I glanced at them, and then I saw a man two people from me. He was Tim DeChristopher, about whom I have written here (*adrianabooks.com/tim-dechristopher-and-civil- disobedience/*). He is the environmental activist who disrupted the auction of federal oil lands in Utah and who went to federal prison for two years. He had said, in his sentencing statement, "This is not going away. At this point of unimaginable threats on the horizon, this [i.e. my going to prison] is what hope looks like. In these times of a morally bankrupt government that has sold out its principles, this is what patriotism looks like. With countless lives on the line, this is what love looks like, and it will only grow."

The car was too crowded for me to move, and I didn't feel I could speak to him over the heads and shoulders of the several people between us. And yet, I knew he might get off, and I would lose this opportunity to speak to a man I very much admired. I was also thinking that every person who gets on a subway train deserves—and has a right—to be left alone.

Finally I spoke. "Tim?" His head jerked around to look for the source of the voice. It was apparent that he really was Tim DeChristopher. He looked exactly like the pictures of him on the DVD "Bidder 70." He located me and smiled. I smiled. Then I said, "Thank you." He grinned and shrugged, and that was all of it. The car was too crowded for anything more. He got off at Harvard Square and went up the Church Street exit, and I went up the main exit into Harvard Square.

Tim DeChristopher had found a way to act in our culture, when action by single people is rare, and most civil action has been taken over by professionals and large organizations. Tim DeChristopher had the courage to accept the culture's punishment for his civil disobedience and has been able to turn it to his own advancement with his sentencing statement and then has been able to use it in political organizing since that time once he was released.

Tonight, I finished supper and sat down to the computer to begin work on this posting when I found that HBO was showing *Angels in America: the Millennium Begins* and *Peristroika,* and, before I could turn off the tube I was sucked into the tragedy of Prior and Louis. The cat came in and lay beside me, his head resting on my thigh. I ended up watching the whole drama, finished after one, this whole stupendous work by Tony Kushner, ending with Prior's famous words, *The Great Work Begins.*

This is hard for many of us, because the "great work" that Prior calls for—the work which will bring full citizenship to gay people, the work of renewal, of living fully, of loving ourselves and others, of "more life" as Prior puts it—seems largely to be over for many people. We don't fear the deaths of all of us from AIDS, and the struggle for our rights has been co-opted by mainstream America. Even our opposition seems to be giving up. Cardinal Dolan said on *Sixty Minutes* yesterday, that the forces for same-sex marriage seem to have won.

The Great Work Begins. Work means Life, and that's what Prior wanted. *More Life.* But what does this mean? A person can write a check or put a gift on a credit card, but there is not much one can do comparable to disrupting a federal auction of oil rich land. Or is it that we haven't thought creatively enough about this new phase of our lives? *Exactly* what can each one of us do to make life better for all of us? Tim DeChristopher found it. Lt Choi found a way to do it, which only he could do—he chained himself to the White House fence, and then did it over and over and over again until DADT was repealed.

Well, then, *what* for the rest of us?

152

…and who they love.
December 13, 2013

Barack Obama, speaking in a stadium filled with South African people and representatives of the world's nations, said Nelson Mandela emerged "as the last great liberator of the 20th century. Like Gandhi, he would lead a resistance movement — a movement that at its start had little prospect for success. Like Dr. King, he would give potent voice to the claims of the oppressed and the moral necessity of racial justice." It was a powerful way to organize our awareness of the history of the twentieth century. In his second inaugural address, he did the same thing for the history of the United States when he referred to the *places* of the civil rights movements in the United States: "Seneca and Selma and Stonewall." By adding *Stonewall* to the other, established civil rights movements, he elevated us and implicitly made a promise to us.

He's done this several times, a practice I am not accustomed to yet. (I am just not familiar enough with being given that level of respect from an unimpeachable source at the very pinnacle of respect in our culture and delivered on the world stage to know how it makes me feel. I think I worry about it a little.)

Now the president has done it again. Toward the end of his eulogy for Mr. Mandela, he said this:

The struggles that follow the victory of formal equality or universal franchise may not be as filled with drama and moral clarity as those that came before, but they are no less important. For around the world today, we still see children suffering from hunger and disease. We still see run-down schools. We still see young people without prospects for the future. Around the world today, men and women are still imprisoned for their political beliefs, and are still persecuted for what they look like, and how they worship, and who they love. That is happening today.

Apparently he is going to do this regularly, give us respect and demonstrate that he understands our situation in America, and it is not going to take a major *gay* crisis to get him to do so. *This is happening today*, he says. I don't know about you, but this has been so long in coming that it's going to take a little time for me to adapt to this new world.

153

The gay protest novel
December 24, 2013

First New Mexico last Thursday and Utah Friday, making eighteen. Life is good right now for LGBT people, but I am reminded of the long years during which we experienced no victories. I remember what those days were like, and the people who didn't make it to see these current victories, and I take a moment to honor them.

I've been reading *Middlebrow Queer: Christopher Isherwood in America,* by Jaime Harker, the University of Minnesota Press, 2013. I've been interested in Isherwood since I was in graduate school in the sixties. Isherwood wrote *Goodbye to Berlin, The Berlin Stories,* the play and musical made from them, *I am a Camera* and *Cabaret* with the stories of Sally Bowles and Christopher in Berlin just before Hitler came to power, and also *A Single Man,* which I read in 1964 and then rediscovered in 2011, and many other novels.

Jaime Harker says that during the Cold War—the period 1945 to 1989—ideas of gender construction and a paranoid defense of heterosexuality got mixed up with national policy and with the struggle against the Soviets. She says this:

> During the 1940s and 1950s, Cold War intellectuals sought to establish the United States culturally as well as politically (and many did so with covert CIA support for key literary journals). The discipline of American studies—established in books by Leo Marx, F. O. Matthiessen,

Richard Chase, and Leslie Fiedler—sought to establish a mythic American spirit; critics in the *Partison Review* contrasted the freedom of highbrow aesthetics with the niggardly realism of totalitarian regimes. These cultural interventions were marked by an aggressive masculinity, any deviance was denounced as aesthetically compromised and un-American. Literary criticism implicitly enforced conservative gender roles and betrayed anxiety about inordinate cultural influence of women and gay men in the United States, an anxiety alleviated through prescriptive and narrow literary norms. (p. 5)

A paragraph later, Harker says, "Michael Sherry's *Gay Artists in Modern American Culture* points out that gay visibility was high in the late forties and early fifties: critics warned of a nefarious lavender menace undermining the masculinity and virility of American culture" (pp. 5-6). The 'masculinity and virility' of American culture were assumed to be critical to fighting the war against totalitarian regimes. Consequently, Harker says, gay novels represented a corrupting force in American culture, and we were subjected to constantly repeated charges leveled against gay men by Senator McCarthy, by many politicians, and by the editor of *The State,* the daily paper I read as a boy in Columbia, South Carolina. There were two stigmas attached to gay men in 1950. One was this charge of corrupting the culture, and the other was the charge leveled against homosexuals by the American Psychiatric Association, that we were "sick." Harker points out that "Cold War intellectuals lumped together and pathologized all novels that touched on gay themes" (p. 14).

To "pathologize" all novels with a gay theme means that it was going to be difficult to justify writing a novel about such a theme. Critics could say that no novel on such a subject can be a good novel. It may be that this is the source of the critical condemnation of gay *political* novels, that they are propaganda for being a corrupting force in the culture.

Christopher Isherwood sought to establish himself as an American writer during this period, a difficult attempt, given that Isherwood was already known as a gay man from his earlier work before he came to America. Isherwood, however, achieved the impossible and wrote major gay novels during this period all of which were attacked for being a corrupting influence on the culture. Harker quotes Isherwood himself in his own defense:

> "There are certain subjects—including Jewish, Negro and homosexual questions—which involve social and political issues. There are laws which could be changed. There are public prejudices which could be removed. Anything an author writes on these subjects is bound, therefore, to have certain propaganda value, whether he likes it or not." [Harker goes on to say] So despite the considerable differences in style and content, I believe it makes sense to talk about this group of gay novels in the late forties and early fifties as the gay protest novel."

To anyone trying to determine his own motivations for his actions during that period—I've done this myself—it is a relief to be reminded that *the writers I was reading,* these Cold War intellectuals, were feeding me bitter bigotry, and I had thought they were wise. And, considering the actions in the last week in New Mexico and Utah, I find that my joy is easily restrained when I calculate that it has taken some sixty-three years for this progress to be effectuated. Observe the damage these "Cold War intellectuals" did in the late forties and fifties: a generation or two of gay people savaged by people they thought they could trust, a generation of gay writers whose works were savaged, but most of all, a critical principle repeated so widely that it became everywhere accepted, that gay novels on serious political subjects can be no more than mere propaganda and not in themselves capable of being interesting and compelling literature. We were told, gay art cannot be high art. That's a crime, to have told us that. We'll never know what literature has been lost to us in the last sixty years because of these "Cold War intellectuals."

154

When it's the government that commits crimes
December 31, 2013

On Saturday, December 28, the *Boston Globe* ran an editorial comment about the British Government's pardoning Alan Turing. The comment is entitled *Britain: Reclaiming the Hero it Maligned.* I wrote about Alan Turing on this blog. In that post, I said, "This posting isn't about quantum computing, and it isn't about Alan Turing and his contribution to the effort to win World War II, but it is about gay people and our tendency to forget the past. Alan Turing was a homosexual."

Well, *this* posting isn't about any of those things, but it is about the things that a pardon does. Once Alan Turing was dead, there was nothing that any of the survivors around him could do to change the fact that the man had killed himself as the result of appalling treatment by the British government. And the *Globe* this morning is wrong when it says, "Alan Turing deserves an untainted place in the history books, and now he has one." Actually, because of government action, Alan Turing was dragged out of the closet into the harsh light of day, then charged with crimes which were not crimes and sentenced to chemical castration. He then committed suicide by eating a poisoned apple, and all of this is permanently hung on the name and reputation of a brilliant man who helped the Brits win the war and helped create computers for the rest of us. None of that is going to be removed by this pardon. The British Government caused Turing untold suffering and changed the things that are said and will be said about him, and none of that will ever be changed. Turing does not need a pardon. He did nothing wrong. I assume the British Government has issued this pardon to put the focus on Turing's life instead of the government's own appalling crimes.

What to do? Leave poor Alan Turing alone. He has suffered enough. What the British Government should do is to get down on its knees and cry, *mea culpa, mea culpa, mea maxima culpa* and do this continually until every one knows exactly how much suffering the government has caused in the name of morality. The *Globe* is correct in raising the question of the 50,000 other men who were convicted under the same law that persecuted Turing. Those that are still alive should be asked, person to person, how they would like the government to respond to its own culpability. I expect a goodly percentage of those who have suffered under this law will say, *Go fuck yourself.* The point is to remove the *government* from the ranks of those who may assume virtue.

And, next step, *What about the US?* We learned this same lesson about our government when it became clear what had happened at the Tuskegee Institute in the thirties, and, of course, the massive persecution of gay people in the last century. Now we know about the hundreds of thousands who have suffered at the hands of government. *What to do?* First, don't forget them. Know where their suffering came from. Try to make their lives better *now.* Think *reparations.* Don't ever believe that there is anything the government can do to make itself virtuous again. *It can't.* The government is successful at building highways and maintaining the safety net. When the government tries to impose morality on citizens or allows itself to be used as the instrument of certain religious points of view, it fucks it up, every time, and then it ends up, not with egg on its face, w*ith blood on its hands.* The pardon that the British government this week extended to Alan Turing gets it backwards. The government should ask *us* for a pardon for its crimes.

*

Read *The Rebel,* by Albert Camus, about assassins in judges robes.

155

A time when gay men could create themselves
January 12, 2014

Bo Ravich, 30, a stage carpenter, is sitting on a roof outside the kitchen window of his apartment on Weehawken Street, off Christopher Street in Greenwich Village in New York, June 30, 1969. During the long, hot afternoon, Bo is talking to Belle, the producer of the play he is building sets for, who is also a friend, and he listens as she tells him her plan: she wants to get pregnant, have a baby and raise a child. The easiest and most personal way would be to find a man.

They discuss the other men who have gathered around Bo during the riots at the Stonewall Inn—Bo's partner, Andrew, a waiter and a politically progressive writer for counter-culture rags in the Village, Joseph, who has just arrived in the Village from the West Coast and a stint with the New Lafayette, the leading Black Arts Theatre in America, and an actor in the play they're producing, and Bo's brother Billy, up from Houston to fight the cops with his big brother. Belle knows she could get an anonymous donor to help with her desire to get pregnant, but she'd prefer something more personal. These men are attractive, and they are good men. Any one of them would make a good father. Very quickly, the conversation turns on the question of whether any of these gay men (even Billy, who is straight) would be willing to provide Belle with the donation she needs. Bo tells her that any of them would take the idea seriously. She says, "I had no idea. I have assumed—"

"That we're gay, and so—"

"Something like that."

"But you know," Bo says, "Billy has been having sex with Joseph the last couple of nights, don't you?"

"Yes," Belle answers, "but they're both so gorgeous—"

"Well, one of them is gay and the other of them is straight. They do what they want, Belle."

"Well, I thought—"

"I think, dear, I know what you thought. But you should remember this. People can do what they want. And I think that, whether they are gay or not, they'll take the question seriously. That doesn't mean they are going to agree to what you're asking. But they will treat the question seriously."

The issue for Belle turns on several things. Do gay men ever have sex with women? And if donating sperm to a friend to help her get pregnant does not violate their sense of themselves as gay men, is it something that fits the lives they are constructing for themselves at the moment? This issue of *getting Belle pregnant* surfaces from time to time in *Adam in the Morning,* down to the last pages, and remains an open question when the novel closes. Bo asks, sitting on the high stoop overlooking Sheridan Square on Wednesday night, when the last riots are over, "—Andrew and I need to talk, but I'd also like to hear what the rest of you think. You're our gang, and I want to know what you think about gay men doing this. *Are* you our family? Do gay men have families? We have a lot to talk about."

Bo assumes that his gang know what a gay man is, and yet a few minutes later Joseph brings up the question that Andrew raised that morning. *"What is a gay man?"* The gang around Bo don't know—or at least are not clear. Michel Foucault said, in the first volume of *The History of Sexuality* (1979) that "[Before 1869] the sodomite had been a temporary aberration; the homosexual was now a species." Gay people, scientists, church people, lawyers, and politicians have spent the years since 1869 trying to discover and describe the characteristics of this new species.

In 2013, we appear to believe that we know. I wrote *Ceremonies* and *Race Point Light,* and wondered when the world view, which was reflected in those novels, was created. When, for example, did we— that is, the gay community generally—begin to think of *gay* and *straight?* When did we begin to think that if you were gay, you didn't have sex with women? Or if you were straight, you didn't have sex with men? When did we start thinking of the closet? When did we begin to elaborate on the identity of a man who had sex with other men? I suspected that these changes happened around Stonewall. I did preliminary research. I found that pressure which came from the political organizing after Stonewall— that is, during the last half of 1969—led to a relatively more coherent and rigid conception for *a gay man*. The gay activists in the first weeks after the riots needed to find ways to increase their numbers, so they made it imperative that all gay men come out. Their political treatises presumed that *being out* was better than being in *the closet*. *Adam in the Morning* was about a small group of men and women who had come to adulthood before Stonewall and therefore were not subject to the binary world we've had since Stonewall. They were more free, not subject to the confinements that gay men were subject to later, even six months later, and have been subject to ever since.

This is one of the things that make *Adam in the Morning* an interesting novel. Bo and Andrew and Joseph and Gus and even Billy can have sex with a man because that was what they want, because that is what their bodies tell them they want. They don't accept confinements either from the heterosexual world or the incipient gay world. And they are capable of fighting to defend themselves, gently against friends like Belle, who wants to impose stereotypes, and violently against the cops if necessary. They are there in Sheridan Square, every night there's fighting against the cops. The refrain in *Adam in the Morning* is, over and over, *They can do what they want.* They create themselves in a way that very few people have the opportunity. There's nothing else like *Adam in the Morning* out there.

*

Michel Foucault, The History of Sexuality, Volume 1: An Introduction. Trans. Robert Hurley. New York: Vintage Books, 1978. (p. 43).

156

At play in Tennessee

January 28, 2014

I was rooting around in my computer, looking for something, when I stumbled into the junk box and there were pages and pages of emails from a man I knew once, slightly, in school. He has gathered around him a group of our classmates, and these men communicate by email. Nowadays, the news that appears to be occupying that group of graduates of a school in Tennessee is obituaries. I read a few, none of men that I know, I don't think. I have a clear memory of only a few people at the school in Tennessee. The tone of the emails back and forth was very complacent. Everybody was happy with the way the dead man had lived his life, and they wrote about how complacent (that is, happy) they felt about everything. All these emails had automatically gone into my junk box.

Today was my day for cleaning our apartment, and while I was picking up and straightening things, and then vacuuming rooms, I was thinking, "I don't know of a group of men that I am involved in that is so complacent." How had they lived their lives where they were so self-satisfied? The country has been through turmoil during the last fifty years, and they are complacent! But the more I considered the issue, the clearer it became. Of course they were complacent. All of these men went to a school that was constructed for them. They were not asked to think, or to analyze anything, or to come up with something new. I expect all their schools were like that. Self- congratulatory. The problem is way bigger than the school in Tennessee. Our whole culture, back there in the fifties and to a large extent today, was built around smart, well-brought up, white, straight, middle-class professional men, and that's what they all are, and they don't know that their whole culture has been built, like a water slide, for them to ride on. They lived their lives, plugging away, and now they can look around themselves and think, "I did a good job." That's what their lives have been like, like riding down a water slide! Wheeeee! Nothing disturbed them at the school in Tennessee, or anywhere else, and so here they are, all of them age seventy-four or seventy-five, undisturbed as they start dying off, one by one. They can send back and forth their self-congratulatory messages. "Gee! This has been such fun!" Of course it was fun. It was MADE to be fun. That's what water slides are for! This school was a theme park designed for straight white men to play in and nothing serious was asked of them. How many times do I have to learn this? You can't expect anything serious from such a place.

157

Some things we can know about the future
March 7, 2014

The last few days I have been reading a book that clarifies where we are. David Brion Davis, writing on slavery in the west, says " dehumanization was absolutely central to the slave experience." The New York Review of Books says Davis' book, *The Problem of Slavery in the Age of Emancipation* (Knopf, 2014), and the two that preceded it, have "shaped history," by which they mean shaped the way we view our past and its effect on the present. Davis' book studies the dehumanization of the enslaved person and the implications for the slave coming into freedom.

    The Problem of Slavery in the Age of Emancipation reminds me that, two hundred and thirty-eight years after the founding of this nation, we—historians, politicians, artists, writers and novelists, black people and white—are still finding the problem of slavery unresolved and are still searching for ways of understanding our past and are still dealing with the consequences of slavery. It is not likely that the problem of queers is going to be resolved any sooner, and that, even if we get marriage equality throughout the United States in the immediate future, or complete legal equality, we will still be researching and talking about and finding new facts and new approaches to the dehumanization to which queers have been subjected all of the years of the history of the United States.

I assume that one of the things that we—lesbians and gays and bisexual and transgender and queer—will come to understand about ourselves is that, for two hundred and thirty-eight years we were dehumanized, that to some extent that is continuing even today from some quarters. This dehumanization has been a psychological exploitation that had implications for individuals and for the community as a whole. Those implications were both destructive and but also the occasion for creative and effective resistance.

Davis's book instructs us that legal equality and freedom will not bring with them an instant end to suffering. We will still have with us the walking wounded, survivors of the long years in the wilderness, who exhibit the effects of wounds received thirty or forty or fifty years ago. We count in our ranks men and women, the recently wounded, who fight in the current wars. Davis's book, published this year but about events in the first half of the nineteenth century, predicts a long, hard, twilight struggle for queers, whatever happens this year with marriage.

158

Influencing the way we are seen
March 27, 2014

Last night I was going to write a post to this blog, when I found that the whole blog had been erased. Simply not there. This morning, after a tense night, I went to Blogger, and to the help forums. A half-hour later, after one query from another user of the help forum, the whole blog—three and a half year's worth of entries—was restored. I was deeply grateful.

In this blog, I usually write about what's happening in national events—Supreme Court decisions, and about the President, Barack Obama—and what I read in the gay press, and about our visits to the houses of relatives, friends, and, once, my partner's and my marriage last September on Race Point beach in Provincetown, events that affect gay people. I also write sometimes about movies and about books I'm reading that affect gay people. I also write about the books I've written. This blog is a casual record of my intellectual life, and of my contributions to the dialogue going on around all of us about us as gay people and about our place in this thing called America. It felt like a disaster when it was deleted.

What drove me to look at my blog last night was that I read an article on Towleroad by David Mixner. He says that the gay community is in danger of losing its past, as the older generation, the activists during the seventies and eighties, reach advanced age and die.

Records are being lost and oral histories go past retrieval. The history of the gay community is being lost.

What's to be done? Publicize the need for gay men and women to give their records and papers to libraries and organizations. Make them available to the next generation of gay people. It is unnecessary for a person to decide whether he or she had an important role to play in fighting AIDS or in achieving marriage equality. It is unnecessary for him or her to say "I was important enough to preserve my papers." Let the next person down the line make that decision.

Think of your "stuff"—whatever you've been saving since you came out and moved to Boston and now is in the basement or the attic or in the back of your closet—as the raw material of history, the data the historian will use to write the story of who we were and what we did.

We can't control the future. But we're a community that has regularly been lied about through most of the decades of the twentieth century, and we owe it to ourselves to save the material that can at least influence the men and women who tell the story of our generation's time on this planet.

159

What is uniquely ours
March 30, 2014

My classmate from the school in Tennessee and I exchanged letters
recently. We've been writing occasionally about relationships—gay,
straight, and otherwise—and looking to understand differences. I had
written at one point, several months ago, "If all gay people were to get
access to marriage, what kind of marriage would it be? I answered my
own question, What kind of marriage do straight people have?"
Actually, what I should have said was, "What kind of marriage do we
already have?" *Look at ourselves*, because, along with every other kind
of relationship, gay people have always had long-term committed
relationships. And those, like Courtney's and mine, were relationships
between committed, I suppose intelligent, experienced men and women
who were not bound by the marriages straight people have. Since these
committed, intelligent, experienced men and women were outside the
bounds of legal marriage for most of the last one hundred and fifty
years, they have been free, over decades, to develop the rules and
customs of their own relationships. It is as if a Constitutional
Convention had been called which was free to write the constitution for
the best government that man had ever conceived, without regard to any
of the ways men had actually been governed in the past. For it's true,
gay men and women have done what everybody has said we ought to do

but have never been able to do because there have simply been too many people who liked it the way it has always been: we have been able to rethink marriage from its roots and, from an experiential basis, have been able to create something entirely new. Courtney and I have a marriage totally different from the marriages of any other person in either of our families, and yet our marriage is not different from the marriages of scores of our friends in the gay (male) community.

The point of similarity is that our marriage, like many marriages outside the gay community, is characterized by deep love, but also, and this is where we differ from other kinds of marriage, a sense of freedom for both parties. Gay people have discovered some things from their time in the wilderness that straight people appear not to know. The two of us don't own each other. Love and lust are different things. A man can be deeply in love with one man, and at the same time experience lust for another. The basic agreement that is a marriage can be talked out between the two people involved. The two people involved can talk out how they are going to handle it when the man has a transient fuck with someone he met on a train. Some guys don't want to know. Some want to know every time, all about it. Each couple can be different. These two men give up betrayal as a tool of relationships, and they conduct their relationship from positions of equality. These are not the ideas of sex-crazed hedonists. They work, they can result in long-term, loving relationships which are not characterized by internal conflict or by a struggle for dominance. They are characterized by a sense of physical and intellectual freedom.

The trouble is, gay people have already—they've been doing it for years—begun to adopt the concepts of straight marriage, abandoning their own history and experience. That's a tragedy. We already know how to have better marriages than straight people, yet we're giving that up in favor of the lesser, older, flawed version. Gay people ought to look at our own experience and hang on to it when entering legal marriage. We know what works. It's been all around us for most of our lives. We may already be *in* a good *gay* marriage. Our task is merely to get married legally and at the same time not let the piece of paper change the way we relate to each other. Let's honor what is uniquely ours.

160

Boundaries around what you can know
April 6, 2014

The only person who can tell what sexuality a person is, is the person involved. Everybody else is clueless.

I was searching for something yesterday on the web when I stumbled on an interview with Kirstie Alley, from a couple of years ago. She was talking about John Travolta and responding to the rumors about his being gay. She said he's not gay. She is quoted saying he is "the great love of my life." And then she is quoted saying, "I know John. With all my heart and soul, he's not gay." Alley is talking about things she knows nothing about. She doesn't know John. Nobody can, but John.

Apparently she had sex with Travolta, and she thinks that gives her authority to speak of his sexuality. It doesn't. Some men can't operate outside their sexuality. Others—many others—can. It works like this: A man knows what his default sexuality is, he likes men, but society brings pressure to bear on him not to like men, which the man gives in to. Or having a relationship with a woman gives the man something he doesn't get otherwise. Or it may be that the man falls in love with her, and he enters into a relationship with her. No one knows what it is but the man involved.

During the whole of the life the man spends with this woman, no one sees evidence of the man's default sexuality. It may be that he will die in this state, or it may be that at some point he will announce that he is leaving his relationship and is prepared to explore sex with men. All of this is so deeply private—it's happening in a place so far removed from any other person's perception—that none of the rest of us can say anything about the process. We can't tell what's happening in another man's brain or heart.

A man I am distantly related to was trying to get his head around parts of my life and having difficulties. He said, worried look on his face, "Well, all those years you were in a marriage, you must have been—" and here he paused, searching for a word, "—at least bisexual." He wanted me to say *yes,* in which case I could be inserted into a familiar pattern, and he could stop thinking about these difficult matters.

But I said, "No. Never during all those years did I stop being gay, and never did I develop a feeling for women. I was never anything more than a gay man." What I tried to go on and explain to him was that *gay* was more complicated than our culture would have it. And some can be profoundly gay and completely gay and yet at the same time can function for a time as something else. It's not that I "functioned" for eighteen years as *something else.* It's that I did what I had to do for *tonight.* And then I did it again tomorrow night. I did this for myself and also because I cared about her. But afterward I went back to being *Dwight Cathcart, queer* the rest of the time even though no one knew about it. *Except me.* Most of the things in life that are worth having are the result of tradeoffs. You give up something important in order to get something more important. I loved her, and, for a number of years I gave up my own sexuality in order to live with her. And to have my children. At that time, that was the way it was often done.

Adriana Books: The Complete Blog
2010-2021, Volume 1
Boston, Massachusetts
Somerville, Massachusetts
Winthrop, Massachusetts
2021

Books by Dwight Cathcart

Ceremonies
Winter Rain
Race Point Light
Adam in the Morning
Earthrise
Adriana Books: The Complete Blog, Vol 1 & 2

adrianabooks.com